"Imaginative and full of action...
continually shifting the quirky plot into places
that are both surprising and fantastical."

- Kirkus Reviews

"Charley has that rare ability to infuse copious amounts
of humor laced through a story that is anything
but funny...his writing style is rich in colorful language...
A completely engrossing and entertaining novel...
Charley Pearson is one very fine wordsmith/artist/poet."

- Grady Harp,
San Francisco Review of Books

SCOURGE

By

Charley Pearson

www.charleypearson.com

CEP Books
Available through Ingram Spark

Scourge

This book is a work of fiction. Names, characters, places, and incidents either are products of the author's imagination or are used fictitiously. Any resemblance to actual persons, living or dead, events, or locales is entirely coincidental.

Scourge
Copyright © 2018, Charley Pearson
Cover Art by Ana Grigoriu
Editing by Catherine Lenderi
ISBN-13: 978-0-997299-3-2-8 paperback
ISBN-13: 978-0-997299-3-3-5 ebook
All rights reserved.

First Edition:
10 9 8 7 6 5 4 3 2 1

Dedication:

This book is dedicated to the CDC
and medical professionals everywhere.
You people fight the real problems.

Acknowledgments:

Multitudinous thanks to all those who provided input on the many stages of this project, from its first incarnation as a screenplay through its evolution into a full-fledged novel. In particular, critique partners included Cindy Rinaldi, Pat Charles, Merry Elrick, JC Walkup, and Sonja Contois. I really needed you guys. (As you well know.)

Heaps of gratitude also go to Misty Williams and Catherine Lenderi, who believed in the tale and assisted with necessary prose-related surgical procedures.

Scourge

Charley Pearson

Disease. Desperation.
Just because you have the nerve
to make tough decisions
doesn't mean you'll make the right ones.

–Professor Sturdevan

CHAPTER ONE

Countdown: Summer,

Twenty Years Before the Scourge

[Year 'T minus 20' (a.k.a. '-20')]

Stacy Romani dashed around minty-smelling shrubs and wild grapevines dangling from a humongous, hollow-trunked *ruk*, probably a white oak. She dodged an evil branch out to snag her dark auburn hair—her bestest feature, with its odd black streaks, even if Mrs. Penfold thought she was too grown-up to say bestest anymore. Not that her nanny was hard to please most days, but she always seemed to come up with new rules.

Faster now. A race atop a fallen pine, a raspberry ripped from a passing bush, a leap across the cackling, stone-filled stream.

A flurry of mourning doves, their wings beating out a warning cry, scattered through the fluffy-leafed trees. Stacy skidded to a halt in the mud.

"Sorry!"

The birds settled higher up, and peace reclaimed the woods. There would be nothing else to scare. Good enough. She flew down the path, arms straight out like wings.

A few minutes later, she plopped down in the far southeast corner of the estate, panted a moment, and restacked the rocks over a tiny grave. Her goldfish Pedro, gone ever since she was a stupid little kid, starved when she'd forgotten to feed him. But now she was almost ten. She'd learned everything she'd ever want to know about death, and it had better leave her alone. She added a stone, got up, and took off.

By the time Stacy had circled the grounds once, she'd pretty much met the requirement to play in the yard. Sort of. It was a huge place, after all. It took her six times throwing a rock to get from the back door to the fence, and even more side to side.

Why did she have to be out here anyway? What was the big secret? Yeah, the house was filling with flat-faced adults, relatives she almost never saw. But that shouldn't ban her from the rec room, not when her parents were coming home from a super-long trip. Her father might play a game with her if he had time, after he bawled her out for breaking her aunt's favorite flintlock pistol, and her mother likely had some cool new science books.

Stacy paused by the rotting sandbox, another leftover from her distant past, and inspected the windows along the rear of the house. No one in sight. Perfect.

She ran to the door, a heavy thing with eight glass panes, the bottom four as spotty as every other window she could reach with her nose. She opened the door nine inches, so it wouldn't squeal, and slipped into the kitchen. No, she was supposed to learn metric. So that would be, um, twenty-three centimeters? Yeah, that sounded right. Practice, practice.

She twisted the knob, pushed the door shut, and relaxed her hold. Not a sound, except the hum of conversation from the front hall. She grinned and tiptoed around a half-height wall into the rec room.

A pink fire engine, an overstuffed gray velvet rhinoceros, and a fancy dollhouse full of tiny figures wearing every different kind of wedding dress she'd ever heard of, lined the wall beneath a map of upstate New York, with a pin showing where they lived. Pieces from giant wood and plastic construction sets made shapes on the floor: angled H_2O molecules, double-bonded carbon dioxide, and six-sided aromatic carbon rings with methyl groups sticking off some of the points. Stacy couldn't believe how long it had taken her to say 'aromatic' right. She went to a periodic chart of the elements laid out on a table, little squares of wood with letters for each of the chemical symbols and atomic numbers in the corner. Scrabble pieces for the terminally introverted.

Stacy giggled. She liked that phrase, 'terminally introverted.' She still remembered the day she'd dreamed it up, playing around with new words, shortly before her mom took her out of boarding school. The teacher had told the class to draw pictures of monarchs. One group of kids were fantasy gamers; they huddled together and drew kings and queens. The others all drew orange butterflies with wavery black lines going every which way.

Not Stacy. She sat alone in the corner drawing a perfect black-, white-, and yellow-banded monarch caterpillar.

Come to think of it, maybe that's why they pulled her out of school. No-nonsense Nanny Penfold didn't waste much time on coloring. Learning was all about books, according to her. At least now Stacy didn't have to listen to other kids laughing at her 'fathead vocab.'

She dismissed the memory, picked up a pair of Monopoly dice, and rolled them four times. "Eight, five, seven, three." She selected the correctly numbered wooden pieces, bearing the letters O, B, N, and Li, and rearranged them a couple of times.

"NOLiB," she read. She separated some of the tiles. "No Lib. No liberation."

A voice came over her shoulder. "That must be the chemical men used before women got the vote."

Stacy whirled. "Uncle..."

"Billy." He leaned on the half wall and laughed. "Don't worry, I won't turn you in. Tend to bend the rules a bit myself."

Stacy relaxed. "Glad Mrs. Penfold didn't catch me." She fiddled with the tiles. "I wish they'd let me have a real chemistry set."

"Not yet," said Uncle Billy. "You're alone too much. That kind of work needs oversight."

He stuck his fingers through the handles of several mugs on the kitchen table, hefted the pot of coffee off the counter, and saluted Stacy with the pot. When he backed through the swinging door toward the front of the house, she heard a snatch of someone's voice. "...be a minor for nine more years."

Stacy sat back on her heels. Who was a miner? Unless they meant minor. She was the only minor here, and she was nine years from being a grown-up. But why would they be talking about her? She crept to the connecting door, waited until the spring hinges stopped bouncing, and put her eye to the crack.

"...great kid, but you know where I live," said Uncle Billy. "An industrial site is no place to grow up."

"You are her closest relative," said an old woman, some great aunt or other. There were so many. "Clan duty. And you are in the best position to protect her."

Stacy gripped the doorframe. It couldn't be her. She had parents. So who?

"After the trustees sell this place, you can expand the factory," said the great aunt.

Sounds came from beyond the mass of adults. The heavy, solid thunk of car doors. The lighter thud of the front door. Followed by odd scraping, hobbling sounds, and faint, watered-down voices. Her mother's, her father's. Thank heaven. They'd been gone longer than ever before, and Mrs. Penfold wouldn't tell her why. And why did they sound so frail?

Uncle Billy's voice came again, softer than before. "Damn doctors. Oughta be able to fix that STD-5 thing by now."

"Super syphilis," muttered the great aunt, spitting to the side. "My own niece."

Stacy pushed the door a smidgen to see her parents' faces. Then she pushed it more, ignoring the growing silence, ignoring all the stares. She took a step toward her parents, or what was left of them. Gaunt frames, deep, pale wrinkles, slack clothes, and big, sad eyes.

After a lifetime, her mother knelt and held out a hand. "Hello, dear."

Her father bent forward in a wheelchair, gasping. His body spasmed and lurched forward. Aunts on either side lunged for his arms, but he tumbled facedown at Stacy's feet, still twitching.

Stacy couldn't move. A single whisper escaped her lips. "No."

A roaring, crackling sound raged in her ears, like the rock-filled stream in the woods risen up in holy fury. Black grabbed her vision, a tunnel, narrowing, centering on her parents, until even they were squeezed from existence. If anyone touched her, spoke to her, held her, she had no senses left to know.

Screaming, howling darkness was all the world held. Nothing else remained.

CHAPTER TWO

Fall, Year 'T Minus 20' (-20)

Three fat crows gave a red-tailed hawk a screeching, off-key tongue-lashing. The hawk never blinked at its impudent inferiors. It plummeted between them and speared a rat near the larger of two freshly painted barns. The crows scattered to distant trees, still complaining, as the hawk soared off with lunch over gently rolling hills dotted here with cattle, there with sheep.

Aatos Pires squinted upward. Mean old hawk. Why couldn't it hunt without killing things? The illogic alarm went off in his head, but he didn't feel like pursuing it. He slogged through an empty pen near the barns, ignoring churning hogs in pens on either side of him, and headed toward his parents' sprawling farmhouse.

He kicked off his muddy shoes by the door, skated on his socks across the linoleum kitchen floor, and pulled his short, eleven-year-old frame onto the edge of a counter. The sun blazed through the window, blasted him, and reflected off the glass. A dark face stuck its tongue out at him, the coloring reflecting most every place Portugal had ever colonized. When you added that to the stupid name his mother had picked out of her Finnish ancestry, no wonder he never fit in at school. It certainly couldn't have anything to do with the fact he couldn't play soccer, hit a ball, or hold his own in a brawl. Or look at a girl without getting red. Or the fact he was smarter than any of the other kids.

Man, his illogic alarm was busy today.

He balanced with one hand, lowered a mug into the sink, and twisted the cold water tap. Outside the window, the hawk sailed into the distance. A few goldfinches and a titmouse fought over perches on a bird feeder; the titmouse was getting the upper claw. Aatos got a knee on the counter, reached out, and tapped the glass. "Stop that."

He froze. There was blood on the windowpane, on the mug, on his hand. It dripped off his arms and pooled in the stainless steel sink. Across the room, red smeared along the doorknob. He wrinkled his nose at the scent. He rubbed his fingers, his arms. When had he put on those long latex gloves? He ripped them off. No cuts, no pain. Strange.

"Hey, Aatos," came his father's voice from outside, near the hog pens. "You sneak off to read again? C'mon, need your help cleaning up."

What had he done? Where had he been? And what was his father talking about?

✧ ✧ ✧

On the fringes of New York City, an elegant old building stood proud and defiant among its taller, younger neighbors. Six lanes of traffic swept past. The building lay farther from the avenue than the modern creations around it, but not by much. What once must have been a pleasant front yard was now cramped, though painstakingly manicured. A small sign to the left of the walk read National Register of Historic Places. A large but tasteful sign on the right read Marshmann Institute for Schizophrenia and Catatonia.

As their taxi pulled in to the curb, Aatos wondered why his parents were so worried. The trip from Ohio to New York should have been fun—his first airplane ride—but not with his mother acting scared just because he'd blanked out a memory for a while. His father peppered him the whole way with simple-minded questions to which he knew all the answers, including the best way to get rid of sick pigs. Cheesh, he'd seen it yesterday. His father had slaughtered every one of them. Blood everywhere. Hogs were normally shipped off live to the butcher, but not when a batch got ill, or so he'd learned.

Leave it to his mother to panic yesterday afternoon when their country doctor mentioned the possibility of traumatic amnesia. His mother grabbed her throat, mumbling about an article she'd seen, trauma and brain damage and catatonia. She flew out of the doctor's office, dragging Aatos, vowing to get the best diagnosis money could buy.

Well, on the bright side, he'd gotten a window seat on the plane, and a great view. That was cool.

Aatos' parents rushed him from the taxi toward the main door of the Marshmann Institute, which opened before they rang the bell. An impeccably-dressed woman welcomed them and summoned a nurse, a genteel fellow who acted like one of those butlers in a British movie. He led Aatos down a corridor while the staffer diverted his parents with questions and forms.

Several hours later, Aatos crouched over a laptop on a bed, fending off furious creatures in one of his many all-time favorite computer games. He didn't know why some people thought 'favorite' implied only one. In any case, they were letting him play instead of plying him with more questions. Big improvement, especially when his mother reduced the anxiety level. And best of all, he was winning. He'd never gotten to level nine before. He'd started seeing screen images way more clearly, his mind filling in depths and spatial relations like he'd grown a 3-D brain, and killing monsters kept getting easier.

"You're sure he doesn't have catatonia?" his mother asked for the eighty gazillionth time.

"Mild amnesiac response to stress," said Dr. Rathmusson, the old guy who'd evaluated him in this classy clinic. "I called your doctor back in Ohio. She says she told you the same thing. I don't know what online medical site spun you up, but there's no such thing as 'a little catatonic.'" He dumped a clipboard of papers in a slot by the door and guided Aatos' parents from the room. "Aatos didn't shut down. He never went unresponsive to outside stimuli." They stopped in the hall. "He suppressed a difficult memory for a while. All that blood. First time he saw anything like it. Perfectly understandable reaction."

"He's too young for butchering hogs," said Aatos' mother, framed in the doorway. She did something with her hands that Aatos suspected was 'wringing.' Weird term.

"Had no choice," said his father. "All eleven were infected."

"And see what it did?"

"I'm fine," said Aatos, hitting quick-save. Level ten. The game was gonna be a drag if the bad guys didn't get their act together.

"He's right," said Dr. Rathmusson. "We'll watch him overnight and release him in the morning."

Aatos' father nodded. "'Healthier stock.' Damn biochemist."

"I'll fix it," said Aatos. "When I grow up. So they don't get sick."

His mother beamed, hands relaxing.

His father's chest swelled. "It's called agricultural engineering."

A heavyset nurse touched Rathmusson's elbow and murmured something. He shook his head as she moved off. "Wish that girl in four-thirteen would respond like this. We're trying two new drugs." He led Aatos' parents away, leaning toward them and explaining God knew what. Adults were always talking.

Aatos waited until their steps faded, then shoved his laptop aside. He'd slain his demons, even if they were only of the computer variety. Maybe he could help with someone else's. Besides, curiosity should never be denied. He clambered out of bed onto the tile.

He let out a squawk and leapt into bed. All right, which of his father's swear words would be appropriate for hospitals with frozen floors? Definitely time to expand his vocabulary. Aatos rubbed his feet, spied his slippers and robe, and hopped toward them on his toes, hissing between his teeth until he felt his feet in the felt footwear. He moaned in relief, savoring a recollection of driving his teacher up the wall with alliteration. But he was older now; time to knock that off. Maybe. He pulled on the robe, stole over to the door, and peeked out.

Nobody as far as the nurses' station, or the walnut and leather office that served as one in this overpriced mecca for the mentally questionable. He snuck down the hall to room four-thirteen, cracked open the door, and popped inside.

The room was a carbon copy of his own, except for the flowers. Something red with a lot of petals, probably roses. Girls were always talking about them. They stood in a fluted glass vase, unless it was that other stuff he'd heard tell of, crystal. Strange what some people liked.

Speaking of girls, one of them lay immobile in the bed, dark auburn hair with unusual black streaking splayed across the pillow. Aatos bit his lip and approached her bed. She'd be pretty if she weren't so much younger than him. At least a year. And if he were old enough to go for that kind of thing. Which he wasn't, thank goodness. No way. So on second thought, she wasn't pretty at all.

Whew.

Aatos put out a hand. He pulled it back before it touched anything, uncertain what he'd planned to do. The girl didn't move. Nor, now he noticed, did she appear relaxed or peaceful.

"You got it worse than me."

No reaction, except a beep from a hunk of electronic gear mounted on the wall.

Some papers lay on the bedside table. Aatos leaned over. "'Stacy Romani.' You fresh in too? You think we're defective?" He grimaced and mumbled. "Don't tell her that, you idiot."

He scuffed his foot against the bed frame. What did you do for someone who wouldn't wake up? Make noise? Find something they couldn't resist reacting to?

"Guess you got money, with a single room."

Nothing. The artificial silence of civilization. Not even street noise could penetrate this sanctum. Nothing like the constant drone of his farm.

"They flew me from Ohio. Where you from?"

Okay, that was boring. No wonder she didn't budge. What else? Oh, of course, except... "If you think I'm gonna kiss you to wake you up, you're really crazy." He shivered.

Stacy didn't move. Not surprising. He wasn't a prince. Now what?

"You see blood too? Dead animals? Get beat up at school? Accident? And where's your folks?"

Stacy's eyelids fluttered.

Aatos grinned. "Your parents! They do this to you? They hit you? That's why they're not here? You got evil, wicked parents?"

The door behind him slammed against the wall. The heavyset nurse spun Aatos around. "What do you think you're doing?"

Stacy's voice scratched behind them, pale yet harsh. "You..." She coughed. The nurse whipped her head around, and Aatos pulled free. Stacy blinked at Aatos. "...bastard."

The nurse pounded a button beside the bed. "It's all

right, dear. You'll be fine." She pounded again and glared at Aatos. "Out."

Aatos inched toward the door. "I woke her up."

"You're taking credit for that? Out. Now."

Stacy closed her eyes. The nurse lifted her, hugged her, rocked her. "No, pumpkin. Sleep time's over."

"My mom. My…"

"I know, dear heart. I'm so sorry."

The nurse kept rocking Stacy. Dr. Rathmusson charged in, and Aatos pressed himself against the wall.

"Does she remember her parents?" The doctor leaned over Stacy, peered into her eyes, and checked her pulse.

The nurse waited until he glanced her way, and nodded.

Aatos sidled out of the room. "I knew it. I knew they were—"

✧ ✧ ✧

"—dying?"

Aatos sat with his parents at their large kitchen table, in the midst of supper, the night after they got home. Dr. Rathmusson had called to complain about his behavior. The doctor seemed to think his medicines had awoken Stacy. Or awakened. Aatos wasn't sure about that one. In any event, the doctor didn't credit Aatos with helping.

"The girl just found out," said his mother. "No idea which one infected the other."

Aatos' brain didn't want to process the information. It kept bounding off in random directions. He had woken her up. He knew it. The poor girl. That is, she hated his guts for what he'd said about her parents, but still.

"I gather they were the center of her universe when they were around," said his father. "She didn't get out much."

Aatos couldn't think what to say.

"Gypsies." His mother shook her head. "Would you close the door?"

His father twitched but said nothing. Aatos got up and went to the door, pausing to gaze at lavender and orange stripes in the sky, a peaceful sunset born from distant volcanic violence. One of nature's many ironies.

CHAPTER THREE

Summer, Year 'T Minus 18' (-18)

Crows were the key. Trinity Schultz could feel it. Even if not old enough, not responsible enough to vote, according to dim-witted lawmakers who related everything to age, she could still outthink everyone in her mother's laboratory.

Schultz Pharmaceuticals might be close to bankruptcy after her father's conviction—as if other companies didn't practice corporate espionage as much as he ever did—but her mother had plans to save the family business. Branching out, she called it. Bioengineering healthy species of livestock.

Sleazy ways to sicken the competition would be more accurate, and Trinity had a knack for that. Just that morning, she'd found the perfect crossbreed of pigs, resistant to a hybridized flu virus that paralyzed every other porker she tried it on.

Of course, her mother had told her to work on sheep. And complained about the cost of replacing test animals. If there was one thing she'd learned long since, her mother would never be satisfied.

Now, crows. They went everywhere, and they could carry her unique flu for days before dying themselves. That should do the trick. Her mother should finally be pleased. Even if it wasn't what she'd ordered, selling the resistant strain of hogs would make her a fortune. Or enough to expand the factory, anyway.

Though why Trinity cared what her mother thought was no longer clear. Why was hurting others acceptable? Not just acceptable, commendable. Exemplary.

That was the word. Exemplary. For it had multiple definitions. And one of them was to serve as a warning.

Forget it. She was thinking too much. Time to document her findings, encrypt them in the Schultz code, and let her mother know.

Something kept nagging in the back of her mind. Some vague notion that what she did might not be proper. Was her mother correct? Did everyone look out for number one, and the devil take the hindmost?

No matter. Back to work.

CHAPTER FOUR
Fall, Year (-16) to Spring, Year (-14)

"That *was* an E-flat!" Stacy slapped her fingertips on the valves of the French horn. It was a comforting sort of instrument; when she got lazy, she could cradle it in her lap like a pet.

"Maybe you're out of tune," said Uncle Billy, rubbing the jaw of the clay figurine he was sculpting. "You know better. You've been playing that thing for what, three years?"

"More. Ever since I moved here." Stacy took a breath, blew a string of notes, then stopped and wriggled her fingers. "Oh."

Uncle Billy laughed. "Good."

"What are you doing, anyway? Growing another ogre?"

"They're elves. Productive little workers, making things people want."

"Ogre babies. I bet they make things people don't need."

"I get no respec'," Uncle Billy muttered. He wiped his hands. "That's it. Enough culture for today. Your lips must be shot."

"Never!" She'd sounded out a tune the other day, much more fun than reading music. The tune had nothing to do with memory flashes of that boy who'd woken her up so many years ago. Foolish girlish fantasies. Nothing whatsoever.

She started in on a rousing rendition of "Here Comes the Bride". A perfect choice for a French horn solo. She broke off after the first eight notes, when Uncle Billy wrapped his hand around her fingers. "Not that."

"Why not?"

"We don't do Wagner."

Stacy gave him her best 'I'm a brilliant teen and you're a moronic adult' look.

"I'll explain when you're older. Part of our Gypsy heritage, you could say. Don't ask for logic."

Stacy made an exasperated sound. "You'll never change."

"What do you mean? We're all about change. We left Europe, stopped being nomads, even learned to follow rules."

"Really?"

"Well, some of them. It's hard, you know."

Stacy laughed. "Yeah, we fit right in." She sprang up and put the circular mass of plumbing into its case. Uncle Billy coughed twice. Stacy pulled the horn out, blew water from the drain hole, and stored it properly. "Anyway, I am older. We used to be adults at fourteen, you told me so yourself."

Uncle Billy chuckled and shelved his sculpting tools.

"I need to get out." Stacy shut the lid of the case. "I'm cooped up all the time."

"You don't like it here?"

"There doesn't have to be anything wrong with where you are for you to want to see other places."

"Ah," said Uncle Billy, eyeing her with approval. "You *are* getting older."

"I want to go to school. My parents pulled me out when I was little, but I want to try again. Mrs. Penfold can't teach me anything new."

"School, huh? Mingle with the *gorjer*?"

"Don't call them that."

"Non-Roma, then. You want to do the whole 'wide world' bit?"

"You're the one who says I need culture. I can't get it from movies and books and seventeen feet of brass tubing."

Uncle Billy pulled off his ball cap. "Yeah." He rubbed sweat into the cloth with his thumb. "Yeah, you're right. Wouldn't hurt to see kids your age either. The crew here don't bring theirs in too often. But if you're ready for that, you're ready for some information first. Can't have you talking to the wrong people."

Uncle Billy didn't say anything else for ages. Stacy couldn't understand the expression on his face. It wasn't one she ever expected to see. Embarrassment? Or grim determination?

"Yeah, it's time. Let's show you what we do here."

He led her past the bunkhouse she shared with half a dozen female employees at the light industrial site she had inherited from her parents, not so very far from where they once lived. The factory, as her father used to say, that Uncle Billy ran so well. Ran it while her father was doing what, playing around? Getting infected with the latest thing in sexually transmitted diseases? Catching something that, face it, amounted to a penalty way out of proportion to the crime?

Why did people have to get sick, anyhow? It was so old-fashioned. They'd been studying medicine for how many hundreds of years now?

She stashed her horn in the bunkhouse and followed Uncle Billy to the restricted area of the plant. The place she'd never been allowed, because of the equipment, the chemicals, the health and safety issues. The place with all the proprietary family secrets.

✧　✧　✧

Uncle Billy let her go off the reservation, as he put it, after she agreed to go by Anastasia and always wear an expensive and quite convincing blonde wig. She couldn't date the outsiders and could never bring anyone home. If a cot in a warehouse could be called that. More privacy than the bunkhouse, and quieter, so better for doing homework.

A month later, she learned houses were not a Hollywood affectation, as rare as her parents' old mansion.

"A house?" said Uncle Billy. "Now you want a house?"

"Well, cottage. Bungalow?"

"Stacy, Stacy, you're driving me crazy."

"Come on. We've got hectares of spare land."

"Hectares?"

"Fine, acres and acres. I'm not certain what a hectare is, anyway."

And they had scads of money, even if she had doubts about the way they earned it. Plenty of good, solid contracts with schools for some of their products, so why make the high-risk stuff?

Uncle Billy caved, like she knew he would, and construction started the next weekend. So, fair being fair and all that, Stacy would comply with his rules. A wig and secrecy provided the security her clan needed locally, especially since they gave her a bicycle and made her take a roundabout way to a school in another town. And sure, learning to walk differently, playing a role, had been fun at first. But it got old fast. She was already sick of playing airhead Anastasia.

New plan. She'd get Uncle Billy to fake some credentials, and wouldn't tell anyone where she lived when she went off to college in a few years. Not a peep. A clean break, separation of research and estate.

Then, back to Stacy. It would be nice to be herself in case she ever again ran into that Aatos boy who had woken her up. Had he grown into someone worth knowing? And why was he in her thoughts? Had she imprinted like a brainless duck? And why would she think of him if it made her mad that she thought of him? Talk about cockeyed.

She pedaled her bike around a bend and her factory came in sight. Smoke burst from one of the stacks. Stacy's teeth ground together. If it was her factory, they could damn well keep it running properly, not set themselves up for an Environmental Protection Agency violation. That would ruin everything.

"Uncle Billy!"

She parked the bike and stomped through snow toward the nearest warehouse, not noticing the cold.

"Hey, who's in charge of the boiler room?"

✿ ✿ ✿

Spring got lost during Stacy's sophomore year of high school. It was the whitest April on record, carrying into May. The late emergence of a highly specific virus, dubbed the crow flu, caught health agencies off guard. By the time they realized the birds carried a mutated form affecting humans as well as hogs, it had blanketed North America. Stacy's school, like many, closed down for over a fortnight.

Fields littered with dead crows filled the news, until they were replaced with videos of corpses laid out in rows, awaiting burial. The boy Stacy had gone out with once, just last winter, was among them. She had one of those momentary, irrational bouts of guilt that it was her fault for dating him when she'd promised never to do such a thing. It took hours for the feeling to pass. Odd how the mind worked.

What they didn't show on television was the way the disease progressed. Stacy could never forget the contortions, the sweating, the torment on the kid's face, going on and on before teachers chased away the students. Who knew how long it had taken for the boy to die?

Stacy didn't sleep that night. She got up when all was quiet, found a satchel, stopped by the kitchen to grab a rack of spices, then collected every alcohol, aromatic compound, and acid in the factory's research laboratory, filling a test tube rack with sealed, labeled samples. She even threw in some leftover Christmas nuts on Uncle Billy's desk—almonds, those dark brown Brazil things, and a few filberts, what other people called hazelnuts. She'd press them for oil. Two racks. Then a third, when she decided to add some bases and a couple of ketones and enols. Some of the things were poisonous, to one extent or another, so gloves and face mask went in too. And pipettes with suction bulbs. No pipetting by mouth. Ever.

She turned around, checking the lab, deciding she had all she needed for now. So out the back way, shutting off her flashlight. She inched across the slushy gravel and slithered beneath a section of fence where melting ice had eroded a gully.

Without her bicycle she thought she could try some shortcuts, but it took forever to cut through woods and fields in the dim light. She reached her school about the time the moon was ready to call it quits. The sky brightened, and someone might see her, but the darn lock on the high school gym... ah, there it went. The athletic types beat on this door all the time, and the frame was so warped it didn't take much to pop it free.

No one would be around for several days. School quarantine, plus a weekend, so even the officious sort would be gone for a while. Stacy crept along anyway. She could have strolled, but creeping felt more appropriate. Besides, it was fun.

When she got to the science corridor, the chemistry classroom door was locked. No way she could jimmy this one. She broke a pane of glass, wincing at the noise, and popped inside.

The refrigerator in the reagent room held a secret she'd buried there, before the teachers sent everyone home yesterday afternoon. Phlegm, blood, and a bit of skin, scraped off when one of the sick students fell against a cabinet. Step one, find the virus that was killing people.

Oh, it was nice having a rich uncle. Or being rich herself, strictly speaking, as head of the clan. But being a minor, it took her uncle to spike the school with third-hand leftover equipment no high school had the slightest need for. Using his shady contacts to obscure the anonymous gifts, one of which was that cool scanning electron microscope in the corner. She'd had a blast using it all year, teaching the other kids how it worked. Today it would finally be more than a toy.

Stacy prepared a variety of samples, uncertain how long it would take to identify the virus. It didn't take much blood or tissue per sample, but she didn't have much to begin with. She set up an algorithm for the microscope, to scan each specimen and record the precise locations where any suspicious shapes appeared. Once it was running, she headed for the halls to look for any more signs of sickness. She didn't have much confidence she'd find viral samples, though; except for the one fall she'd witnessed, by one sick student, any other blood spatter or skin abrasions may have resulted from the panicked evacuation, not from stumbling by an infected soul.

It took all day to identify the virus, the one shape that wasn't present outside infected tissue. Scanning eight other blood scrapings she'd found here and there yielded one with the same virus, though most samples appeared degraded. Too warm in the corridors. No clue whose blood it was, and no way to warn the victim—it wasn't like she had DNA samples from everyone in the school to compare it to—so she tried not to obsess over that unsolvable problem.

She dared not continue working at night. People drove

by the building now and then, and the place was supposed to be empty and locked up tight, so lights shining in windows would be a rather bad idea. She broke into a couple of vending machines—cash for the machines, right, she knew she'd forgotten something—and made a night of it in the basement, holed up in a corner with her flashlight and a notebook, planning the next day's assault on the virus.

Saturday was a bust. Saturday night was another sleepless waste.

Then came Sunday, and more luck than anyone had a right to. Some of her acids and bases were more than capable of destroying the virus, splitting it or dissolving sections, but she wasn't sure why she'd bothered proving that. The chemicals were too deadly to be cures. Testing them mostly just filled time while waiting for other results.

But then the most curious thing in the world happened.

None of the kitchen spices she'd collected had any effect, nor the nut oils, nor any of the combinations of medicines she'd stolen from the nurse's station at the school. But wintergreen, a.k.a. checkerberry, seemed to be deadly to the virus, for no clear reason she could think of. Not mint or spearmint or peppermint, not cloves or sage, not anything else, but the exact aromatic compound in wintergreen oil reacted with the viral coating and split that baby wide. Which meant the virus couldn't reproduce, which meant the body's immune system could get it under control, which meant people might survive. And who needed FDA tests or government approval to eat wintergreen?

Ha! Take that, foul plague.

Stacy typed up her notes on the school computer, documenting procedures and failures as well as the one success, and fired them off to the Centers for Disease Control. Then she realized she should have waited a bit, in case CDC traced her IP address and sent someone to the school.

Or maybe someone was already coming. It was Sunday evening and she'd had to turn on a light to finish her report. All her plans for staying hidden had flown from her head when she got excited about finding a cure. She wiped the keyboard, ran around the room cleaning fingerprints off everything she'd touched, collected trash from her candy bar diet in her satchel, and glanced around. Any clues left as to who she was? It would spoil Uncle Billy's secrecy paranoia if they caught her. She didn't even have her wig with her.

A siren. She'd better have been thorough. No more time. Certainly no time to head back to the gym and exit the way she came in. She went to a window, pried it ajar, shoved the satchel outside, and scraped through the gap as the siren rounded the side of the building and cut off.

"Hey, you, stop."

Yeah, that was likely. Stacy ran from one patch of woods to another, dodging in shadows. The growing dark was perfect, enough light to keep her balance but not enough for them to follow. She sloshed through a stream for a long way, heading the wrong direction, then used a tree limb to pull herself from the water. A long swing to a long drop far away to obscure her scent, then follow the rocks to pavement and away. Two miles of roundabout hiking got her back on the road to the factory.

Way overkill. A minor vandal would never warrant the kind of search they did on television for serial killers. But it was hilarious to know she could do it, and kind of a celebration at her success over the flu.

When she approached the factory gate and the guard recognized her, her elation ended. The donkey doodoo hit the rotary impeller, and Uncle Billy read her a riot act longer than she'd realized they could last. Partly for running away without leaving any word, partly for stealing lab supplies, partly for engaging in dangerous work alone, and more than anything for endangering the whole clan by trying to help strangers who'd never done a thing for their family. Stacy tried to claim that a cure for the flu helped the clan as much as anyone else, which sort of mollified him, but not much.

"You should have kept your work on-site and not risked exposure."

"But we don't—"

"Never mind the site doesn't have a scanning electron microscope. That's not the issue."

She'd never been so grounded in her life.

But the news was fun to read. Authorities were testing wintergreen. By the time summer dried up the world, the epidemic had died out.

Stacy had one final, sad thought on the whole affair. Hundreds—no, thousands of years they'd been studying medicine, trying to cure diseases. And what had they learned? How far, really, had their knowledge advanced?

They barely had the cap off the reagent bottle.

CHAPTER FIVE

Summer, Year (-13)

"Quit sulking. There's someone you ought to meet."

"I'm not." Trinity set down her wine. "Sulking, that is. And by the way, who? And why?"

Her old friend Chad slid into the booth beside her, trapping her in the corner of the bar. She'd not seen him since undergraduate days, but he'd jumped right in as if no time had passed.

"You never made a secret what you thought of your family," he said.

"I did too. I mean…"

'Chain-smoking' Chad laughed. As skeletal as ever, and still with a boy's high-pitched voice. "We all had problems. I told you how I used to rip off freshmen." He lit a fresh cigarette.

"Are we any better now?" Who had given him that nickname, anyway? Surely it hadn't been her.

"I am. Are you?"

"I don't know what you're talking about." Was he allowed to smoke in here? Eh, who cared? Trinity picked up her wine. Somehow the glass had gotten empty again.

"Has your mother put you to fixing any of your bugs?"

"No profit in it. Besides, she knows I don't do cures."

"Right. So what are you working on?"

"I can't talk about it."

"Or won't. Remember why we drifted together in the first place? From cheating and corruption to neo-Nazis and sarin gas, people suck. Including us."

"Thanks for making me feel better."

"Until now."

Trinity pulled down her arm. Maybe she didn't need to signal for a refill. "Now?"

"Come with me. Meet this guy. He's got a way to fix the world."

As much as Trinity waited for it, Chad didn't blink. "Fix it?"

"Just listen. See what you think."

He still hadn't blinked. How did he do that? She put money on the table and pushed herself up. Chad grinned and took her hand.

CHAPTER SIX

Spring, Year (-12)

Stacy managed to be first out of the parking lot after her high school graduation. She tossed the diploma onto the back seat of the sad, decrepit vehicle Uncle Billy let her use, and drove past the town's two-hundred-year-old park. Sunday afternoon, with mothers and strollers, and fathers pushing swings. Real families, like on TV. Kind of cool, if not for her. Not anymore, anyway. Or not yet.

Or, here was an idea—quit moping. If she wanted a family, she knew what to do. Let the elders select a suitably distant cousin, give up her career plans, and become such an old-fashioned cliché she'd go stark raving, with a side order of homicidal maniac.

When she reached the factory, Uncle Billy waved from across the lot and resumed a discussion with two of the younger workers, getting the place ready for their big environmental inspection tomorrow. The workers—quiet Franky and bubbly Theresa—gave Stacy a thumbs-up and went off toward one of the groundwater monitoring wells. Their pal Rudy followed, going out of his way to ignore her. On the plus side, at least one guy around here didn't think she was marriage meat.

"Do I get a new car for graduation?" Stacy wished she had the kind of 'gimme, gimme' flirtatious smile some of the girls at school had. Even though it made her sick when they used it. And nauseous when it worked. So never mind, maybe it was just as well.

Uncle Billy fumbled through his papers. "Would you take it if I gave you one?"

A smile? Oh, no, he meant a car. Stacy hesitated, and dropped her shoulders. "I guess not. Some of this stuff we make..."

"You know why. How many countries have Roma been chased out of, everything stolen, our people killed?"

"America never did it."

"How many nations could one time say the same? You can't trust governments." Uncle Billy signaled another worker and pointed at Franky's group; the new person went off to help with the wells. "We make as much money as we can, we hoard, and we take care of our own."

"Standard lecture seventeen-B," said Stacy, trying on her exaggerated pouty look.

"Which I shall repeat until you stop pestering me." Uncle Billy flipped up another paper.

Okay, the pouty thing was about as successful as her flirty smile. Very 'un.'

"So how'd it go?" said Uncle Billy.

Stacy beamed. "They made me valedictorian."

"Damn. I suppose that means we have to celebrate." He peeked from the corner of his eye. Stacy waited him out. After a moment, he tossed down the clipboard and gave her a hug. Stacy laughed, squeezing as hard as she could, until her uncle made grossly fake gasping sounds.

"Not that you had a lot of competition," Uncle Billy said. "Such a small school."

Stacy shook her fist in his face. He put up an open hand and backed a step.

"All right, I give up, you're exceptional. Oh, wait. Here." He slipped a plastic card from a pocket and gave it to her. "Debit card for the Big Apple. Get yourself some decent clothes. Don't want you embarrassing us at that fancy university."

Stacy took the card in both hands. "Cool. Thanks." It would be nominal, not like a car. This, she could accept.

"Just keep your ostentatious spending down there where no one knows you."

"Aye, aye," she said, prancing off toward the main gate.

"And get changed. Then check the emissions monitoring logs for the smokestacks."

"Will do."

"And try to be more modest."

Stacy couldn't help grinning. He'd gotten her a present. He always did, though he said he wouldn't. But this time it was one she could keep. And on top of that, he'd done everything she asked, cleaning up the place and reading regulations and buying gear and pushing everyone to get ready for tomorrow, after he'd given in and let her call the New York State Department of Environmental Conservation to schedule a voluntary compliance review. After all, NYSDEC was going to visit every company in the state sooner or later. This way Uncle Billy could show off how good they were and forestall any surprise inspections when they might not want visitors.

And she was getting new clothes.

In her world, it was as close as she could get to a perfect day.

CHAPTER SEVEN

Spring, Year (-8)

The tall, angular man chose his names carefully. From his oldest follower to his newest, that Trinity girl, not one knew him by the same moniker as another. That was as it should be. His true identity should never be associated with his good work. Such would be vanity, and an undertaking tainted by a quest for glory held no spiritual reward.

He chuckled. Undertaking. He was an undertaker. That was a good one.

They were wonderful people, those who accepted his wisdom, who considered ways to forward the cause of earth's deliverance. Not sufficiently creative yet. Not as dedicated as he would like. But they tried.

Ah, yes, they were truly turning into believers. This glorious world could be saved. The trees and the bees, the oceans and deserts, every beautiful aspect of creation had its place, and could be made again to flourish. All it took was the removal of a single bad influence, for which he needed to instill a touch of fanaticism, perhaps, to find the ultimate solution.

Terrible word, fanaticism, and one he usually reserved for his enemies, religious zealots and political extremists. He should know; the things he had done when younger... well, no need to churn up that sediment.

Now the scalpel must do its part to save the patient.

The ecosystem. One good cleaver would do it all. His people must search harder for ways to craft the necessary tool. And with enough passion, enough reason, enough patient explanation, all mankind would understand his goal, and accept it. The disease could be expunged.

The disease of humanity.

CHAPTER EIGHT

Spring, Year (-8) to Fall, Year (-8)

Another day, another graduation. Stacy flipped her diplomas in the air and caught them. Two degrees, tied for highest grade point average in college history, and plenty of grad school offers. Not to mention an award for identifying the gene that made some people immune to the crow flu. Sure, they'd long since developed a vaccine for it, as if her wintergreen cure weren't enough, but her time-consuming senior project had genetic implications for the whole immune system.

Hmm. Maybe Uncle Billy had a point about being more modest.

Nah.

A week after Stacy's homecoming, she had her car reloaded and ready to leave. She bid farewell to Franky, Theresa, and especially Rudy, who'd warmed so much over the years that today she had to pull her hand free. She locked the little cottage Uncle Billy had built for her back in high school and crunched across the gravel between two warehouses, scratching a mosquito bite with the corner of a folder, surveying the ten-acre sprawl of her factory. Not that she was more than a figurehead, she spent so little time here. She couldn't think when she last had a walk in the surrounding woods.

When did she metamorphose into such a workaholic? There had been a caterpillar inside her, once upon a time.

Somewhere, somewhen, a chemistry hobby had become a career. Maybe she was just lucky.

Piping snaked overhead between the buildings, four-to-six-inch carbon steel lines suspended from pipe hangers. Along the ground ran insulated eighteen-inch steam heating lines supported on stanchions, with sharp elbows for expansion joints when the temperature changed. It all looked fine. Clanging, hissing, and an occasional earsplitting whine entertained a score of workers hurrying about. Greenish-yellow smoke burst from one stack, but quickly dissipated; that was one to tell her uncle about.

A door creaked open behind her. Stacy turned.

Uncle Billy flicked one of the odd dark streaks running through her auburn hair. "You never did dye this stuff to match."

Stacy ducked away, laughing. "It's my dark side."

"Nah. Only animals have multi-colored fur. Proves your roots."

She pointed at the gray on his temples. "Yeah. You're showing your own."

"Hey," said Uncle Billy, "that's my light side." He rubbed his bushy brown hair, more or less hiding the gray. "Shoulda outgrown puns by now."

Two guards sauntered by with old NATO-standard assault rifles slung across their backs. They didn't wear uniforms, but all the guards had plaid shirts, black M-P Gas ball caps, and silver badges different from the IDs on other employees. The guards nodded, Stacy smiled, and Uncle Billy half saluted.

Stacy pointed from their caps to the sign above a small building: Multi-Purpose Gas, Inc. To one side, hundreds of compressed gas cylinders in all sizes and colors were stacked on pallets, receding into the distance. "When are we getting the new logo?"

"Can't decide how much to put on it. 'Exotic Gases,

Precision Mixtures, Accuracy Guaranteed' seems a bit long."

"I suppose." They strolled around a corner toward the entrance. The machinery whine came again. "I thought you fixed the radial bearing?"

"That's a stator thruster," said Uncle Billy. "All the compressors need replacing."

"Ah. Expensive." Stacy watched a local pesticide subcontractor spray around the wheels of their single decoration, a vardo imported from England, a Gypsy Ledge waggon by the famous Bill Wright. "Anything from NYSDEC lately?"

"Our rep wants a few new groundwater monitoring wells and a bunch of soil samples." Uncle Billy kicked an oversized stone off the path. "Nice lady, but I don't think she believes we're as clean as we say."

"Suspicion is their job. Speaking of which, did she ever ask why we have so many guards?"

"Yeah, and I told her," said Uncle Billy. "What else you gonna do with a bunch of unemployed nephews, leave 'em on the street? She laughed at the family resemblance."

Stacy rolled her eyes. "Your moral compass never budges, does it?"

"Glued to the spindle, pointing at 'kin.' This place is our salvation."

Stacy took a few more steps. "Yeah, salvation. You'll never take me off the deed, will you?"

"By our laws, you're head of the clan," said Uncle Billy. "Besides, 'Anastasia Romani' has class. Where would we be with 'Good Ol' Bulldog Billy' on the prospectus? We ship all over the world now."

"Don't."

Uncle Billy frowned. "You disrespect your parents. They worked hard to build this business."

Stacy made a face. "They certainly provided well for

us."

"They'd be proud what you're doing with it. Top honors and graduate school. Bet you cure cancer."

Stacy snorted. "I wish."

"Either way, you'll do the world good."

"And, as usual, the end justifies the means?"

Uncle Billy shrugged. "Why not?"

Stacy chewed her lip, studying the facility. "The means are here, regardless." They continued toward the gate. "And on that note," she handed him the folder she'd been carting around, "here's the changes you need to make to products C-137 and D-14."

Uncle Billy opened the folder and flipped a couple of pages. He got lost in the details, until a non sequitur popped out. "You dating yet?"

"Me? No." She glanced at the factory.

"Don't be silly," said Uncle Billy, "you won't find anyone here. All those World War II stories from your great aunts, lectures about the horrors of racial purity, and then they say marry within your culture. Surely by now you've given away that dead hog."

Stacy smiled. Where his expressions came from was beyond her. If she was lucky, it would stay well beyond. "Yeah," she said, "it's rather hard to miss the contradiction. But still."

"But nothing. In the absence of your mother, I am duty-bound to bug you."

Stacy laughed. So that's why he pretended she could consider outsiders. She didn't for a nanosecond believe the family would ever accept one, and she wasn't about to admit her selection of graduate school was predicated on Aatos Pires' choice, that strange boy she'd been thinking about since age ten, and whose academic progress she'd tracked since freshman year.

"Fine," she said. "I stand bugged." She grabbed her

uncle's arm and towed him to the parking lot.

Uncle Billy harrumphed and went back to reading the papers.

When they reached her car, Stacy said, "So then, I'm off."

Uncle Billy pulled himself out of the folder, slapped it shut, and opened the door for her. "Aye, aye, milady. And don't come back."

They grinned at each other and spoke in unison. "I mean that in a good way."

Stacy squeezed his arm and got in.

✡ ✡ ✡

A month after Stacy began at her new university, she got a letter from Uncle Billy. She tore open the envelope and a slip of paper fluttered to the floor. A rectangular thing, a bank draft from one of Uncle Billy's secretive offshore accounts. No big deal until she retrieved it and saw the number. It took one point seven seconds to find her cell and punch speed dial.

"What the hell is this?" Stacy gave the check a snap. Sure, he couldn't see it, but he'd darn well know what she was talking about.

"It's your living allowance," said Uncle Billy.

"What do you expect me to do, buy the whole damn college?"

"I read up on your field. You'll be doing a lot of research. Don't want you mouse-milking because you can't get the right equipment."

She ran her finger along the zeroes. "I don't need this much. They've got good facilities here."

"You'll find a use." Uncle Billy sounded so smug when she couldn't slug him.

Stacy let him stew a bit. He knew she might tear it up. She almost did. But no, not this time. Maybe he was right.

Maybe she could find a use.

"All right," she said. "Thanks, I guess."

"Ah, I love it when you're grateful." He chuckled till she closed her phone.

It took a couple of weeks to figure what to do, mulling over options in the tiny cracks between classes and homework. Eventually, she opened an account in one bank, withdrew large fractions, and deposited them in some other banks and the school's credit union. She bought a townhouse outright and eliminated references to the old Dynamore Delicatessen, long since burned down—the artificial home of record she'd used in undergraduate days. And she cruised nearby towns and surfed the Internet until she found what she wanted. Three charities should do it. And oh, all right, she'd hang on to a little mad money. Macy's had a turquoise Chinese cheongsam she'd been wanting.

The first charity was a reforestation project. She'd always liked the woods. Then off to the nearest branch of the STD Hospice Network. Yeah, that one was a bit obvious.

Her last stop took her back near the campus. She parked several blocks from her goal and walked, turning at a few corners to make sure she was alone. She stopped once when she saw a familiar face come out the front door of a day care center. Voices spurted from a window.

"Goodbye, Mr. Pires."

"Robert, sit down."

The man gave a little wave. Aatos Pires. The boy she'd researched and followed to university. What could he be doing here? Stacy loitered past the building, but she was out of earshot for anything he might have said.

So that was him. Interesting. Perhaps she'd learn more over the coming months. He hopped down the stairs two at a time and caught her eye.

Bad move. Didn't want that, not until she knew more

about him. Stacy let her vision slide away, lingering on nothing, and disappeared around a corner.

She confirmed Aatos didn't follow and went on to her third bestowee.

This choice was admittedly a little more obscure, if any of her high school friends ever learned of it. It had taken time and a spot of research, but she was pretty sure she'd picked the best facility. She delivered her donation to the local and rather impressive substance abuse rehabilitation center. From all she'd read, they certainly seemed deserving.

When she came out, she saw no one she recognized. Just in case, she took a roundabout way to her car.

✿ ✿ ✿

Officer Nadya snapped a picture as Stacy left the substance abuse center. Stacy never looked at the police surveillance van parked down the block. Nadya rolled up the van's tinted window, dropped the camera, and tapped numbers on her cell phone.

"This is horse dung."

The phone rang through. No one answered.

"I don't care what the lieutenant thinks. We'll never catch users this way."

She let it keep ringing.

"We must have thousands of shots by now. All they do is stuff 'em in a file cabinet."

The call went to voice mail. Nadya hung up.

"Screw this. I'm taking that job with Homeland Security."

She started the van and drove off.

CHAPTER NINE

Summer, Year (-5)

The blast was louder than the angular man expected. Dirt and rocks burst from the earthen dam. One shard clipped his arm and two of his followers swore at injuries. But water ran through the cove once again, the balance of creation restored, and the night's mission a success. Or the knight's mission, for was he not a crusader, the most sterling of advocates for the recovery of nature?

Flow increased as the dam crumbled. Water gushed, pulsed, then poured downhill as the structure gave way. Not exactly smashing down the trees, scarcely more than annoying to the people below from mild flooding, but still acceptable. Sweeping away the village may be what Jamie had promised, but none of his people had achieved such skill.

"It's not enough," said a mousy young woman, his latest recruit. "One river at a time, one hamlet's worth of people, will never get the job done."

"Yeah," said another. "Jamie was supposed to get three times that much dynamite."

"You should talk," said Jamie. "You were promising poison gas."

The angular man raised his arms. "Patience, dear ones. We are the best our species has to offer. We shall not bicker amongst ourselves. We shall not accuse. Perhaps Trinity is correct, and the technology does not yet exist to accomplish our beneficent goal. But someday we will prevail. Seek on, and in the meantime, continue your smaller acts of distraction. Ecoterrorism, some may call it, but we know better. Any action to slow the destruction of habitat, to forward the path of Luddism, is honorable."

A bit of moping, but mostly nods. Glorious people, his disciples. Even that skinny Chad boy, with little academic training to contribute to the cause, could make a fine soldier should they ever need one. It shouldn't come to that, of course. Peaceful extirpation of the human species was the goal. Well, as peaceful as they could make it. Dynamite made a charming exception now and then.

Time. That's all it would take. Eventually, one of his people would find a means to secure the final objective. Perhaps Trinity. Far more competent than any other he led, and her dedication grew with time. She had not cried about the necessity of killing people in months.

By the way, where was she? It was past time for them to hightail it out of here. He looked around.

Trinity came pounding up the slope, seconds before the flood rose to cover her path. She clutched a snake in each hand, right behind their heads so they wouldn't bite.

"What did you—"

"They had a pet store." Trinity leaned over, took a few gulps of air, and released the snakes. "I couldn't let all those puppies die."

Jamie scoffed. "I thought you killed animals for a living."

"You really are off-the-wall, you know?"

"Enough," said the angular man. "We have to leave."

They crammed themselves into a nondescript van that Chad had stolen. They would split to the winds when they reached the deserted drive-in movie theater a few miles away. And now he thought about it, he should probably not gather his disciples like this again. Too risky, potentially losing so many followers at once should they be caught. And as tonight had shown, groups were self-defeating. Too many egos and lone wolves. They should each work their separate plans.

But that Trinity, daring what no other had when she expected everyone in the village to drown. Most laudable. Indeed, she had nerve and perspective as well as intelligence. She could be the one to accomplish their true goal.

Yes, perhaps Trinity would find the way.

CHAPTER TEN

Fall, Year (-5)

Two hundred university students mingled in the auditorium of a newly renovated conference center. Aatos hopped off the stage and began the obligatory welcoming routine among his younger colleagues. The center got a lot of use, being a short drive from the massive state university where Aatos had earned both a bachelor's degree and, a couple of months back, Ph.D.

Doctoral candidates from around the country were present, and few knew each other, so they danced the minuet of self-confident youth out to meet and greet. Clicking reverberated throughout the room. At the lectern on stage, white-haired Professor Sturdevan slapped the microphone. One student laughed.

A fifty-plus-change reporter—Joshua Grimm, according to his name tag—meandered through the crowd clutching a memo pad and scribbling notes. "Stupid science," he mumbled, as he wandered past Aatos. "Hated it when I was their age. Hate it now. Damn editor."

Aatos did a double take at Grimm, then noticed a woman, one of the students, eyeing him from across the room. He finished talking to another attendee, straightened his shirt across his much heftier waist—vowing for the forty-seventh time that week to get some exercise—and worked his way over to the girl. She wasn't one of the out-of-towners; he'd seen her around campus, floating down halls lost in contemplation, or haunting labs late at night. And one time, he could swear she had given him the once-over. But contrary to Professor Sturdevan's predictions, his ego hadn't gotten big enough to walk up to strange ladies and inflict himself on them.

Or not very often. He was a guy, after all, and a certain amount of that kind of thing was expected. This time, the target—er, the woman in question—was point-blank staring at him. And after all, it wasn't every day a pretty girl gave him that much attention.

When he reached her, his mouth blurted out an opening line that did not, in any way, resemble anything that had passed through his brain. "I sense a high probability, approaching certainty, that 'have we met before?' would not solicit an affirmative response."

The woman looked at him askance, one of those dubious faces they must teach girls in middle school. "You *are* a post-doc."

Aatos gestured at the stage. "Guilty. Helping Professor Sturdevan."

The woman seemed to be fighting down a smile. "And I fear you have jumped to a conclusion."

"What?" He drew himself up. "I never jump to conclusions."

"Oh?" Another one of those doubtful airs.

"Certainly not," Aatos said. "I may leap with wild abandon. Take a blind dive off a cliff without checking for rocks. But I never merely jump."

"I see," she said. "You're Olympic class."

He pretended to beam with pride. It had no perceptible positive impact. Okay, add that to the list of ways not to impress women.

"The point is," she said, "you're wrong, Aatos Pires."

Aatos shut his mouth. No, she wasn't familiar. Or was she? "I managed to forget someone like you?"

"No. Someone like me fifteen years ago."

Fifteen? What was she talking about?

"I owe you for waking me up."

The light caught her hair and Aatos stepped back. Dark auburn with a few black streaks. Stacy. Stacy Romani. He'd dreamt about this girl for years. Woman. Girl. One and the same? "You... how'd you know it was me?"

"My family taught me to check out suspicious contacts."

"But your parents..."

"Extended family."

Aatos processed the concept. A stalker? Yeah, right, he should be so lucky. "You've been here for years. Why didn't you say anything before?"

"Wasn't sure you were worth knowing. A childhood cr... chaotic memory can be misleading. But the profs like your work, and you do more volunteer stuff than anyone I've ever met. I guess you can't be all bad."

"Oh. Um, thanks. I think." No way. There was no conceivable way she had almost said 'crush.'

"So, biogenetics?"

Professor Sturdevan cleared his throat at the microphone. "Please take your seats."

"Agricultural engineering." Aatos pinched his crush-crazed mind, willing it to settle down.

"Really? You're a farmer?"

Sturdevan shuffled papers. *"I'd like to welcome all you would-be doctorates."*

Stacy and Aatos sat. "You'd be surprised." Aatos lowered his voice as everyone quieted. "The fields aren't much different anymore."

"You're here because you are the elite of biochemistry," said Professor Sturdevan. *"Our hope for tomorrow."*

"Designer plants?" Stacy asked.

"You'll be seeing a lot of each other over the years,"

said Sturdevan. *"We're a small community."*

"Designer immunity. For healthier livestock." What did Stacy want? She wasn't coming on to him. She scrutinized him like a laboratory specimen. He dared not make a move.

"So pretend you like each other." The audience gave the professor one of those short, dutiful laughs. Grimm put a hand over his eyes, across the aisle.

And Stacy just kept studying him.

✿ ✿ ✿

Later that morning, in a small conference room, Professor Sturdevan threw up his hands and leaned on a lectern. Aatos sat up front near Sturdevan, while Stacy and a dozen fellow students laughed at the professor's delivery. Aatos tried not to watch Stacy more than any of the others. A remarkably difficult objective.

"So yes," said Sturdevan, "screw the poets. It's not love or kindness, not a sense of humor or playing games that make us human. You see all that in nature. And animals think, plan ahead, sometimes use tools. It's the extent to which we use rational thought that defines our humanity. Retention and expansion of knowledge. We don't need emotion for that. Now could I please be allowed to get back on topic?"

The students laughed again.

"Thank you," said the professor. "And I agree, ethics is boring. What can I say? Even logical people can take the same information and reach very different conclusions. So who but us should regulate us? Who else knows what we do, and how powerful we become, manipulating the stuff of creation?"

The students got serious. One said, "So there is no situation in which randomized double-blind testing with placebos can be run on humans?"

"Not at all," said Sturdevan. "You can test. But you

can't add the element of surprise, because they must consent. And that affects results."

Stacy raised her hand. "Yet it's okay to use knowledge gained immorally? Like primitive anatomy from vivisecting prisoners, or Nazi medical experiments?"

"Well, once the knowledge exists, however horridly obtained, it seems a shame not to use it."

"Then we should use illegally obtained evidence to convict criminals. Censure the police later if you have to."

"They'd never punish cops enough," said another student. "Goodbye, civil liberties."

"That's fixable," said Stacy.

"Please," Professor Sturdevan said. "Your points are related. But we're off track again. The issue is the future, and the people in this room. What kind of research will you do? What is your goal? Why is it fair, principled, and of benefit to the world?"

"And why," said Aatos, "should someone give you a pile of money to work on it?" That got yet another, if rather predictable, laugh. And that one was on the professor's head, Aatos told himself. The prof was the one who said you had to keep the audience awake or you'd never teach them anything.

"Ah, grant money," said Professor Sturdevan. "Or profit motive." He pointed at Aatos. "I'll let our alleged expert here address those after lunch. Me, I'm hungry."

The students chattered, rose, and headed out.

Aatos paused by Stacy, wondering if he could find out more about this girl, or if he should even try. "So," he said, "sometimes it's fine to skirt the law?"

Stacy recoiled like he'd stabbed her with a pencil. "Sometimes it's too late to worry about it."

She brushed past him and left. Aatos watched her glide away with the grace of a gazelle.

No, not a gazelle. Forget her. She didn't ask for

anything, didn't offer anything, and didn't leave the slightest hint if he was in trouble or she was grateful for the past. No invitation of any kind. So leave her alone. Walk away.

No gazelles.

CHAPTER ELEVEN

Spring, Year (-3)

Seasons flickered past like butterfly wings. One evening, more discouraging than most thanks to a decisive experiment that exploded her latest theory, Stacy leaned back in her cubicle along the wall of the chemistry library. Or... wait, if that theory didn't work, there were some rather intriguing implications. And one of them, regarding immune response, could help a lot of people. If it were true.

Stacy kicked back, squeezed between two bookcases, and pawed through massive books on a table in the open area beyond. She stalked across the room and revised a formula on a giant whiteboard, erasing, replacing, erasing, expanding. She went to her cubicle, bit a thumbnail, and fondled one of Uncle Billy's ogre babies on the corner of the desk until the paint coated her fingers. Then she sat and scribbled notes so hard the paper ripped.

The janitor levered open the door and started turning off lights.

"No, thank you," said Stacy with a decimal of her brain.

The janitor laughed, turned the lights on, and backed out, rattling his rolling trash can between door and jam.

Stacy jerked up her head, looking from the sound to a clock high on the wall. "Shit, not again." She tapped a pen on her notepad and mumbled. "Sorry, guys." So much for the group dinner and alleged night drive into the

Adirondacks. Why she thought she could maintain a friendship, she didn't know. What social skills she had degenerated the older she got.

Wait, what skills? And don't even ask about dating. She had the emotional acumen of a sixteen-year-old, if she wanted to be honest about it.

Friends or not, she could use a break, though. She needed exercise. Shopping counted, didn't it? Easter was coming. That janitor, Akeem, loved bragging about his brood and celebrated every excuse to buy his kids candy. Stacy could add to the wealth, and probably receive another lecture from Akeem on how family was the only important thing in life. Forget countries or religions or, she supposed, right and wrong, to listen to him. Pretty much the same spiel she got from Uncle Billy or anyone else in her clan.

But how could that be true? Whatever happened to loyalty to a cause? Anyone who dared say 'greater good' anymore was an automatic bad guy. Like they'd never heard of triage. And she was a party to it. She kept her mouth shut about what her clan was selling. As bad as the Mafia, as bad as Hatfield and McCoy feuds in the hills. That's what 'family first' got you.

Damn, she was in a dark mood. She grabbed her sweater and headed for the door. It was her blasted experiment going wrong, that's what had her down, and set her ruminating over the bonds of family and the consequences for outsiders. Forget the dumb candy, time for serious shopping. Toys for those kids of Akeem's, that would prove she could break the mold and think about others.

So what did kids enjoy these days? Did girls still play with dolls, or was everything on computers? That would be sad, dreaming of weddings on a two-dimensional screen, without the tactile feedback of satins and ribbons sliding through your fingers as you dressed your favorite character for her big day. Breaking one bond and forging a new, while retaining links to the past. Selective merging of new and old, keeping and discarding and... *where on earth was she going with this?*

Her hand clasped the doorframe, and she focused on the whiteboard with all her equations. Toys, families fled her mind. This was important. If she could selectively break that one bond deep inside the immunoglobulin she'd been working on, open it up and merge in a certain string of amino acids to shape it better—or start afresh, and code DNA to create a new chemical with that modification—she could control the immune response in the manner she dreamed, and help people. A lot of people.

She tripped back to her cubicle, mind churning. Somewhere along the way, she lost her sweater. She could look for it later. This was too critical.

She dropped to her chair, opened her laptop, and began typing, faster and faster.

CHAPTER TWELVE

Winter, Year (-2)

"**I** tell you, I almost have it," said Trinity. "The design is nearly complete, and I've got a few new ideas on how to synthesize what we want."

"You've been optimistic before," said the angular man. He checked out the window for any sign she'd been followed.

The abandoned church they met in these days was about the fourteenth different hideaway since Trinity had met him, and she was always careful. Insulting, the way he didn't trust her.

"It's clear out there," she said.

He dropped the heavy blackout curtain. "Just being cautious. So you're gaining confidence?"

"Definitely. There's this guy I work with—"

"Stop!" The man jumped up and loomed over Trinity. "You have not divulged our purpose outside my ring of disciples? Tell me you have not."

"I wouldn't do that," said Trinity, pushing her mentor away. "He's a blind fool, an inventor with no conception what his ideas can lead to."

"Ah. Very well, then. And you think you are finally close?"

"Well, I'm getting there."

The angular man took off his reading glasses and set down the monograph Trinity had given him. "I do apologize. 'Tis easy to counsel patience, yet hard for oneself."

"It's coming. I can feel it."

"Do not rush it, child. Do it right. Time is on our side, and we may only get one chance."

"Don't worry, sir," said Trinity. "We shall triumph."

The man smiled. "You're quoting me now?"

"Always."

"My thanks. There is one thing I meant to bring up. You need to stop raiding pet stores and releasing all the merchandise."

Trinity pouted. "Why? Caging animals for pleasure serves no useful purpose."

"I appreciate the propriety of helping man's domesticated species revert to a feral nature. But your research holds far more importance to the world, and you must not jeopardize it by risking incarceration for petty crimes."

Trinity huffed, then bowed her head. Boy, when this guy pontificated, he was a real stuffed shirt. "You are right, of course. Could another disciple take up my hobby?"

"I will ask. Perhaps someone will volunteer." The man shook his head, as if indicating how unlikely that would be.

Trinity gave another moue. "Poor things. Well, I suppose this will give me more time to concentrate on the main project."

"That's the spirit. You do know, we are all counting on you."

CHAPTER THIRTEEN

Spring, Year (-2)

From a rise two blocks away, the Clingman's Dome Conference Center had a roof shaped rather like the top of the Great Smoky Mountain peak it was named for. That is, massive and without distinguishing features. More importantly, from a commercial standpoint, it had a revolving restaurant in a tower mounted atop the building, superficially matching the tower on the real Clingman's Dome but much larger, with escalators looping out in open space instead of a ramp. There were also elevators for the handicapped, and a dozen spare wheelchairs so the faint of heart could pretend grave illness and ride up and down, to the highly-publicized ridicule of the staff. Well-rehearsed and colorful abuse had its own audience. In any event, the view justified the restaurant's affectations and mountain-high prices, or so Aatos had always heard.

The conference facilities far below were more utilitarian, with nearby sandwich shops, and suited the scientific community quite well. Until recently, Aatos had found them more than adequate.

Today would be different. He was well out of the university, gainfully employed for several years now, and still surprised every time he saw the numerals in his paycheck. The private sector blew away university salaries. To top it all, his pride and joy, his latest project, had landed him the role of central speaker. He could hardly wait to try out the tower restaurant when he was done.

First things first, though. Aatos passed a simple, stark placard reading April 10: Practical Bioengineering. A bit incongruous, what with Easter decorations adorning shop windows to either side. In one of the plate-glass windows, his reflection superimposed on a giant blue bunny in the display. His neat little goatee granted him a bit of maturity his years had so far failed to accomplish, and an expanding waistline proved his university years were a thing of the past. Probably a slowing metabolism. Or the typical post-collegiate problem of having money. His refrigerator was so well stocked, thanks to an inability to leave things on the grocery shelves, that whenever he opened the door all he could think was 'what a shame not to put all that good food to use.'

Okay, maybe he wasn't as wide as the bunny, maybe he was only fat in comparison to a cornstalk, but that midline bulge was definitely noticeable.

Aatos smiled, straightened his tie, and entered the conference center.

An hour later, he pranced across the auditorium stage. A screen behind him showed professional video of row upon row of long, shallow ponds, each surrounded by corrugated metal fencing. The complex was covered by an array of two-inch piping with spray heads for foam fire suppressant, suspended with pipe hangers from a vast array of scaffolding.

"Algae vats," said Aatos. "Fire safety is key. You'll see why in a few minutes."

On the screen, the ponds faded. A large biochemistry text opened.

"I'll go slow, for benefit of the press."

Scientists in the audience chuckled.

"You all know the early stages. Breaking the genetic code. Four different kinds of deoxyribonucleic acids in DNA strands, and each set of three codes for a specific amino acid."

A spinning DNA double helix on the screen unwound in the middle. A long sequence of the letters A, G, T, and C appeared along one unwound strand, at random.

"Or more properly, DNA codes for RNA, and that's the blueprint for amino acids."

A ribbon labeled RNA grew along the unwound DNA strand, separated, and flew toward a giant molecule nearby.

"And enzymes use that blueprint to pick between the twenty amino acids and create a specific, sometimes very long sequence of those building blocks. That is, a specific protein molecule."

The RNA strand passed through the giant molecule. A protein strand grew from the other side. As it emerged, it folded upon itself to create a new molecule.

"RNA to code for any protein can be inserted into benign viruses. Those viruses infect the target, make DNA, and add it to the organism's original DNA."

A virus on screen penetrated a cell wall and opened up. The RNA shot out into the cell and migrated to the nucleus, where it passed through a happy, chugging little factory with a smokestack, spinning out a corresponding DNA strand. The cell's DNA unwound, and the viral DNA inserted itself.

"And if you think this is what it really looks like, you're in the wrong field."

The scientists laughed. Aatos saw Stacy come in and sit down in the back of the room.

✧　✧　✧

In the middle of a broad, level field, fences surrounded rows of shallow ponds, the algae farm in Aatos' video, complete with greenish water, scaffolding, and pipe hangers.

"But that's history," said Aatos, continuing his far-distant lecture.

Countryside stretched beyond the ponds: farms, woods, and highways. An interstate wove around swells in the ground and disappeared into the distance.

"Now, with computer graphic modeling, we can understand precisely how enzymes work."

Well down the interstate, off a major intersection, and a short way down that road, lay a mammoth building. A sign read Schultz Pharmaceuticals—Designing the Future. Trucks lined a loading dock on one side of the building. No smoke or noise marred the pristine factory.

"Computational chemistry reflects the strengths of van der Waals dispersion forces and dipole-dipole attractions, not to mention hydrogen bonding."

Inside the building, banks of glove boxes stood in long lines, linked by Plexiglas tunnels for passing things from one to the other. Workers stood at several, arms inside the rubber gloves installed on rings in the sides of the boxes. Numerous windows in the stainless steel let them see what they were working on inside. Bright blue machines stood to the side, one labeled DNA Sequencer, another Enzyme Production.

Along a wall near the sequencer were several computers. Thirty-four-year-old Trinity Schultz sat down at one and smoothed the pleats in her skirt. She shoved aside a computer printout dated March 26, pushed up her green satin shirt sleeves, and let her fingers skate across the keyboard. After a moment, she continued one-handed and reached for her mouse.

"Knowing this, we no longer have to copy nature. We can design enzymes to synthesize exactly what we want..."

Trinity's computer screen showed a complex protein, lengthening and twisting. With her last few keystrokes, the protein stopped growing. Two small molecules floated in from the side. One stuck to the upper left of her large molecule. The other flipped and stuck to the upper right.

"*...and test them out.*"

The central enzyme contracted, bringing the small molecules together. The screen flashed, and the two reacted and combined.

"*And if it works as planned...*"

The screen enzyme released the new molecule, the combination of the two little ones. Once released, the large central protein, the enzyme, snapped back to its original shape.

"*...we can go into production.*"

Trinity hit a key sequence. Her screen flashed the words: Viral Production Started. The DNA sequencer beside her came to life. Lights on the enzyme production device flashed. Inside the first blue container, tubing carried colored liquids. Switches flipped, arms twirled in tiny mixing vats, and peristaltic pumps pulsed away.

"*So decide what you want. Break it down in pieces and create designer enzymes for each step of the synthesis.*"

Inside a chamber, DNA helices grew and twined. DNA swirled to the side. An enzyme opened it up and created an RNA strand.

"*And that's what we did. We chose the product, designed the enzymes, coded the DNA/RNA, and created a virus.*"

Inside the viral production equipment, an RNA strand swirled into a helix. A bell-shaped protein coat grew, wrapped the RNA, and created a virus particle. The phage swept down a tube and ended up in a chamber, amidst thousands of other identical virions.

"Witless," Trinity groused. "Virus particle, phage, virion, fully-formed virus dude.' How many words do you need for the same damn thing?"

She filled a syringe from the chamber and thumbed the

sliding plastic cover over the needle. She walked across the laboratory, through wide double doors, and down a hall to a vast room laden with the scent and sound of a dozen barnyards. Inside were rows of large, clean cages holding a variety of animals: hogs, calves, sheep, and a few chickens. She went to those lining the far wall.

"The virus infects algae, and algae makes our desired product."

Trinity opened the door of a cage on the second tier, soothed the pig inside, and gave it the injection. She closed the latch and nodded in satisfaction.

✿ ✿ ✿

On the stage in the conference center auditorium, Aatos drew himself tall and pointed to the algae farm on the screen behind him. Man, he had this audience in his pocket.

"Oil! Or any grade of gasoline or hydrocarbon you like."

The audience murmured, a growing buzz.

"This is the engineering part of bioengineering. Making a product with value. With enough farms like this, and proper safety precautions, we can eliminate our dependence on foreign petroleum. Or, for that matter, make anything else you like. Questions?"

Hands shot up.

✿ ✿ ✿

In the bowels of Schultz Pharmaceuticals, Trinity turned off her computer, lined up the reference books on the shelf, and pushed her chair under the desk. She brushed stray goat hairs off her linen pant suit and went across the lab, through the double doors, down the hall, and across the room with the rows of cages.

The pig she had injected two weeks before lay on its side, dead. Hogs in other cages were inert or kicking feebly. Her hand went to her throat.

A door shut in the distance. Camille Schultz's

distinctive high heels clicked on the linoleum. Trinity's hand dropped to the cross on her necklace as Camille approached, gray hair in a rock-hard chignon rubbing her jacket collar.

"I succeeded," said Trinity.

Camille eyed the cages. "Thought you might. You're a walking disaster."

Trinity's jaw tightened.

"Been telling you that ever since you poisoned the cat."

"I was ten, Mother. It was a chemistry experiment."

"And you're so much better at it now." A hog coughed twice and lay still. "Where's the cure?"

Trinity swallowed. She shook her head, slipped around a pillar, and hurried away.

Camille backed from the cages.

✿　✿　✿

With Aatos' lecture over, the auditorium rapidly emptied. A few stragglers stopped inundating him with questions and ambled toward the exit, chatting among themselves. Aatos breathed a sigh of relief and followed. He couldn't resist checking the rear where Stacy had been.

She was still there, obviously waiting to catch his attention. She glided across from the far aisle, along the central row of seats. "So," she said when she got close, "what's your control circuit? They just churn out oil?"

"Self-regulating," said Aatos. "Oil kills the algae if we don't harvest."

"And it's carbon-neutral. Takes in as much carbon dioxide to make the fuel as given off when it burns."

"Oh, right. Green energy."

"You should have mentioned that."

"True. You always all business?"

Stacy smiled. "Sorry. Hi. Good to see you again."

"You too. It's been what? Since one of Professor

Sturdevan's Christmas parties?"

"Holiday parties. You know him and religion."

Aatos laughed. "Right, right. A year ago."

"Two," said Stacy.

Two? She cared enough to remember? No, it didn't mean anything. She had a good memory, was all. "I hear you're getting a name in immunology."

"Only theory. You're the one who's production-oriented."

Aatos lifted a shoulder. "Pays well. But it's not medicine."

"Ah, that," said Stacy. "Life takes odd roads."

"So true." Aatos hesitated. Oh, why not? Take the plunge. "Speaking of paths, there's one up to the tower restaurant. Want to avoid the crowds down here and indulge?"

Stacy's tongue made a lump in her cheek. It rolled around.

"I mean, my treat," said Aatos. "It's supposed to be good. And we have a break. I mean, it's lunchtime. Well, you know that. If you..." Babble much? No, not a chance. Not me.

Stacy tilted her head the smallest fraction of a millimeter, draining another liter from his confidence level. "Okay," she said. "I guess."

Wow, that was an auspicious beginning. But hey, it was a yes. He led her to an elevator.

☼ ☼ ☼

Three hours later, Aatos and Stacy had covered personal histories, though hers sounded rather abridged. They'd dissected a trio of movies and solved the world's latest monetary crisis. And promptly forgotten how. Somewhere in there, he had complimented her hair or eyes, hopefully both, but he couldn't say anything else now for fear of repeating himself, and she had noted he used to be in great shape before the extra weight. Favorite places had blurred into favorite foods, which were glossed over in favor of jokes about how people they knew used to eat them, most notably triple-decker ice cream cones. Pistachio seemed to be a featured part of that discussion, but his mind kept drifting into the sparkling river of her eyes and getting lost in the eddy currents.

He'd never seen her so relaxed. He'd never seen her wear that soft, gentle smile. They migrated back to personal stories, and he embellished a couple of his unclassier moves in middle school. She countered with a childhood tale that tinted her pink, until he laughed so loud it silenced the other diners, which deepened her hue to that of the beets she hadn't touched.

And somewhere in there he had taken her hand. And she must have accepted that, because now she was tapping his palm with a finger.

No, wait, now she was stroking it. Good God, did she have any idea how many nerve endings were in the palm, and what it was doing to him?

Then the overhead music, a medley of moldy oldies goodness knew how ancient, moved on to Three Dog Night's "Old Fashioned Love Song".

☼ ☼ ☼

Stacy woke from a dream. No, heavens, it was a nightmare. A love song? And what under the sun was her nail doing to Aatos' hand? She yanked back her arm, pinning the offending finger against her belly.

"I have to go."

Aatos jumped from surprise to confusion to hurt so fast she'd have missed the whole thing with one blink. She rose and whisked phone and wallet and what turned out later to be a napkin into her purse.

"Did I say something—"

"No," said Stacy. "I have to go. I can't do this. I can't be with..." She made a vague motion that couldn't explain anything, since she didn't know what it meant herself. "I'm sorry. I didn't mean to lead you on."

She bounced off an older, perfectly-coifed woman.

☼ ☼ ☼

"Excuse you," said Camille, recovering her balance. She stepped around Stacy and speared Aatos. He knew the look. Business, nothing but. "You trying to hide up here?"

"Hello," said Aatos, standing up. "Stacy Romani; Camille Schultz, of Schultz Pharmaceuticals. My boss."

"Pleased to meet you," said Stacy, backing away, torn between her precipitate departure and the polite introduction.

"Yes." Camille didn't waste time on her. "Got a project for you." She nodded at the remains of Aatos' lunch. "I assume you're done?"

"Yes, ma'am."

"Good." Camille tilted her head toward the door.

Aatos threw a silent question at Stacy. She gave him a half-hearted smile and turned away.

What else could he do? He followed Camille at her customary brisk pace. He'd never find out what had spooked Stacy. He'd done something wrong, that was for certain, and it didn't appear fixable. And to think it all started because she came to the conference to see him.

Oh, all right, probably not. This was a professional conference in her field of expertise, not far from the university she still inhabited. Of course she would be here. And as much as she'd briefly warmed, she detached again as fluidly as ever. Was she always this distant? Was she leery of him in particular?

He glanced back before the door of the restaurant

closed behind him. Stacy was locked in place, gazing across the tables to the view over the city.

Nope. Not a hint. He would never learn what she thought of him.

✿ ✿ ✿

Stacy drifted along the halls of the chemistry building, missing her corner and ending up on the terrace above the quadrangle. She'd finished Aatos Pires' latest article and couldn't get her brain free. If his research, his findings, his future plans had captured her imagination, that would make perfect sense. Getting intrigued by science she could understand. But it wasn't that. It was him. His stupid, lopsided grin. His fumbling reaction when she had made herself known. He was the boy who woke her up, and he had grown into a genius. It could have been a friggin' fairy tale if she dared let it.

And she almost had. She almost went too far. With an outsider. Someone the clan could never trust. Until his devilish boss had materialized and dragged him off. Saved by the hell.

Dammit, she needed to scrub her mind and reenter reality.

"There you are."

Professor Sturdevan. Thank heaven. He would snap her out of it.

CHAPTER FOURTEEN

End of Countdown:

Spring, Year Zero of the Scourge (Year 0)

"Ma!" Judy struggled to support her gasping Papa. They stumbled across a stream, past twisted, stunted trees, and through a rocky, sloping field. Limp gray clouds drizzled the remains of an early spring storm across the battered landscape, not a blade of grass still vertical in the unmown yard around their home. "Ma!" They reached the small, weather-beaten farmhouse before Ma came out and helped lift Papa up the steps.

Inside, Ma and Judy maneuvered Papa onto a crude wooden bed. His fingers writhed like snakes on a pitchfork. Judy sagged down beside him and wiped blood from his ear.

"We gotta do somethin'."

Ma went back to scrubbing dishes in a chipped porcelain sink. "Ain't nothin' to do. Papa hates doctors. Cain't afford one nohow."

"We could get some medicine."

Ma stopped scrubbing and leaned on the sides of the sink. "Wouldn't know what to get. Never seen nothin' like this."

Papa continued to twitch. Judy clutched his hand, unable to still the spastic fingers. Blood seeped from the other ear, coating the pillow.

☼   ☼   ☼

"Did you see the news, Trinity?" said the angular man. He dressed as a reverend these days, the role he most certainly deserved. No one need know he had failed the seminary. He sidestepped, blocking Trinity from her car in the lot of their favorite bar. "It is beginning."

"Are you sure?"

"I will inform the other disciples. You are going to be famous."

Trinity fiddled with her pendant. "The fleeting fortune of fame." She slid the cross inside her sweater. "But no. Our work is secret."

"They will learn, eventually. Too late to matter."

"I rather liked anonymity."

"I can identify." He touched her chest where the cross lay hidden. "Rest assured that with time, it will matter no longer."

"Yes. That is the whole point, isn't it?"

Trinity slipped from the man's awkward attempt at an embrace and drove back to her mother's laboratory.

☼   ☼   ☼

Joshua Grimm sprawled in a chair in front of a desk in the worst-decorated office of his news agency. No excuse for it, far as he could see. The need for austerity measures was long past, now they'd built a robust Internet presence. He savored a memory of his latest chance to scoop the majors. That fire was a godsend—empty building, no casualties, lots of drama with no risk—and he'd even talked the insurance rep into sponsoring a pricy ad. Win-win.

He sniffed. Old dust and fresh mold. Boss-man Cranbrook clung to abstinence like nirvana. A framed print, not quite up to the quality of Motel 6, hung askew on the wall behind his desk; seven drab-colored coffee mugs crouched atop dictionaries, piles of papers, and an open thesaurus; and a single dingy curtain drooped from the tilted rod on one side of a window whose glass must, presumably, have once been transparent. The lingering odor of expensive cigars might take years to wear off, or so Cranbrook said, and therefore 'it didn't matter' if he defied the smoke-free workplace regulations with the raunchiest cigarettes available.

Grimm snapped a lighter on and off, in time with the ticking of an old analog wall clock designed to run backward. He compared it with his watch and tapped the dial. A flurry of activity beyond the door proved everyone else had an assignment. A siren wailed outside, always a good sign since the police station was close and the hospital far away.

Cranbrook charged in and slammed the door against the wall. The knob passed through a gaping hole in the wallboard and the door wedged in a matching, long vertical crack. He ignored Grimm, smashed his bulk between the armrests of the swivel chair behind the desk, and dug into a bottom drawer.

"No more science crap," said Grimm, standing up.

"Fine." Cranbrook surfaced with a handful of notes and a broken cigar. He held up two strips of paper covered with the claw marks of a deranged rooster or, perhaps, Cranbrook's handwriting. The editor glanced from one paper to the other, rubbing his tongue along his lower lip. Grimm scratched his back against the doorframe and waited.

Cranbrook slapped down one of the papers and crinkled the other. "There's reports of unusual animal deaths in the Midwest." He tossed the wad of paper in the general direction of a pair of waste cans.

"Blech," said Grimm. He straightened up and tucked in his shirt. "And/or, yuck."

Cranbrook rooted through a pile of manila envelopes

on a rusty sheet-metal credenza below the window and pulled one from the middle. "Okay," he said, "try political analyst." He waggled his little finger at the corner of his desk.

Grimm scanned a tiny note stuck to the desk with a speck of jelly and made an accepting grunt. On his way out, he caught a blurb on the monitor in the office across the hall. Their canine-breath rival, the infamous Sniffer Dog website, was topping the charts with hits on their latest story, 'Corruption in the Feds!' That sounded like a political issue, if the Dog didn't have their facts wrong again. Cranbrook's election–evaluation chore wouldn't take long. Maybe Grimm could do a follow-up on the Dog's claims as well.

It took a bit of sleuthing later in the afternoon. The video accompanying the article's purple prose depicted an ornate grandfather clock and other lavish furnishings in the local FBI field office. The view bounced around like someone filming with a cell phone hidden in their hand, and the commentary fumed with virulent claims of fraudulent spending. The anchor for the report sounded like a rabid used-car salesman. No wonder the site got so many hits; it was hilarious listening to this guy. But was it accurate? WFA—waste, fraud, and abuse in government—were perennial favorites, and accurate often enough, but how had the Dog gotten wind of something no one else had heard of?

Grimm visited the FBI branch depicted in the article and, after a half hour of stalling, was allowed to view the office in question. The occupant was away, and no, they wouldn't tell him who it was. A public affairs geek claimed the room's appointments were all private property, not taxpayer-funded, and they'd explained that to the Sniffer Dog. Grimm got more dirty looks than he could count from random staff and agents who probably figured he was throwing acid on the wound. That evening, he slummed a nearby bar and bought a few whiskies for a couple of potentially disgruntled employees. Still nothing to back up the Dog's accusations. So what was the original source?

Time for the fun stuff. Or what he'd thought was fun when he was younger. Now? More in the scary category. He was too old to see the upside of a criminal record.

Getting into the Sniffer Dog's offices at 3 a.m. wasn't too hard, considering. It wasn't his fault the idiots running the place had such outdated door locks you could pop one open with a credit card. Well, after he opened the two dead bolts, that is. That part did take several minutes. He hadn't engaged in such dubious evidence-gathering activities since his junior days in the press, and lock-picking skills got rusty with disuse. Good thing the alley was deserted.

He crept inside and poked around until he found the author's desk. One computer, still on, with the access password stapled to the bottom of a drawer. Seven versions of the offending article occupied a file folder, the older ones filled with 'track changes' comments. Grimm started with the oldest and read every one, jaw sagging with disbelief.

The first draft had been a useless piece identifying plush decor and no evidence of wrongdoing. Editorial comments included 'BS,' 'they suckered you,' and 'spice this up.' Ensuing rewrites got progressively stranger, with inserts from over a dozen people adding more and more outrageous claims of government deceit and foul practice. The whole thing read like a joke gone wrong, reporters having fun with each other, until somehow the final product got released as news because, well, it would draw so much attention, and garner so much cash. Advertisers paid by the number of hits on your website.

A disgusting blight on journalism, that's what it was. Whatever happened to the Walter Cronkite tradition? News as an honorable profession, free from the control of money-grubbing MBAs? Maybe Grimm was too old. Nowadays every company, every industry from cars to beer was lodged in the hands of business majors, not the engineers or brewers who first started them. It was ruining the world.

Not this time. He wouldn't let the Dog have the last word on this one. He tried not to dwell on the fact he had resurrected one of the worst tricks of his journalistic youth, breaking and entering, to expose failings of the press. Irony was so overdone.

Grimm downloaded copies of everything and returned to his own office when dawn was a sickly glow in the eastern smog. He pounded out his revelations regarding Sniffer Dog and planned an assault on Cranbrook. He had more arguments marshaled in support of publication than his editor could possibly resist.

In the end, he never got to use the rationale. Cranbrook jumped on the scoop with both feet and one well-honed nose. They ran their website retaliation in time for the noon releases, copying the Dog's style: 'Corruption in the News!'

CHAPTER FIFTEEN

Summer/Fall, Year 0

Three Bunsen burners flamed atop a long workbench, one of the twelve lined up across the immense chemistry laboratory in Schultz Pharmaceuticals. Colorful reagents bubbled, all but one of which had no purpose except to provide a bit of atmosphere. Figuratively, that is. Aatos would be darned if he'd put up with a dull, normal laboratory, not after all those science fiction movies he'd ingested, tested, and digested.

On a more practical note, rows of bookcases, gas chromatographs, mass spectrometers, and other tools of the trade packed the space, nearly concealing the view out the two windows on the west wall. Aatos shut both windows, blocking the roar of trucks pulling away from the loading dock, the mind-numbing thrum of a lawnmower, the overwhelming aroma of fresh-cut grass, and most importantly, a rich crop of ragweed pollen. He sneezed for about the five hundredth time in the past half hour and dumped an empty tissue box in a waste bin.

He went to the bench, adjusted an analytical balance, and turned off a burner. He surveyed the work area, then went over to a large green, red, and yellow parrot in a cage on another bench. He pulled a plastic bag of apple wedges out of a drawer and held one up to the bird.

"Come on, Mr. Praline, you cannot live on seeds alone." The parrot bobbed his head a couple of times, sniffed at the fruit like a dog, and took a nibble. "Now if you'd just learn to talk." Mr. Praline tilted his head and nibbled again.

Aatos heard Camille's unmistakable spike-heeled footsteps. Her voice carried across the room. "I take it you haven't finished."

Aatos kept feeding Mr. Praline. When the steps got close, he said, "This latest infection is rough. How come you've got the sickest hogs this side of the prime meridian?"

Camille sniffed at one of his fake reactions. "We stress them. Constant improvement or we lose market share."

Aatos frowned. "Stress? Animal testing is supposed to have a beneficial purpose."

Camille wrinkled her nose at Mr. Praline. "Trinity's bugs and your cures make the healthiest stock on earth."

The apple snapped in Aatos' hand. "She's creating new viruses?"

"Of course. Or rather, modifying existing ones, making them more aggressive. Nothing nature wouldn't do sooner or later through mutation. Like I said, it gives us a leg up in the market."

"There is no 'of course.' Nothing stops it. You're killing your own market. You can't let her use my equipment that way. She's too damn clever."

Camille's pen split an errant birdseed laying on the bench. "Clever." She got an enigmatic smile. "Yes, I believe she is."

Aatos tossed down the bag of apple slices. "Thank goodness it didn't spread to humans."

"True," said Camille. She inspected a fingernail for damage. "If word got out we did it, lawsuits would be overwhelming."

"God, is everything money with you?" He grabbed the parrot cage and stalked away.

Camille pinched her lips. He opened the door.

"Aatos. Don't you want to cure it?"

He gripped the handle.

"We ship hogs all over," said Camille. "How many farmers you want to bankrupt?"

Bankrupt? Aatos sneezed again. Faintly, tentatively after all these years, his illogic alarm tried to wake up. But it was so very, very rusty.

"Two months' salary, bonus when you fix it."

Another long pause, then Aatos shut the door.

And walked back toward Camille.

☼ ☼ ☼

Trinity Schultz rocked from foot to foot in front of Camille's desk, the errant student called on the carpet. Her mother had no idea how it made her feel, or more likely didn't care.

"Tone it down," said Camille. She sat behind her desk filing a fingernail, holding it up against the light for inspection now and then.

"I did what you wanted. Batch 458A of the hogs are carriers of the new virus. Ship them where you like."

"Killing off competitors' stock so people buy ours means our own must stay healthy. Your newer viruses are too virulent. If Aatos can't fix them, we can't make money."

Destroying farmers who didn't buy her products. How could she think like that? How could anybody? Yet, people were all alike.

With rare exceptions like her mentor, the angular reverend with a million names. Such an inspiration. He had turned Trinity's life around, and now she was doing her part. She had been a pawn in her mother's machinations, but now she was a pawn under her mentor's guiding hand, and this time she would delight in what a pawn could do. It could reach the end of the board.

It could even end the game.

☼ ☼ ☼

Six months dribbled by, until one day snow flitted around a mid-sized urban hospital, coating lamp posts, cars, and shrubbery. A siren split the silence, howling past a climax and descending to a whimper. An ambulance skidded up to the emergency room door. A flurry of white coats around the rear of the ambulance took but a few seconds to evaporate into the building.

An hour later, Grimm hiked down an austere corridor and found Cranbrook glaring through a plate-glass window into the intensive care unit. A technician adjusted respiratory equipment at the head of a bed obscured by a plastic tent; he pulled his hands out of one pair of glove ports, slid them in another pair, and worked on a piece of gear inside near the pillow. A younger nurse stuffed a cardiac resuscitator into a bunched-up plastic sleeve to get it safely into the tent.

Grimm studied the apparatus. "Is this why you called me? Medical story?"

"This is my nephew."

Grimm sobered. "Sorry. What's wrong?"

Lights started pulsing on two instruments. The technician punched a button.

"Immune system," said Cranbrook.

A senior nurse in a full anti-contamination suit, complete with respirator, entered the tent from the back. The technician pulled his hands out of the way.

Cranbrook growled. "Nerdy kid played computer games nineteen hours a day. No way he could get a sexually transmitted disease."

Doctor Nielsen walked past on his way into the ICU. "You think we'd do this for AIDS? Other things affect immune response."

The door shut behind Nielsen, muffling sound. The nurse took over operation of the devices inside the tent and pulled the resuscitator out of the sleeve. Nielsen stuck a hand in one of the gloves and pointed at a tray. The nurse set the resuscitator on a table, went over to the tray, and prepared a syringe.

"So what do you want me to do?" said Grimm.

The patient's limbs began flailing. Blood splattered inside the tent. Alarms went off on three different machines. Two more nurses rushed into the room. One helped the other into an anti-contamination suit. The heart monitor flatlined and the body went slack. The nurse in the tent dropped what she was doing and started CPR. Red lights appeared on another piece of equipment.

Nielsen said, "Give lidocaine, then epinephrine." He rattled off dosages so fast Grimm didn't catch them.

The nurse went to the tray, prepared the drugs, and injected them into an intravenous line.

Cranbrook leaned in, beating slowly, softly on the frame of the ICU window. "Find out what it is. And what they're doing about it."

CPR continued as the second nurse, now suited up, entered the tent. A flurry of needles, orders, and furtive glances. But there came a point when the doctor told them to stop. Grimm thought they'd given up awfully fast, until he saw the time. He reached out and put a hand on Cranbrook's shoulder.

Cranbrook's fist slid to his side. He watched the nurses put away their tools. Their every act monopolized his attention.

Grimm pursed his lips. More words held no value. He shook his head and left.

CHAPTER SIXTEEN

Spring/Summer, Year 1

Spring had attacked the metropolis. Pale green leaves vied with blossoms on the slender trees in planters along the street. Outside the large conference center, taxis disgorged scientists in suits. Nothing tailored or expensive. Plain department store merchandise that academics found more than acceptable.

Stacy mingled and shook hands, a trifle incredulous she was numbered among such an elite group, giving her first postdoctoral paper. She passed a sign reading Bioengineering the Future. And to think she had once had to beg for a chemistry set.

Two hours later, the auditorium stuffed with three hundred professionals from around the world, Stacy crossed the stage toward the podium. She aimed a laser pointer. The screen showed brilliant protein molecules, rotating to expose all sides, each element a different color. "In conclusion, phospho-apatase-D and gamma-ferronase, in conjunction with immunoglobulin-G, react to the chemical characteristics of intruders, and develop receptors to support identification and destruction of new infectious agents."

Stacy flicked off her laser pen. Lights in the room came up. "Of course, as always, further research is warranted. This is a recording."

That broke the polite silence. The audience chuckled

and clapped, and Stacy smiled, satisfied she hadn't embarrassed herself. Now to get something to anesthetize those butterflies. Something special for lunch, perhaps. And maybe she could update her diary; that was always relaxing. As long as no one ever found it, of course; such was the nature of diaries. Or—

Ah, she had it. That janitor she was always giving a hard time, making him leave the library lights on. Akeem something. He had what, eleven children? Easter was coming. Time for some major candy.

Wait, hadn't she been planning to do that once before? Good grief, that was like four years ago. She was heading out to buy stuff for his kids, and completely forgot the impulse when her research reared its head. Thoughtless, and lost in her own little world, like always. Even if her research did save lives.

Not this time, by God. She was buying toys, and that was the end of it.

☼ ☼ ☼

Cranbrook threw documents in the air and chased two junior reporters out of his office. Grimm got out of their way, grinned sourly, and followed Cranbrook into the room amid the swirling papers.

"Spill," said Cranbrook, lowering himself onto a folding chair behind his desk and balancing on the narrow seat.

"It's not just your nephew." Grimm watched the papers settle around him. He wondered if today's version of a guest chair was worth risking.

"Didn't figure it would be unique. Diseases rarely are."

"Six cases in the U.S., perhaps, but not clear all symptoms match. One in Mexico, one in China."

Cranbrook wrinkled his brow. "That's a little far afield."

"No good info, and I may be suffering med-student syndrome, seeing correlations that aren't there." Grimm nudged the chair with his foot. It quivered. "CDC's not gearing up, whatever it is. Too much flu this year, or too little money."

"Both, likely enough. Well, see Special Agent-in-Charge Chou Lee Lin at the Eighty-Eighth Precinct."

"There's a police angle on this?"

"Different story. And he's FBI, not police." Cranbrook stood up and examined the wobbling chair. "Odd thing is, they asked for you by name."

"Huh." Grimm tiptoed between the scattered papers and out the door.

✿ ✿ ✿

Grimm scanned the docks as he approached Special Agent-in-Charge Chou Lee Lin, a.k.a. Doctor Lin Chou Lee if you gave him his civilian title and Chinese-style surname. A cracked and oil-blackened concrete quay, sheet metal warehouses, stacks of Sea-Land containers, and scattered collections of fifty-five-gallon drums filled the scene, illuminated by thirty percent of the mercury lamps installed overhead. Someone must be working hard to keep that many lit, he figured. The rest of the lamps had spikes of glass poking out of the sockets.

Blinking red and blue lights from police cars failed to cast reflections off the two rusty freighters sagging on their mooring ropes against a short, stubby pier. Clanging metal punctuated the dull throb of diesels, the long boom of a crane hauled cargo from one ship, and rotting fish and garbage contended for atmospheric dominance. Quite the delightful place for a late-night adventure, Grimm decided. He drew closer.

Dead bodies littered the place. Okay, maybe not so delightful. Uniformed police herded four handcuffed toughs toward an unmarked car and two black-and-whites.

Grimm was mentally composing copy the moment he

spotted Chou Lee. When was the last time a severe, well-seasoned FBI investigator showed up at a crime scene in a silk suit?

Chou Lee chewed an unlit pipe, tapped it on his cheek, then pointed at the bodies when Grimm stopped beside him. "Story's a bit worrisome, Mr. Grimm."

Interesting, thought Grimm. A tall, thin, Chinese-American dandy who jumped straight to business with a third generation Bronx accent. He could forget using 'Doctor' or Chinese word order when this article went to press. It was 'SAC Lin' all the way.

"This is an NYPD bust. Aren't you FBI?"

Chou Lee didn't bother confirming it. His credentials made it clear. "Seems there's cocaine on that freighter." He pointed to the ship with no active crane. "First, it's Columbians and ships. Then Afghani heroin and planes. Then Mexican dope with trucks and submarines. Plus a few more sources getting into the act. Now the Columbians are making a comeback, and budget cuts reduced ship inspections, so we're right back where we were years ago."

"Disturbing," said Grimm. "Disenchanting, even."

"Problem is, the locals didn't want it. Reneged on a contract. Sellers got unhappy."

"'Curiouser and curiouser, said Alice.' Dealers getting all moral and upright?"

"Could be. Could be." Chou Lee rubbed the empty bowl of his pipe. "Or suddenly getting cheaper stuff elsewhere."

"Ah," said Grimm. "That would be a worm in the ointment."

"Thought those were flies."

"Aren't flies in pudding?"

Chou Lee took a pointless puff. "Never did like pudding."

Grimm grunted and offered him a light. Non sequitur. There was a more than even chance he was going to like this guy.

"Cops are doing fine, I guess," said Chou Lee, watching the organized confusion unfold around him. "And we're too busy." He looked at Grimm's cigarette lighter, at the empty bowl of his pipe, and back at the freighter. "By the way, thanks."

"What for?"

"You're the one who cleared my office of those corruption charges, after that Sniffer Dog article. Why do you think I called your editor?"

"No biggie. You weren't guilty."

"Well, figured you might be the rare bird we could trust on a case or two. We'll see what happens. I don't expect a whitewash, but if you give us a fair perspective, maybe we'll try this again someday."

"Thanks."

"If you get in the way, you're out."

Grimm pocketed his lighter. No reply called for. That was a given.

☼ ☼ ☼

Aatos figured he must be slipping. Or worse, Trinity was getting a whole lot better at her bugs. That infection last year took four months to cure. This time it took him till the end of summer, over eight months, to fix her latest virus. There was still something peculiar about it, something he didn't understand, but the pigs were recovering.

He couldn't believe he'd almost asked her out when he first came to work here at Schultz Pharmaceuticals. She was only a few years older than him, after all. But one conversation was all it took to send him running. A fanatical vegetarian who espoused the benefits of animal testing, an eco-extremist who didn't think it mattered if the company's environmental discharges were out of specification, and a population control advocate who thought human procreation should be a capital offense. At least that last one wasn't oxymoronic.

At two o'clock he met Camille at the entrance to the huge second-floor laboratory. A researcher dashed in front of them to silence a beeping device on a glove bag. Aatos led Camille past the equipment to a lab bench near the back and handed her folder after folder. "Reagent orders, repair bills from overuse of various paraphernalia, replacements for test animals."

She scowled. "Bottom line?"

"Something funny going on. I'll get security to check on possible theft." Aatos handed her a different-colored folder. "The good news is I fixed the hogs."

"What? You neutered them?"

Aatos laughed and removed his new glasses. "No. That virus of Trinity's. No outbreak in weeks."

The apprehension left Camille's face. "Wonderful!"

"Yeah, you're in fat city. Literally." He tapped his belly, sticking it out as far as it would go.

Camille nodded. "The world is safe."

☼　☼　☼

An ambulance screamed out of the dark to the brightly lit entrance of the mid-sized urban hospital. The wailing siren sputtered to a stop. A young emergency medical technician hopped out and opened the back.

"Keep him steady," said the driver, helping the younger EMT remove a gurney. A middle-aged, tuxedo-clad man gasped through an oxygen mask, fingers gone spastic. The two technicians wheeled the patient inside.

A few minutes later, the older EMT watched through the door of the trauma bay. A nurse turned off the monitors around the blood-spattered patient and nodded to Dr. Nielsen.

Nielsen came out of the bay and removed his glasses. He tapped them on his thumb. "You know who he was?"

"Of course," said the EMT. "Picked him up from his limo."

Nielsen kept tapping. "I've seen this before." He rubbed the glasses back and forth along his thumb. "How many were exposed?"

"The whole convention, I imagine."

Nielsen tapped. And rubbed. And tapped.

And stopped tapping.

"I'm calling CDC."

CHAPTER SEVENTEEN

Fall, Year 1 to Spring, Year 2

Valerie Slotowski juggled a stack of reference books all the way from her undersized SUV to the front door of a tall, utilitarian building in Atlanta, Georgia, sitting on a half-landscaped hill appropriated two years back from its prior owners. A large sign read Centers for Disease Control and Prevention, Research Annex. The new facility didn't have security fencing and the parking lot was unpaved. Promises and excuses aplenty, but the budget had yet to fix those oversights.

Trees flashed red and orange leaves. Where had the summer gone? Valerie tried to open the top treatise in her pile and check out where her own article got placed, but reading and balancing simultaneously was challenging.

An hour later, her supervisor, Marcel Ngono, a hefty Cameroonian with a bushy mustache, hung up the phone in his small enclosed office. He stood up and shouted across the room—a cavern full of three dozen cubicles, desks, filing cabinets, and five-foot-high partitions. "Yo, Valerie! You got more work."

Valerie peered over numerous stacks of reports, two computer terminals, and thick glasses. She quit typing, shoved a thick ponytail over her shoulder, and pulled a pen from her mouth. "Oh, goodie."

☼ ☼ ☼

Grimm climbed out of an unmarked car in front of his

news service and tossed a semi-salute at the interior. SAC Chou Lee waved an empty pipe out the window and merged into traffic. Grimm trotted inside the building, galloped down a warren of halls, and pulled up in Cranbrook's office. He grinned, ignoring the other reporter lounging across from Cranbrook in an unusually sturdy guest chair.

"You gotta keep me on police work, boss."

"Drop it," said Cranbrook. "You're back on science."

Grimm opened his mouth, but shut it when the other reporter reached over and handed him a sheet of paper.

"Your contact at CDC called," said Cranbrook. "They're finally tracking my nephew's affliction. Already sent out three Epidemic Intelligence Officers."

Grimm read the note. "Disease detectives." He took a breath, held it a moment, and let it out. "Right. I'll be in touch."

Cranbrook's voice came from behind. "This could be Pulitzer material."

Grimm made a disgusted sound. He put a hand on the doorjamb. "Let's hope to hell it's not."

✧ ✧ ✧

Barren trees flashed a stunning display of ice all around Schultz Pharmaceuticals. Sunlight glittered off every pile of snow, fallen leaf, and metal pole. The perfect silence was shattered by a salt truck firing up.

Five protesters huddled near the largest of the trees. A reverend of some Protestant sect, from his collar and blue-gray robe, raised a sign reading The End is Nigh. Another sign said Biochemistry in a red circle with a red slash through it. Most of the protesters were unrecognizable in parkas and balaclavas.

A gust ripped away the tall, angular reverend's sign. He pursued, but it cartwheeled over the snow faster than he could run, even if he hadn't had to contend with all the slipping and falling.

Aatos turned from the window of the second-floor laboratory. Camille Schultz stood on a small crate across the room, regaling a dozen researchers loosely congregated before her.

"Good news," said Camille. "You missed a holiday bonus this year when the company had stock difficulties. Of course, in our case that means animals, not Wall Street."

Half the researchers appeared amused; the others remained mute. Beyond them, overfed movers loaded Aatos' DNA sequencer and enzyme production machines onto rollers and pushed them toward the doors.

"But we're past that. New contracts. Not merely breeding stock to Argentina, New Zealand, and Kenya. We've now got Malaysia, Ukraine, and Germany."

A portable television on Aatos' workbench mumbled through the weather and skipped on to sports after a commercial about pickup trucks. Next to it, Mr. Praline rubbed a foot with his beak. "Oh, fords. Pining fords."

"Fjords," murmured Aatos. "They're not cars."

"Fords. Cars," said the parrot.

"This not only funded brand-new synthesizers," Camille said, "designed of course by our very own Aatos Pires."

Double doors crashed open. A ridiculously well-timed interruption. Aatos squeezed behind a technician and darted over to check on the movers rolling in his latest inventions. Larger, shinier, more streamlined yet complex machines. One was labeled DNA/RNA Transcripter. Another, Synthesizer 1000. Clanging doors didn't really worry him; the support frames would protect his contraptions as the movers jockeyed them into position. Not that Camille appreciated his calling such expensive hardware 'contraptions.'

"Perhaps more important," said Camille, "next

paycheck you'll see those bonuses."

The researchers gave a subdued cheer and returned to work.

When Aatos got back to his bench, Mr. Praline shuffled to the side of his cage and chewed on a bar, probably meaning he was hungry. A news anchor on the TV said, "Returning to our top story, the baffling new killer disease is spreading around the globe, from China to Argentina, with no cure in sight."

Red lights flared on an animated globe, one spot after another, even in the arctic.

☼ ☼ ☼

Mud coated the countryside around Stacy Romani's gas production facility. Or possibly her Uncle Billy's, or the whole clan's, if she could convince herself of that, despite her name on all the papers. Globs of snow crouched in corners, and stiff winds whistled through naked trees. A stark beauty embraced upstate New York in winter, if you appreciated the sterile nature of it all.

Stacy trailed along the edge of the facility. Beyond the warehouses, bulldozers smashed down trees. The woods she had so enjoyed, once upon a lifetime ago. Closer in the ground was already cleared and the elongated pits of a new algae farm were going in, as pictured in Aatos' lecture. And she would never have the nerve to tell them to stop, to overrule her uncle, to blow off their contracts and promises and all the money they brought in. She thought she saw Franky a couple of buildings over, and maybe Rudy, but she wasn't in a mood to be sociable.

She didn't respond to the crunch of footsteps on the gravel path. She knew who was coming.

Half a minute later, Uncle Billy planted himself beside her. "Impressive, huh? We read those articles you sent."

"I didn't mean this." Stacy pointed at the bulldozers.

"There's more woods. Plenty of wetlands to the south. NYSDEC inspected the pit liners and we got all our permits."

"Don't be fractal." Another tree fell. "You know that's not it."

Uncle Billy scratched his nose. "Yeah. Well, then we called that Schultz place."

"And made them an offer they couldn't refuse, I imagine."

Uncle Billy chuckled. "That tackle of theirs is impressive. And these algae farms won't just make hydrocarbons."

"Don't say it."

"The competition will hate it. That's why there's more guards."

Stacy shuddered. "This isn't survival. You're way past protecting the family. This is greed."

"I prefer to call it insurance. Can't have too much of that."

"Can't you limit your products?" She could hear the pleading in her voice and hated not being able to block it. "There's plenty of money in the university trade. We don't need to risk making the..."

"Dangerous stuff? We can handle it."

Stacy took a deep breath. She lifted one hand toward the new farms, waved a finger, then let it drop. "I can't."

"Can't what?"

"No more free gear," said Stacy. "No more 'research grants.'"

"You need—"

"I can't take money from this!"

She strode through the middle of the complex toward the parking area, speeding up every step. Uncle Billy followed, quelling with a look every worker who acted the least bit curious. She raced out the gate and opened her car door, taking in the factory one last time.

"I love you. All you guys. My family." Stacy held her stomach. "I'll sign financial things. I'll review your specs, keep your products safe." And then, at last, she made eye contact with Uncle Billy. "But I won't come back here. I can't."

She got into the same clunker she'd been nursing along for years, dug her nails into the steering wheel, and drove off, shunning the rearview mirror until she was miles away.

☼ ☼ ☼

A farmer limped from behind a hillock at the edge of a small Peruvian village, legs quivering. "Help me," he whispered, "help me." He tottered into the middle of the street near a fountain with a pitted marble Madonna. "Doctor." He dropped his walking stick, hands twitching.

A street vendor screamed, scooped up a handful of her scarves, and backed away. A withered old man pointed and yelled: "Plague." He stumbled over the rough cobblestones with his cane. A younger man helped him. Two women snatched their children's arms and pulled them toward a church. A tourist dropped his camera, grabbed a pole, and poked at the farmer, keeping him away.

The farmer fell on the stones, arms and legs convulsing. A militiaman ran up. Blood erupted from the farmer's ears; he twitched faster and faster, rolling in the dust. The militiaman unlimbered his rifle. One sharp crack, and the farmer went still.

A few locals came out of a nearby tavern. One man pushed through the other people. "Ric? Rico?" He took a step closer to the body and whispered, "Ricardo?"

"Gasolina!" yelled the militiaman, shooing him off. "Dangerous. Dangerous." His voice caught. He swallowed once and tried again. "Get gasolina!"

CHAPTER EIGHTEEN

Spring, Year 2 to Summer, Year 2

Forsythia and daffodils burst around the periphery of Franklin Liberation Memorial Park, a plot of land barely larger than its name. Less than an acre. A pair of eight-year-olds splashed in the fountain, oblivious to the temperature, while their parents read on a bench nearby. Three dogs who could not possibly have a single gene in common cavorted in the water with the children.

Stacy couldn't get enough of the image. She strolled along a cinder path beside Professor Sturdevan. "I need to go off-campus more often. I never knew this place existed."

"Told you so." Sturdevan inhaled until he had to unzip his jacket, and touched the odd petal, here a late crocus, there a dogwood blossom. "That immunology work you're doing is Nobel quality. You need to publish again."

They rambled a few more paces.

"It is kind of unique, isn't it?" said Stacy.

"Cracking the body's database of 'safe proteins' so organ transplants are never rejected? Gee, let me think."

Stacy smiled. "Okay. I'll present my other paper, then go full tilt on this one."

They reached the end of the park. Stacy took the professor's elbow and forced him into a U-turn, so they could wander through it again.

☼ ☼ ☼

Grimm juggled a stapler, tape dispenser, and pair of

scissors in Cranbrook's office. He caught them once or twice and scooped them off the floor the rest of the time.

"Dammit, it's a plague," he said.

Cranbrook pored over a proof sheet, marking words, slashing out copy, and circling items. "CDC, World Health Organization, and the U.N. haven't classified it yet."

"Since when do we care what experts think?"

Cranbrook made a *wigett* expression. *Well, I guess that's true.* Grimm fumbled the stapler and scissors onto the desk. He nudged the tape dispenser out of sight with his toe.

Cranbrook shifted in his new easy chair. It seemed the most uncomfortable thing he'd tried so far. Too low, if nothing else. "Anything more on the drug front?"

Grimm shrugged. "Couple shootings. And the new stuff is designer shit."

Cranbrook kept marking copy, so Grimm left. At this rate he'd retire before he got out of the science business. Where was a good police chase when you needed one?

✿ ✿ ✿

In the middle of a fluorescent-filled, eighty-foot square CDC laboratory, Valerie focused a microscope. She raised her head, popped off her stool, put on glasses, and dashed over to pull one printout from a mass spectrometer and another from a gas chromatograph. She opened a small glass door on the latter and flicked the needle on the graph paper. It flopped down.

She tapped a pencil against her teeth, let out a breath, and shook her head. Her cell phone alarmed. She checked the wall clock, swore, and chased out the door.

Valerie emerged from the building into swirling fog, went to the nearest parking lot, and stationed herself at a spot marked for M. Ngono. She rocked from foot to foot, shivering, twisting a diamond engagement ring on her finger while she waited for her supervisor. About the twelfth time she checked her watch, Ngono pulled into the space she was standing in. She backed into a bush. He barely stopped before she jumped out and opened his door.

"The data are plain weird," said Valerie. "Maybe it's me." She handed him a folder on their way to the building.

"I got everything you emailed up to thirty minutes ago," said Ngono, "and two voice mails. That's it so far?"

"Yeah."

"How many victims have you checked?"

"Over a thousand. Everyone we've got samples on," she said. "Blood, marrow, liver. I stole a few technicians to help me."

Ngono shuffled through the folder. Photo after color photo of contorted victims showed a consistent pattern of twisted limbs, uncontrollable fingers, and blood showering from eardrums.

"Some nosebleeds," said Valerie, "but not many. I'd have expected more, with all the spuming from ears."

"That could help ID patients. Nothing wrong with idiosyncratic features."

"But useless for finding the cause of the problem."

They pushed past a couple of other people, entered the building, and stormed down the hall.

"Maybe you can see something in the spectra," said Valerie. "I can't."

"Nothing?"

"Oh, killer reverse transcriptase, making DNA out of the viral RNA and immune to everything we've tried. Except stuff that kills the whole cell."

Ngono waited a second. "And?"

"A pea-soup of nasty proteins, destroying mitochondria and starving every cell."

"But what's the source?"

"That's just it," said Valerie. "There is none. All the

normal bugs are there. E. coli, a dozen flu varieties, reaction to bad food."

"Over a thousand patients and nothing ties them together?"

"Except not a one has anything unusual."

They crashed through a door labeled Pathogenesis.

☼　☼　☼

Eight protesters marched in an oval outside the main entrance of Schultz Pharmaceuticals. The reverend's battered sign still read The End is Nigh. A second sign said Humanity Sucks, and another, Plague 1000, Biogenetics 0.

Trinity Schultz came out of the building with two of her associates. The protesters came at them, brandishing their signs like weapons. The associates hurried toward the parking lot. Trinity followed, then stopped when she saw her mother driving in.

"Retribution is at hand!" yelled the reverend.

Trinity twiddled her fingers at the reverend. He held back another protester and all eight reestablished their oval demonstration outside the building. Trinity rejoined the associates.

Camille got out of her car, nodded thanks at Trinity, and went inside.

☼　☼　☼

Upstairs in the main lab, Aatos slammed a *Handbook of Chemistry and Physics* on the bench and went to a bookcase to get another volume. It took a lot of oversized references to sag the metal shelves, and once Aatos worried enough to insert slabs of wood halfway along each shelf to prop them up. Today, though, he knocked the wood aside when it got in the way of something he needed.

Camille inspected the laboratory from the doorway, a daily habit everyone watched for. Maybe she did it to gauge efficiency, or progress on the various tasks, but most people figured she wanted to see if they were busy, so they put on a show. Aatos never understood people who only worked to pay the bills and goofed off half the time. Chemistry was an adventure, not a chore. Either that or they were normal, and he was the one who wasn't, but that didn't sound likely. And why did it bother him today?

When he dropped a thick copy of the *Journal of the American Chemical Society* on top of a *Handbook of Biochemistry and Molecular Biology,* from a height of fourteen inches, that proved too much for Camille to ignore. "Problem?" she said, when she got near.

"CDC won't hire me," said Aatos.

"You're job hunting?"

"Not anymore. They won't touch anyone who's worked for you. They claim you 'steal information for commercial gain.'" Aatos kept slamming books around and ransacking their indexes.

"So what's all this?"

"That new epidemic, or whatever it's turning into. They're out of their depth."

"You're wasting my money on a minor human disease?"

"I've got a clue," said Aatos. "They don't. And it won't stay minor."

"I did not authorize—"

"Call it an investment. If I succeed, you'll make a bloody fortune."

Camille's anger blurred, transforming into speculation. Aatos pulled two more manuals off a shelf, opened one, and lost himself in it. A background clatter rose as the other researchers returned to work. Camille must have given them her attention.

✼ ✼ ✼

Heat shimmered off the asphalt pavement outside the

Clingman's Dome Conference Center. Shirtless kids skateboarded past the entrance, weaving among all the suits. Today, 'suits' again included Stacy. She was getting rather used to this, which could well horrify Uncle Billy if he learned of it. It wasn't exactly low profile. At least she never let any of the other attendees hit on her; that would really fry his bacon. Not that she was saving herself for some obscure cousin someday. She'd never met a single one of them she had anything in common with. So unless she could figure out a way to transmute Aatos Pires into an honorary Roma, she'd have to be content with the pleasures of solitude.

Good grief, what had made her think of him? Oh, right, this conference center. Stacy pulled out her notes and forced herself to review her speech again.

In the cool auditorium sometime later, Stacy finished delivering her latest paper with a flourish of an arm at the screen. A spiky green blob surrounded and almost obscured a yellow, equally spiky blob. Scientists clapped.

After answering a smattering of questions and shaking herself free of other attendees, Stacy started up the aisle. On stage, Trinity Schultz flashed a laser pointer at a title on the screen: Despeciation.

"The eradication of an entire species," said Trinity. "Nature does it. So do humans."

Stacy smiled at Professor Sturdevan and two graybeards as she passed them.

"Let me play devil's advocate," said Trinity. "Are there not species so purposeless or dangerous, the world would be better off without them?"

A woman popped out of a seat and blocked Stacy at the door. "Valerie Slotowski, CDC. Oh, wait." Valerie lifted her right hand a centimeter. She seemed surprised when a heavy briefcase dragged it back down. She stuffed folders from her left hand under her right armpit and wrestled a wallet from a right-hand pocket, so she could flash her ID. "Liked your paper on phospho-apatase-D."

"Thank you."

Beyond them, Trinity's voice swept over the audience. "*How can nature fail to make the occasional mistake?*"

Valerie put away her wallet and pointed at Stacy's briefcase. "This one was okay. Not as deep."

"Um, thanks again?"

Lights flickered as Trinity's slides changed. "*I know, you're thinking smallpox.*"

"We've got a problem," said Valerie. "You're one of the best in the field."

Stacy put out a hand. "Pleased to meet you."

"Oh. Yes. Hello." Valerie shoved her glasses up her nose and shook Stacy's hand.

"*But go beyond smallpox,*" came Trinity's voice. "*Perhaps there are others.*"

"Nice rings," said Stacy. A wedding band nestled against Valerie's engagement ring. "Let's go outside."

Valerie nodded and followed Stacy through the double doors.

✿ ✿ ✿

Stacy and Valerie squinted when they reached the sidewalk. They donned sunglasses and sidestepped skateboarders.

"...and AIDS attacks T-lymphocytes, yes?" said Stacy, continuing a discussion that had trailed through lobbies, hallways, two elevators, and a restroom. This woman was fun to talk to. Sharp as a shark's tooth.

"And other cells," Valerie said. "It inhibits the immune system meant to fight it."

"Right. So what's the issue?"

"This new pandemic."

Stacy stopped walking.

"Yeah, it's a plague," said Valerie. "Can't control it, no idea how it's spreading, and one hundred percent fatal so far."

Dragging steps resumed.

"Guess I was hoping the press was out of control again."

"Those videos on television? Fits, seizures, and enough gore for a Torquemada movie? Sorry, all accurate."

"Ouch."

"Yeah, and here's the rub," said Valerie. "This doesn't inhibit the immune system. It eats it."

Stacy stopped again.

"Actively seeks out lymphocytes. Uses them for parts to spread itself." Valerie looked to the side, realized Stacy had stopped, and walked back. "This is to AIDS what AIDS is to flu. And flu can—"

Valerie stared into the distance.

"So you want me to think of ideas," said Stacy. "A way to stimulate an immunological response that can survive an attack."

"Flu. No, it couldn't be."

"Hello?"

"Oh God, if that's true..."

Stacy waited for more, but it never came. "Are you all right?"

Valerie took off down the sidewalk. "Thanks for the help. Later."

So was she supposed to do something, or not? What a strange woman.

CHAPTER NINETEEN

Fall, Year 2

"As you can see," said a television anchor, "a mere smattering of people dot the sidewalks, and Christmas decorations are at a record low along this multilane avenue, deep in the lungs of the city. The traffic is so light you'd think the place had emphysema." Available parking spaces abounded, a rarity no one remarked on. One in every five store fronts was boarded up or covered with metal gratings, despite the fact the holiday shopping season should be in full swing.

Parents pulled children close, and tight family clusters drifted along, widely spaced islands on a sea of concrete.

A boy touched a dead flower in a cast-iron vase. His mother gripped his hand. "No. You could get infected."

☼ ☼ ☼

Grimm perched on the corner of his editor's desk. Cranbrook fiddled with a TV mounted on the wall opposite. On the grainy screen, people rushed along the city street. The mother hauled her boy away from the cast-iron vase.

"Lungs?" said Grimm. "Emphysema? What moron wrote that?"

The anchor's voice continued: "Cases of Random Immune Assault Syndrome, or RIAS, have shot up the past two months, from hundreds to thousands."

The TV switched to a graph showing an exponentially rising curve. The image wavered worse than the chairs in

Cranbrook's office. "Panic isolationism isn't limited to the individual level. Governments are forbidding travel and embargoing trade."

Cranbrook slapped the side of the TV. The image cleared, then went even more haywire.

"The World Health Organization, and multiple national groups like CDC in Atlanta, are at a loss."

Cranbrook snapped off the video. "Nice copy. That'll keep the panic going."

"True, though," said Grimm.

"So get your ass out there and make them find a cure."

Grimm laughed and got up. "Wouldn't it be cool if the press really could manufacture news?"

"Yeah, spiffy cool," Cranbrook muttered, slamming the door behind Grimm.

✿　✿　✿

Aatos pored through computer logs of equipment usage, spread across the expanse of a laboratory workbench. He compared handwritten ledgers showing operational times of 2 a.m., 3 a.m., 4 a.m. Scribbled notes filled his sink.

He stuck out a leg to halt a passing lab assistant. "How come Trinity is never around days, anymore?"

"She avoids you. Calls you the Evil Designer."

"Where'd she come up with that? I'm the one with the cures."

"Hey," said the young woman, pushing down his leg with her clipboard, "I just work here."

Aatos snapped up loose papers and crushed them into wads. "I need her help to figure this thing out."

The lab assistant shrugged. "Trinity is heir apparent. She does what she likes."

Aatos glared as she scuttled away. He couldn't believe what a child she was. How could they let people out of college at that age? When he got his baccalaureate, he was a mature, sophisticated adult. At least, it had felt that way. This couldn't be the first sign of aging, could it? Maybe that's why he wasn't dating anymore. It had nothing to do with obsessing over memories of Stacy Romani. It had everything to do with younger women being children and mature women being too old. That was it.

What was that faint, scratchy alarm in the back of his brain?

Aatos dragged his mind back to the problem. No Trinity. No help. What he needed was someone like Stacy. For research, that is. Research. Was that when he stopped dating, after he'd run into Stacy again at that conference? No, there was no correlation between those two data points. Or not much. A one-to-one correspondence, possibly. After all, how many women were that smart and that pretty and that nice?

And that thoroughly, unapproachably distant, when you came down to it.

Never mind. Get to work. No more daydreaming.

✧　✧　✧

Ngono shook distinguished old Commissioner Zelog's hand outside CDC headquarters, and Zelog's aide helped the commissioner into a black, unmarked limousine. As soon as they were gone, Ngono hastened inside and barged into Valerie's lab. A couple of researchers moved aside as he made his way between the benches, to where Valerie was poking a vial back and forth with an empty pipette.

Ngono stomped over to her. "The Commissioner's getting heat."

"That's nice." Valerie shoved away the vial. She set down the pipette and hunched her shoulders.

"What's wrong?"

Valerie rolled the pipette left and right, then aligned it

with the edge of the lab bench.

"Valerie?"

She flicked the pipette, sending it rolling across the bench, and slouched on her stool. "Is denial an acceptable scientific methodology?"

Ngono reached for her notebook and flipped through the latest few pages.

"It's not in there yet," said Valerie. She peeled herself off the stool and led Ngono to a machine in the corner. "Watch this."

She turned on the device and adjusted a few settings, then pointed at a screen. An image of a virus appeared. It rotated, and the coating opened as if hinged, revealing a grayish mass inside.

"Let's ignore the guts for a moment." Valerie hit a button, and the grayish mass disappeared. "Then characterize what's left."

A complicated spectrograph replaced the viral image, about a hundred and fifty peaks of various heights streaming from left to right in bright red.

"There. That's our capsid, our viral coat." She punched a few keys. Another complicated plot joined the first on the graph, this time in green. It matched the red jagged line, except it had a few extra peaks. "And that's the Sumatran flu coating. A benign beast."

Ngono leaned forward. "That's why you called me." He studied the display, then absently hooked a toe around the foot of a stool, drew it over, and dropped down. "You know what this means. Hence the denial."

"Coatings unique as retinal scans," said Valerie. "This baby's man-made."

"With the spiky parts cut off. No immune response."

Valerie traced her finger across the matching green and red. "Someone stuffed a new toy into an old box."

Ngono pulled out his cell phone. "Somebody doesn't

like us."

☼ ☼ ☼

Grimm took a deep breath, trying not to pant. Chou Lee stalked down the sidewalk toward the local FBI building, slipping between other pedestrians, and Grimm needed extra steps to keep up, partly because he was dodging sideways all the time, taking the long way around when Chou Lee's gap in the crowd closed up too quickly.

"You think the FBI will take this one over?" said Grimm.

Chou Lee brandished the stem of his unlit pipe. "Got to. It's too deadly. Homeland Security may stick their nose in too."

They headed inside to Chou Lee's extravagant but cramped office. The same one Grimm had investigated a few months back. Mahogany furniture, crystal desk lights, and gold-framed oils on the walls were so grossly outside the Federal GSA purchasing catalog, even for senior executives, that Chou Lee had clearly done his own decorating, and there had never been an excuse for that Sniffer Dog nonsense. Chou Lee offered Grimm coffee in a china cup. Grimm took it and plunked down in what was not so much a chair as a small leather throne. It smelled new.

Chou Lee sat behind the desk. "Two different cartels pissed off about a 'tio' something. More shootings. And more drugs on the street than ever."

"Still designer stuff?"

"Over half of it. There's never been a lab capable of a fraction of that output."

Grimm pulled out a lighter and snapped it on. "No glimmer where it's coming from? And you want me to print that?"

Chou Lee glared at the flame. "Goddamn it!" He flung

his pipe across the room. "The public can help us find these guys. Call us idiots for all I care if it helps nail 'em."

The phone rang. Chou Lee answered and listened patiently for almost a whole second. "I don't have time for medical mysteries. I've got a—" He listened some more, then sat up straight. "BT Event? Yeah, yeah, bioterrorism. How the hell do you know that?"

✧　✧　✧

"Because every intermolecular bond vibrates at a different frequency," said Valerie. She and Ngono stood by her computer. The image hadn't changed; it still held the red and green viral coating spectra. Chou Lee studied the display while Grimm hovered in the rear.

Valerie traced the jagged lines with a finger. "You know how if you drive an old clunker, sometimes it vibrates like mad at, say, forty-seven miles an hour, but stops at fifty?"

Chou Lee nodded.

"Resonance. Same for chemical bonds." She hit some keys, separating the peaks by a fraction of an inch, then merging them again to highlight not their similarity, but their identical nature. "Same fingerprint. Same chemicals. It's not natural; it's artificial."

"Wait," said Chou Lee. "Doesn't that mean the plague is a variation of the flu?"

Valerie shook her head. She hit more keys, and the spectra were replaced by a complex, twisty RNA. "Another thing. Here's our RNA." She kept typing. Another chemical shaped up on the screen. It wound around the RNA, aligning perfectly, creating a smooth, single body. "That's the protector protein to keep the RNA in shape, to minimize mutations."

"So?"

"Viruses don't have protector proteins like this, inside their shells," said Ngono. "That's why they mutate all the time. Even if this was something new, like we first thought—" He leaned forward and pointed along the length. "—it's too perfect. Nature never is, especially for a mere virus."

"I wouldn't call this one 'mere.'"

"Maybe that's the good news," said Valerie. "This thing won't evolve fast, so when we find a solution, we won't be facing a host of variants."

Chou Lee rubbed his jaw. "But you're saying..."

"Man-made," said Ngono. "Somebody attacked us."

Grimm grabbed the doorframe. "Can you contain it now?"

Valerie grimaced.

"It's airborne and widely spread," said Ngono. "No symptoms until it goes fatal. And we can't find it without a lab like this to take apart samples."

Grimm looked at Chou Lee. "Terrorists? Or the Columbians?"

"If Columbians could do this, they'd make designer drugs. Not get pissed off about not selling the natural stuff."

Grimm huffed a couple of times, in confusion or frustration. Either way, he gave up after barely a second and left, slamming the door.

Chou Lee hesitated. He knew what he ought to do, by procedure. He was under the Criminal Investigative Division, and he ought to hand this off to Counterterrorism. But he knew what would happen. He was agent on scene, everyone was strapped for manpower, and the powers-that-be would second him to Counterterrorism and tell him to handle it.

The bean counters could straighten out the paperwork later. For now, Chou Lee pulled out a notepad.

"So," he said, rubbing his cheek with the point of a stylus, "who *is* able to make stuff like this?"

CHAPTER TWENTY

Winter, Year 3

Forty acres of algae farms surrounded the original ten acres of the Romani gas production facility. The bulldozers were gone, and construction was complete. Piping crisscrossed the area, with netting to keep out birds. Near the periphery, a pair of workers yelled directions to a third in a cherry-picker navigating alongside the last of the new power lines.

Stacy stood beside Uncle Billy, counting the ponds, taking it all in. Her uncle remained silent. Production was clearly underway on whatever products he needed this week. Stacy kicked a small pile of snow, scattering it across the road. A lone crow cried defiance at the winter.

Two EMTs emerged from a building, manhandling a gurney over the gravel path. A bloody sheet hid the occupant. Rudy and Theresa followed them out and stayed by the door. Theresa's shoulders quivered. Stacy didn't expect it was from the cold.

After a long minute, Uncle Billy said, "Thanks for coming."

Stacy scuffed her shoe. "I wish I'd been in time."

"Franky knew you were trying."

"He's... he was only a year older than me." Of all the cousins who'd hit on her over the years, he was the shyest, the nicest. She made the EMTs pause and put a hand on a clean part of the sheet. She hadn't broken down yet, but it was coming. She could feel it down there, building. Why did she need to hide it in front of her relatives? All she could think was, let me make it home first. Let me cry in peace.

The EMTs continued on. They reached the ambulance and put the gurney inside. Rudy stepped toward her, but Theresa took his arm and pulled him inside.

Uncle Billy scratched his temple. "You know anything about that pandemic?"

"You said it was food poisoning."

"EMTs think otherwise. They said we're lucky he was our first."

"That's... oh. I get it." The EMTs slammed the back door of the ambulance and got in the front. "It's worse than the bubonic plague in the fourteenth century," she said. The ambulance drove off, out the gate and down the road, shrinking, fading against the gaunt trunks of trees until it disappeared around a curve.

"Guess this really is your last visit," said Uncle Billy. "Don't come back."

Stacy put a hand on his arm. "Thanks. But it's everywhere."

Uncle Billy nodded. He laid a hand on hers and squeezed it gently.

✿ ✿ ✿

Outside Schultz Pharmaceuticals, the reverend and a dozen other protesters carried new signs in their mittened or heavily gloved hands: Biogenetics = Devil Worship, Mankind Will be Judged, The Price of Arrogance, and Plague is Our Retribution. An unmarked black van pulled onto the shoulder of the access road, short of the parking lot. Binoculars glinted through the windshield, pointing toward the protesters. Inside, Chou Lee sat beside the driver, Agent Nadya, a dark-haired Slavic woman serving as liaison from Homeland Security.

Chou Lee lowered the binoculars. "Interesting protesters, Nadya."

"Why here, Charlie?" she said. "None elsewhere. We've been three places. Our people, a dozen more."

"It's Chou Lee. Good question."

"That's what I said. Call for backup?"

Chou Lee patted his pockets. Nadya handed him an empty pipe.

"Probably should." He got out. "Let's walk from here. Don't want to be stuck in a van near that group." He shoved the door closed and started up the road.

Nadya punched one more digit into her half-dialed cell phone. Chou Lee was getting away. She slid the phone into its case and caught up.

✿ ✿ ✿

In the second-floor laboratory of Schultz, Aatos slid a finger across ledger entries and a computer screen. "Did you tell Trinity to make another killer virus?"

Camille Schultz tossed a folder on the desk. "Not after the hog fiasco. She's doing research for publication."

"This much? You see the cost for animals and reagents? Log time on the machines?"

"She said it was you, wasting time on plague research."

Aatos couldn't think how to respond to such a flagrant lie.

Camille went to the window. "I don't know who's doing what, but I've half a mind to... Oh, crap, now she's talking to those people." She pounded out the door.

"The protesters?" Aatos checked the window. Sure enough, there was Trinity among the signs, near some tall, bony guy in a religious collar.

The door clicked shut. Aatos shrugged and returned to the lab bench. He sorted through Trinity's printouts and handwritten notes. One word, retribution, appeared repeatedly. He went to another computer and entered the standard company activation code. The screen lit up with a spinning viral particle. A nasty, spiky mass. A legend read 'Hog-Human Prototype 178-B.' He typed 'Trinity' under 'restricted user ID' and moused to the password line. His fingers hammered the keyboard: 'retribution.' The screen dissolved to blackness.

Aatos grinned. "Finally."

A new screen flared open, titled 'Project Trinity' in crimson letters, with a picture of the 1945 Alamogordo, New Mexico atomic bomb explosion in the background. Aatos paused at the mushroom cloud before he noticed small print shooting across the bottom of the monitor: 'Project Trinity Security System: secondary password:___.' A 30-second timer appeared next to the underline and started counting down.

Aatos could see the whites of his eyes reflected in the screen, growing large, full of nothing. Not one single idea.

✧ ✧ ✧

Outside, Chou Lee crammed his pipe in a pocket. He blew on his fingers and stuffed them in his pockets as well. "Beautiful day, Agent Nadya."

Nadya removed the sunglasses from the top of her head and put them on. "Too much mud. Better when it's colder."

"You are so Russian."

Nadya shivered and pulled her coat tight. "Not really."

They walked up the drive toward the building. Camille Schultz banged out the front door and headed for the protesters. One of them heaved a sign at Camille. Another pointed at Chou Lee and Nadya and yelled.

"Hey, wow, the cops finally figured it out."

Nadya started jogging. Chou Lee lengthened his stride.

✧ ✧ ✧

Aatos typed and hit Enter, over and over. 'God,' 'justice,' 'Satan.' The on-screen countdown continued.

He pawed through Trinity's papers again, flinging one after another to the floor. A pair of words caught his attention, and he pounded the keyboard. 'Cleanse,' 'rebirth.'

No reaction. 'Despeciation.' Nothing. He swore, soft and eloquent.

✢ ✢ ✢

Camille marched up to Trinity. "I told you these people were poison."

The reverend stuck his sign between them. "Thou shalt not—"

Camille batted away the sign. The reverend pouted.

Trinity lifted her chin in proud defiance. "They are the Way!" she shouted. "And I am their Instrument."

"You're the what?"

Chou Lee and Nadya hurried closer.

"It's time the truth came out. Thanks to the Evil Designer, the earth shall be purged." The protesters flourished their signs and cheered Trinity's words.

Camille spun toward the building. "What is he doing?" The reverend smirked. The other protesters did their best impression of righteous.

"Whatever it is, it's too late," said Trinity.

Camille looked at Trinity, then at the second-floor window. Confusion creased her forehead.

✢ ✢ ✢

Upstairs, Aatos kept typing. Pointless, useless typing. The countdown reached zero. He glanced at the wall outlet, but there was nothing there, nothing to unplug before it was too late.

The computer screen blanked, then flashed a single line: 'Files Erased. Project Terminated.'

☼ ☼ ☼

Chou Lee and Nadya pushed through the group in front of the Schultz building and flashed their ID badges. The protesters were slow to give way. Nadya broke one of their signs; that helped.

Chou Lee's attention slid over Trinity, reflected off the reverend, and centered on Camille. "Ma'am, are you in charge?"

"Stand firm, my child," said the reverend.

Camille moved forward. "Yes, I am."

"Not anymore," said Trinity.

A window squealed open on the second floor. A man leaned out and shouted. "She made a virus. Files gone."

Camille's jaw dropped.

Nadya pointed upward. "He the evil designer?"

Trinity leered. "Not *a* virus. *The* virus!"

"When a scourge brings sudden death, God mocks the despair of the innocent," cried the reverend. "Job 9:23."

Camille whispered, "The plague."

Trinity yanked a revolver from her bag and held it aloft. Chou Lee and Nadya drew their own guns and held them low.

Trinity laughed. "So little you know."

Chou Lee circled the group. Nadya kept an eye out for more weapons.

"You hired me to help, Mommy."

Nadya said, "I thought that guy up there was the designer?"

"You mean Aatos?" Camille staggered back. "Him too?"

"She's gotta have backup files," said Aatos.

Trinity twisted around, twitching her gun. Chou Lee eased sideways.

"But I was never meant to heal."

"Trinity!" said her mother.

"Put it down, miss," said Chou Lee, from opposite Camille.

"My purpose is to cleanse."

Nadya squatted, getting a safe angle up at Trinity.

Aatos yelled. "Don't shoot."

Nadya's aim didn't budge. "I am disinclined to heed that advice."

"We need what she knows." Aatos kept disappearing from the window, then reappearing, as if he wanted to flee but couldn't make up his mind.

"Hold your fire," said Chou Lee.

"Humanity will pay for its hubris."

"Trinity!" said Camille again.

"Starting with him." Trinity swung around and aimed up at Aatos. A crack echoed off the wall of the building. Aatos flew back from the window.

Everyone froze.

Trinity collapsed. Blood pooled beneath her chest. Camille screamed and leapt to stem the bleeding. Chou Lee kicked away Trinity's gun.

Nadya lowered her own, smoking gun. "You think she had a cure?"

"You nuts?" said Chou Lee. "Seal it off. Find that designer guy."

Nadya held her gun hand close, pointed up, and flicked her finger at the protesters. They cowered, creeping around Trinity's body. Nadya herded them toward the building.

Chou Lee helped Camille staunch Trinity's bleeding.

"I've got it," said Camille. "Call for help."

Chou Lee freed one hand and punched his cell phone.

✿ ✿ ✿

One story up, Aatos scrambled off the floor. The police were coming. Thanks to Trinity, they thought he had something to do with the virus. She tried to shoot him to shut him up, they'd think, as if he might break under pressure. And he was the only one who had ever cleaned up her messes. Where the hell could he go to work on this one?

He grabbed printouts, shoved CDs and a picture of his parents under an arm, and tossed a thick, double-folded blanket over Mr. Praline's cage. The parrot squawked a protest.

He picked up the cage and raced out the door.

CHAPTER TWENTY-ONE

Winter, Year 3

Grimm entered Cranbrook's office and watched him beat on his TV. The plaster around the wall mounts crumbled, releasing a musty scent.

"Your story's on," said Cranbrook, pushing in a piece of loose plaster.

Scratchy, incomprehensible voices mixed with static. The sound gradually cleared; Cranbrook kept playing with the picture. An anchor's voice said, "—same outer coat as the Sumatran flu. Hence, it is practically undetectable. When asked what that means—"

A burst of static heralded the arrival of a crystal-sharp picture of the virus.

"Rather have the sound," said Grimm.

Cranbrook glared and readjusted. The picture went crazy.

"—origin to Schultz Pharmaceuticals. The owner and employees have been taken into custody. CDC hopes their records will lead to a cure, but—"

Static blared and the picture cleared again, showing CDC Headquarters.

✵ ✵ ✵

Aatos skulked through a dark alley past a variety of trash cans, dumpsters, and two squalling cats, to the back of his townhouse. In one arm, he clutched printouts, CDs, and his parents' photograph. He set down his birdcage, pulled out a key, and fumbled it toward the door. One of the CDs slid off into a bush. Better not be his Big Band Era collection; he didn't have time to go fishing for it.

A flashlight beamed inside. Aatos snatched back the key. Through the side window, two men—they had to be FBI agents—mauled his books and papers.

Aatos lifted the cage and slunk to the alley.

There was one place left to go. He might not be welcome. He had no slightest reason to believe he would be, especially if the police wanted him. But he had to try. It was that or sit around and watch the epidemic go ballistic.

☼ ☼ ☼

A computer monitor glowed in Stacy's university laboratory, granting her a rather ghoulish cast when she caught her reflection. She sat on a stool by her lab bench, chin in hand. Her other hand tapped a computer mouse, over and over.

Around her, the thirty-by-forty-foot laboratory was swallowed in shadow. At one end, bookcases made a nook filled with two desks and three computers. The main expanse included a variety of chromatographs, centrifuges, analytical balances, and rows of sinks with vacuum lines, gas outlets for Bunsen burners, and the computer Stacy was currently using. Or, if she felt like being accurate, the computer she was currently *not* using, thanks to a lack of inspiration.

The door opened. Professor Sturdevan stuck his head inside. "It's night, Stacy. Customary to turn on a light."

"I'm coming." She didn't move. Her thoughts skittered from one piece of equipment to another, from one text to another, slippery as hot grease on icebergs.

Sturdevan tried again. "You have a pet."

Stacy's brain stored the comment without processing it. "I have a pet."

"Didn't know you had a dog."

"I have a..." Stacy raised her head. Something about that seemed to require attention. "A dog?"

The professor waved a hand at the gloom. "A black lab."

Stacy made a disparaging noise.

Sturdevan chuckled and lit up the room. "Pondering evolution?"

"Evolve. Change?" Her eyes glazed over again. "Slow. What if it's survival of the species?"

"Stacy? You sick?"

"What?" Stacy clawed out a handful of awareness, then another. "Oh. No. Not me."

"I see," said Sturdevan. "A hundred thousand others."

Stacy nodded. "CDC needs a new biosafety level. They only go up to BSL-4, for smallpox."

"What are you thinking? Skip over five and call this six?"

"Maybe. Or two-pi, full circle for the human race."

"Well, I won't tell you to rest. Or take it easy. If you got any ideas, work your friggin' ass off."

Stacy smiled. You could always count on the prof's bedside manner. "Aye, eyesore," she said, perfectly content to descend to his level of humor.

Sturdevan grinned and left. Stacy dropped her chin onto her palm. She drummed a pen, then flung it down and slid over a bright red plastic pencil case. She slipped open the cover.

A tapping roused her. Stacy slammed the cover and shoved the case away. "Forget something?"

The door cracked a fraction, a hair more, then popped the rest of the way. Aatos sidled in and shut it. He dumped his papers on a stool.

Stacy gaped at him. "You!" God, yes, of course it was Aatos. Stupid thing to say. But he couldn't be the monster the news portrayed. "What are you doing here?"

"I need your stuff," said Aatos. "For that matter, I need you."

"You've been on TV."

"Yeah, that figures."

"Did you help that woman?"

"No!"

Stacy narrowed her eyes.

Aatos fidgeted. He cleared his throat. "She used my synthesizer. My computer modeling. My designs. And I taught her everything."

"Ah. That's not helping."

Aatos jammed the CDs and picture on the papers, cleared a space on a bench, and set down his birdcage. His finger caught the edge of the blanket, whipping it off the cage and onto the stool. The photo clattered to the floor and came to rest by Stacy's foot. "I don't see how the inventor of a medicine is responsible when someone's killed with an overdose."

Stacy couldn't move. Aatos was right here. Spouting metaphors. "Okay, maybe not. But—"

"We can debate guilt later," said Aatos. "Right now, you've got the equipment we need to figure out what's going on."

Right here in front of her. And he wasn't going away. "We're supposed to call the FBI if we see you."

"You know that won't help," Aatos said. "We have to stop the plague."

"We?"

"CDC doesn't have the expertise."

"Us?"

"I'm the best in the world at design and synthesis. You're damn near best at theory. Immunology."

"You and I?"

"We can do this." Aatos waited, watching her. "You said

you owed me."

And then he stood there. He'd apparently shot his wad, fired his bolt, and completed half a dozen other clichés, if she could remember what they were.

Mr. Praline scraped at a piece of cuttlebone. "Owed. Eau de fjord."

Stacy had no idea how to react. She closed her eyes and massaged her temples. Owed him. Right. That was hardly the point. At least, she didn't want it to be the point. The point was: Aatos. If it were anyone but him, she could do the right thing and turn him in. If he were anyone but Aatos, she would never consider the possibility they could pull off a research project of such a magnitude. Solving the plague, just the two of them. Insanity.

Except she'd solved a minor one, once, and she knew tons more now than when she was a kid. And Aatos had long since proven his genius. Who else in the world had a better shot? So maybe they could.

Even his parents joined the plea, laying there by her instep, hugging. His father in comfortable sweats, his mother in a silk party dress; a male fantasy if she ever saw one. And what did they know about science, anyway? Why were they siding with Aatos? Which was her silly imagination butting in, stamping reality on a picture, for goodness sake.

The thing was, Aatos had a point, even if he hadn't spelled it out. If she didn't help him, if the police found him, his knowledge would go to waste, and all humanity would suffer. It didn't matter how little chance they had, how unlikely a cure might be. Any effort, however long the odds, should be attempted.

Stacy took about as deep a breath as she'd ever taken in her life. And then she took another.

"We give CDC everything," she said at last, "as soon as we have it."

"Can't," said Aatos. "Anything from us, they'd have to verify. They'd tear your lab apart and we'd never make it to the next step."

"An independent effort? Not efficient."

"If they do anything on their own, fine. Call us backup."

Stacy kept rubbing her temples.

Aatos listened at the door, peeked out, then shut it again. "What else you got to do?"

Stacy turned to her computer screen: 'Controlled Immune Response: Updating the Database.' The research project Professor Sturdevan thought would win her a Nobel.

She sighed and clicked it off.

CHAPTER TWENTY-TWO

Winter, Year 3

Outside the local FBI office, a food vendor in a wafer-thick coat hopped from one foot to the other. A sign on his cart read Plague-Free Half-Smokes. Three pedestrians hurried off. A fourth scoffed and crossed the street. A fifth said, "Are you sure?" and bought one without waiting for an answer.

Upstairs, Chou Lee glared out the window, phone to his ear. "Yeah, I know you tapped his parents' phone. But not a single credit card hit? Who are his friends? Where did he hang out?"

Agent Nadya dumped a folder in his in-basket.

"Screw the excuses. Keep showing his picture." Chou Lee slammed down the phone. "Can't find one lousy chemist. What kind of a name is Aatos anyway?"

"My ancestors only invaded Finland," said Nadya. "They didn't try to figure out the names."

"They invaded my ancestors too. No, wait, mine invaded yours. Maybe it was both."

Nadya showed him two fists. "Wanna fight about it?"

Chou Lee tugged an earlobe. "Think it would help?"

Nadya dropped her hands. "Unlikely. But it might have been fun."

Chou Lee scraped frost off the window. "We should have kept all those protesters while we had 'em."

"Nothing to hold them on. Peaceful picketers."

"For all we knew. Then half their names turn up bogus."

"Easy to fake college IDs. Homeland's working that angle. Too late for us."

Chou Lee went back to scraping frost. Down on the sidewalk, people inspected each other, shying away from anyone whose ears were covered. They might be hiding blood. A bearded man in a face mask that could not possibly have had any value, crushed atop his whiskers like it was, opened his coat and revealed rows of pockets with four-ounce brown bottles. He bellowed so loud Chou Lee could hear him through the glass.

"Get the cure. Only ten bucks."

A woman gave him the finger. She went to a kiosk, passed a bill, and ripped a magazine from the vendor's rubber-gloved hand. She wiped the magazine with a tissue.

✿ ✿ ✿

Valerie shooed Ngono out of her oversized CDC laboratory, turned to an assistant, and pointed. The assistant started up a massive three-foot square, floor-mounted centrifuge, and a strip-chart recorder connected to a nuclear magnetic resonance spectrometer. Rows of lights flashed along the top.

Valerie plunked herself at a desk. Her fingers sailed over a keyboard. Images of viruses chased across the monitor. She worried her ponytail and snapped a pencil in half with her other hand. "Come on, brain. Work."

The instruction had no discernible effect. After another hour and a half of pencil abuse, she dragged herself out of the building, through the frozen dinner section of the local mart, and into the bungalow she shared with her fireman husband.

"I'll stick those in the fridge," her husband said, taking the grocery bag. "Macaroni's already on. So's that movie we were gonna watch. Nothing like cheese and violence to help you think."

Valerie couldn't help laughing, much as she didn't feel like it. "Your version of human chemistry is astounding." She tossed her coat on the floor by the door.

"Thanks," said her husband. "Or not. You gonna change?"

"No. I'm too tired to relax." She folded onto the couch, scraped the shoes off her feet using a leg of the coffee table, and wiggled her toes.

"And you say my logic is iffy." He swung her legs over and rubbed her soles.

A half hour later, the first of the sniper scenes came on. Two men with rifles, side by side, took out a man inside a high-rise office building.

"Why did they need two shooters?" said Valerie.

"The glass," her husband said. "Layer of protection. So two phases, two steps. The first guy breaks the glass, but the bullet gets deflected. The second attack kills the guy."

Valerie grabbed the remote, paused the film, and put her feet on the floor. "Two steps?"

"Yeah. Why?"

Valerie didn't answer. She got dreamy and ricocheted toward the front of the house, picking up keys, coat, and a hip bruise on the way. Her husband stopped her before she went out and held up her shoes. The concept of shoes drifted through her brain. If the shoe fits… but would it? Was she on the right track?

"Never mind," he said, "I'll drive you." He slipped the shoes on her feet, helped her into her coat, and guided her to the car.

Twenty minutes later, he led her to the main entrance of her CDC annex. She was functioning well enough by then to say, "Thanks," and kiss him goodbye before she disappeared inside for another two days.

CHAPTER TWENTY-THREE

Spring, Year 3

Desolate prairie stretched hundreds of miles in every direction, broken by the occasional scraggly tree. A one-room church with peeling paint stood watch at the crossroads of two dirt tracks, its once tidy graveyard now sprawling beyond a sagging split rail fence. A small group of people clustered around one of several new, short, simple wooden crosses outside the fence.

The image blurred, then cut to another cemetery, this one on a rocky, windswept hillside. Two Mongolians stacked stones on a cairn.

A desert. A veldt. A swampy patch near a forest. A shaded grove with Mount Fuji in the background. Each with its own group of mourners, its own growing accumulation of human remains, its own religious symbols. A news anchor said, "The plague is still accelerating. Four hundred thousand dead worldwide, that we know of."

The picture jiggled. Cranbrook banged on his TV set.

"How much money you make?" Grimm asked.

"Shut up." Cranbrook whapped the recalcitrant cube again.

On screen, the anchor said, "The World Health Organization still has no answers. The Save Trinity Foundation preaches obliteration, but others see reason for optimism."

"Optimism my ass," said Grimm.

"Nothing from CDC?"

Grimm shook his head. Cranbrook squeezed behind his desk and leaned on his fists, glowering up at the TV. He didn't sit. He had no chair today.

☯ ☯ ☯

Stacy entered her laboratory, one hand filled with papers and the other with hamburger and drink. She shut the door with her hip and nodded to Mr. Praline.

"Pretty bird," cooed the parrot.

She swiveled toward the back corner where Aatos was working. Had he taught the creature to recognize her? No, don't be ridiculous. No way he had the bird that well trained. Or that inappropriately. Though it was kind of cute.

No, shovel that. It was not cute. It would be quite unacceptable. She needed to keep her head straight, not go wishing for distractions. She gave herself the proverbial mental slap and went to the corner.

Behind a bookcase, Aatos compared data points on graph paper with a book of tabulated data in fine print. Stacy dumped the burger. Aatos stuffed it in his mouth without pausing.

"Any progress?" Stacy asked.

"Smtsrs slphgr."

"Nice to know." She took a sip and set the cup by Aatos.

He swallowed as fast as he could, washed it down, and tried again. "Man, you're a good cook."

"You have no idea."

"Oh?"

"Believe me," said Stacy. "And you don't want to learn."

Aatos gave a 'tsk.' "Sounds familiar. Too much cooking in chem labs to want to do it at home."

"Bingo."

"What I said was, symptom suppression. That's all I've seen so far. Ukrainians figured how to control the shaking in most victims."

"In other words, nothing significant?"

"Right."

Stacy reached above his head and pulled a thin stocking cap off a shelf. She tossed it beside him. "You can't keep sneaking to the bathroom. Wear that all the time so you don't forget. It's a common affectation. With your new glasses, and since you quit shaving, no one around here knows you well enough to recognize you."

Aatos pulled the cap over his head with one hand, still plotting data points with the other. "Am I handsome now? Mysterious and sexy?"

Stacy figured it was her turn to make the tsk-ing noise.

✿ ✿ ✿

On a walkway near the front of CDC headquarters, Grimm and other reporters held up microphones, trapping Ngono and Valerie against blossom-covered bushes. Late March, and the Atlanta-area flower festivals were beginning. Rather surprising, considering how many cancellations the plague engendered, but this time tradition beat out paranoia.

In the street beyond them, an ambulance activated its siren and pulled away from the curb. A sight becoming so common, or so painful to think about, no one reacted.

Grimm put on his best aggressive-reporter face for the benefit of the camera. "You call this slow? Half a million dead in a year?"

"More like two years," said Ngono. "Possibly three, but what may have been early cases aren't well documented, as usual."

"That's still not slow," said Grimm.

Ngono bristled. "We have reason to think it could have been worse."

"The problem is the phase one airborne version," said

Valerie.

Ngono started. Valerie shrugged.

Grimm stuck his microphone at her. "Phase one?"

Valerie watched Ngono for permission to continue. "We got confirmation from World Health, Japan, and India."

"Already?" He tugged his mustache, then signaled.

Valerie stepped forward. "You know it's airborne and undetectable with normal screening. It's hiding in at least three different modified common flu coats. But we got suspicious. We started testing healthy people."

The reporters went silent.

"All positive. It's all over the world. Probably has been for months, even years." Valerie twitched, suppressing nausea. The reporters edged back.

"Relax, she's pregnant," said Ngono. "Anyway, that's why no pattern, monitoring symptoms. It's virulent—highly contagious—in a benign phase one."

"Then it goes to phase two in some people," said Valerie. "Then it kills."

"Why? How?" said one reporter.

"No logic." Ngono snarled, a pit bull in search of a target. "No common thread."

"It's weird," said Valerie. "Like it's got a time delay."

Grimm shook his microphone under her nose. "So how will you contain it?"

Valerie gawked at him.

Ngono scowled. "Don't you listen? It's everywhere. We're all infected. There is no isolation."

"As for who it hits next," said Valerie, "it's a crap shoot."

Grimm needed confirmation on that one. "Random?"

☼ ☼ ☼

TV news played on a spare computer stuffed at the end of a workbench in Stacy's lab. She turned up the sound. In the background, Aatos moved from one piece of equipment to another, checking dials and recording data on a legal-sized clipboard.

"Random?" Stacy clicked on a portable recorder and tapped it against her jaw.

Ngono appeared on the TV. "Completely."

Aatos pumped his fist. He jotted more notes.

Stacy muttered to herself. "What in nature is random?" She switched off the TV.

Aatos waved his notes and tossed them aside. "Got it." He opened Mr. Praline's cage and stroked a wing.

The bird sidestepped away along the perch. "Got it. Don't got it."

Stacy kept mumbling. "Breaking chemical bonds. Forming new bonds."

Aatos opened a box of tiny crackers and a jar of peanut butter. "Not her style." He scooped out peanut butter with a cracker and offered it to the parrot.

"Huh?" said Stacy.

Mr. Praline bobbed his head and crunched away. He tried to speak again, but the peanut butter garbled it.

"Trinity. She's elegant," said Aatos. "Leaving phase two to a random loss of protector protein is too unreliable."

"But it could work."

"Doubtful. This thing is stable as U-238." He licked a speck of peanut butter off his finger and held out a grape to Mr. Praline. The bird snubbed him, beak in the air.

Stacy stopped tapping the recorder. Stable, sort of. But not perfect. Far from it.

"It'll last a billion years," said Aatos.

Stacy murmured into her recorder. "Radioactive decay?"

Aatos shut the cage and slapped his notebook. "So there, I got the whole virus sequenced, and every protein characterized. What you got for theory?"

She picked up her red pencil case, glanced inside, and set it down.

"Stacy?"

She pointed at his notebook with her recorder. Her tongue rolled around her cheek. "Won't make everything at once, will it?"

"Not if it's got a phase two."

"So what's it make first? What's in people during benign phase one?"

Aatos made a note. "I'll get the CDC data. Or World Health's. Somebody's posting it."

Stacy nudged his notebook. "And of all the stuff it does make..."

"Yes?"

"...does anything use trace metals?"

"Um. Let's see."

He flipped through the notebook. Stacy dropped her recorder, got up, and went to the refrigerator.

Aatos checked another page. "You need blood?"

"No." She opened the freezer part of the fridge.

"Tissue sample?"

"No." Stacy pulled out a candy bar. "Frozen chocolate. Want some?"

CHAPTER TWENTY-FOUR

Spring, Year 3

Dr. Nielsen stopped in the doorway of a hospital room. Two nurses moved between four patients on beds—two beds and two cots—crammed into the small space. Heart monitors on the windowsill, and IV drips on poles stashed behind the beds, trailed lines to each patient. The sheets quivered; each patient, strapped to their bed frame, suffered continuous spasms. Nielsen entered and plucked the chart off one bed.

"We finished the protocol," said one nurse. "No response."

"I know," said Nielsen. "Keep them comfortable."

The other nurse tightened the hook-and-loop band over a patient's wrist. "That's it?"

Nielsen let out a breath, replaced the chart, and stepped outside. The first nurse followed him out.

The second tried to stuff a bloody bandage into an overfull biohazardous waste bin. She gave up, juggled it in her hand, and headed for the door.

Nielsen looked from the bandage to the main desk. "Don't we have a single blessed Candy Striper left?" No one answered. He stalked down the hall to find the nursing supervisor.

The window at the end of the hall stopped him. Outside, ringing the hospital in row after row, families stared up at the building. At him, at every other window.

They clutched tissues and flowers and bibles. The silence was eerie. Likely some were crying, or cursing, or demanding some unspecified action, but the glass was thermal double pane, and nothing got through.

Cars crowded every conceivable surface, with barely a gap for ambulances. Security guards roamed about, chasing away anyone trying to dump their vehicle in that one remaining corridor. As he watched, more people left cars in the distance and approached on foot, joining the throng, making yet another arc around the hospital. They huddled in their grief, hopeless, watching. Waiting for the inevitable.

"No wonder they canceled visiting hours."

"What?" said a passing orderly.

"Nothing."

A pandemic of this magnitude was something Nielsen had never considered. Something they never mentioned in medical school. A disease unlike anything nature had ever unleashed, leading to a situation no one could have planned for.

Everyone in the world had phase one. It was just a matter of time till they graduated.

He released a breath and returned to work.

☼ ☼ ☼

Chou Lee entered an interrogation room and sat down behind a wooden table. Camille Schultz sat, stone-faced, across from him.

"Your daughter can't talk yet. Not coherently. Prognosis not good."

Camille showed no reaction.

"Aatos Pires' log-in times to the building don't match machine records. Can't tell if your daughter had help, or if she used him to cover her tracks."

"Trinity couldn't do this alone. She was never that ambitious."

"That reverend character is motivation. Got a whole cult and a dozen Internet sites. 'Cleanse the world. Let God start over.'"

Camille said nothing.

"The one thing that's clear is Pires wiped all the records off Trinity's hard drive when he saw she was caught," said Chou Lee. "Do you know why he would do that? Did they have a relationship?"

"I don't know."

"Did she play him? Did they conspire? Did one of them betray the other?"

No reaction. Chou Lee let the silence linger, but Camille didn't seem uncomfortable enough to fill it. He pushed aside his notes. "You had no knowledge of all these activities in your own company?"

"Apparently not."

Chou Lee pulled out his empty pipe and tapped it against his palm. "We hear you encouraged Trinity to design nasty viruses. Why?"

"If you heard that, you know why."

"You don't think nature provides sufficient challenges?"

"You have to anticipate problems, not wait for them."

Chou Lee sputtered. "Anticipate. Wouldn't this be more in line of create?"

Camille slid a nail along a crack in the wooden desk. "Perhaps."

He watched her finger repeat the motion. "How many viruses did Trinity make?"

"That I am aware of?" She crossed her arms. "I'd have to check our records."

Chou Lee tapped his pipe again and set it down. He unfolded a piece of paper, smoothed it, and leaned forward. "Are you aware the intentional creation of harmful biologicals is a Federal offense?"

Camille uncrossed her arms and straightened up. Chou

Lee played his follow-up card.

"Aatos Pires erased the plague files, but we found another drive with encrypted information about your other ventures. Homeland security is working with ciphers. Anything else you'd like to tell me on your own?"

"I... no. Not without a lawyer."

"Well, then, can you at least tell me something about Aatos Pires? How did you meet him?"

"At his parents' farm. I'd heard about him from Trinity. Seen his work. He told me his version at a company picnic once, after a few beers."

☼ ☼ ☼

Coming up the long driveway, fresh from his first year in graduate school, Aatos watched his father march past their two barns, past the long, low metal workshop, and into a muddy field. An elegant woman kept pace, her tailored suit complemented by heavy work boots. A flunky stumbled in her wake, pushing a wheelbarrow. None of them paid the least bit of attention to the thin, wispy sprinkle still falling.

Aatos pulled up beside the house and parked his third-hand pickup truck next to a Schultz Pharmaceuticals van. He got out, kicked off his good shoes, and waded into the field. After three steps, he was barefoot. Note for the future: mud is quite effective at stealing socks.

Twenty yards off, his father stopped near a brown lump puddled by the fence. A cloud of flies lifted off the carcass of a sheep. "There's your 'Wooly Health.'"

The woman signaled the flunky, who spat something Aatos hoped was tobacco juice. Otherwise the guy packed more saliva than Aatos had ever seen. The flunky donned rubber gloves, warded off the flies, and heaved the body into the wheelbarrow on the second try.

"You'll get a full refund," the woman said.

"Oh? Thanks. Hey there, Aatos, welcome home. Say hi

to Camille Schultz."

Aatos tossed his father a salute, grabbed the front of the full wheelbarrow, and helped the flunky get it moving. The dead animal was truly ripe. No wonder the flies were out in force, despite the drizzle.

"Aatos Pires?" said Camille. "You're working on a doctorate now, right? My daughter Trinity showed me your senior thesis. She's in the same field."

Another rut, another push. "I thought you were a drug company."

"That's how we started. Now we're one of the top bioengineering firms in the country."

Aatos' father grunted. "That's why I figured you'd have a better product."

Camille grimaced. "Generally, we do. Far superior to the competition." She pulled out a card when they got to the driveway and passed it to Aatos. "Maybe we need more help. Look us up if you're interested."

Aatos stuffed the card in a pocket. "Gonna be at the university a while yet." He helped the flunky get the sheep and wheelbarrow in the back of Camille's van, then steered himself toward the house and a very hot shower. He retrieved his shoes on the way inside.

That Schultz woman had made an interesting offer. She was awfully well-dressed. There had to be money in her industry. And any woman who could mix high class with practicality was kind of cool, despite being his parents' age. If he could help animals and get a good salary besides, perhaps academia wasn't the only option.

✡ ✡ ✡

Chou Lee drummed his fingers when Camille finished. "You expect me to believe he thought you were hot?"

"I'm not that old."

Chou Lee kept drumming.

"All right, he may have been sucking up. I *was* his boss."

"Yeah, that I could buy. It'd fit the picture for this jerk."

CHAPTER TWENTY-FIVE

Spring, Year 3

Ngono stood silent in the doorway of Valerie's giant laboratory. She sat on a lab bench twenty feet away, ankles crossed, rapping her heels on the cabinet underneath. A dozen other CDC researchers propped themselves against stools and benches in front of her, brooding over shoe color or cracks in the tile floor.

"Don't tell me about better ways to suppress symptoms," said Valerie. "So what if we control tremors in the early stages? I want something that matters." She glared around the room. "Come on, people. What have we got?"

After several moments of silence, a few started listing points. "It kills every immunoglobulin we try." Feet shuffled. "Every poison that works on the reverse transcriptase shuts down healthy cells." Someone dropped a pen. No one picked it up. "Same for the coat inhibitor. Thought we could stop the spread if the virus couldn't make a coating."

"That one wouldn't matter, would it?" said Valerie. "Everyone we test already has it in them."

The third scientist blenched. "Might save babies."

Valerie put a hand on her belly. "Nice idea. But they get it in utero, direct DNA transfer. Don't need a coating if it's already in germ cells."

"Did we get anything from Sandia? The bioterrorism unit?"

"No. With the damn thing all over the world, controlling the spread is next to irrelevant. And catching Trinity's accomplices is secondary at this point. I can't imagine those who did this put any effort into an antidote."

A return to silence.

"Think! How do we stop this thing from going to phase two?"

They all avoided eye contact. No one said a thing. The shuffling stopped, the sign of total discouragement.

Ngono came forward. "That's it. I've heard enough."

The researchers flinched like naughty children.

"I want you all out of here. Now."

Alarm circled the room.

"Go home," said Ngono. "Relax. Sleep. Don't come back for twenty-four hours."

The alarm was replaced with relief, if somewhat tinged by guilt.

"Out!"

The crowd headed for the door, more lively than they'd been in some time. Valerie pulled into herself.

"You too," said Ngono.

"I don't know what to do."

"I told you. We'll try again next week. How's the baby?"

Valerie slid off the bench and slogged toward the door. "Normal," she said, voice numb. "I'm having her checked twenty times more often than they recommend, which is about never this early on. Everything is perfectly normal."

"Her? You know already?"

"It's just an expression." Valerie teetered out.

Ngono sat on a stool and dropped his head to his hands. One hand shook. Then the other. Jerky and slow at first, then faster. And faster.

He lifted his head. His fingers kept speeding up, and his face went slack.

☼ ☼ ☼

Aatos' fingers danced along a keyboard, an image he couldn't shake no matter how much he tried.

His computer monitor lit up the back corner of Stacy's lab. A twisted mass of protein wound across the screen. Spots of it were black, green, yellow, or red. He traced along to a white spot.

"Carbon, oxygen, nitrogen... sodium."

"Sodium cracker," said Mr. Praline.

"Soda," said Aatos, tapping his chin. "Soda cracker." He nibbled a fingernail.

The parrot nibbled his cuttlebone.

☼ ☼ ☼

Outside, a couple of hundred yards away, Stacy dropped onto a bench on the quadrangle. She ripped pieces off one of last year's leftover maple leaves, bit by tiny bit, and scattered them on the ground. When the last flake had landed, she pulled her portable recorder out of a pocket.

"CDC reports rapid progress when the disease migrates to phase two. Random breaking of chemical bonds doesn't fit."

Birds cried mating calls and staked out domains in the trees. Hardy early bees hummed among the hyacinths. Nature carried on, blissfully unaware of any crisis.

Stacy tapped the recorder on her knee. Students meandered across the quad, a ridiculous number of them still wearing face masks or carrying boxes of hand sanitizer. She put the recorder to her lips. "No trace metals in the enzymes or other products formed by the virus. So there's no way to alter diet and restrict intake to inhibit the thing." She lowered the recorder and tapped it a few more times, then raised it again. "Not to mention, if there are no trace metals, there's no naturally-occurring radioactive isotope of one, to decay and set off phase two."

She got up and strayed between the buildings.

Two hours later, Stacy stuffed her recorder in a pocket and entered a grocery store. She wandered down an aisle, shoving a cart with one hand and tossing in boxes now and then. She kept mumbling to herself; other customers kept away. "Phase two. Random. Chemical bonds breaking and forming, or radioactive decay. Nothing else in nature is reliably random."

She accumulated six identical boxes of stuffing mix before moving on to the next row. "Aatos has got to be wrong. Bonds break all the time, that could be it. Or maybe there really is a trace metal and he missed it."

Stacy lingered by the beef jerky and drew one bag after another off the rack. She had a vague notion she didn't like it, but the impression evaporated into mist. "How likely is it Aatos would screw up?" Or did he? Could he really be guilty of helping Trinity, and regretting it, trying to fix it now, so hiding knowledge of...

No, that made no sense. If he wanted to fix things, he wouldn't hide information. And she couldn't believe he was responsible. Nothing in the way he acted fit that.

"Yet if it's not a trace metal, what else decays?" She passed into another aisle and pulled out her recorder. She had to click it twice. It must have already been on. "Tritium is too rare. Carbon-14 is rare, plus you can't count on it for structural stability, then controlled failure."

She fumbled the cart, the recorder, and a box of cereal while avoiding a small boy. His mother apologized, scrubbing the boy's fingers after he touched a shelf. Stacy nodded absently and mused over the condiments. "So radioactive decay is not the—"

Stacy blinked. She stared at the salt. Big cylinders of salt. Iodized salt. Sea salt. Salt substitute.

She centered on the salt substitute. She lowered the recorder and kept staring. "Potassium-40."

The mother tried to reach around without touching her. "Naturally radioactive."

"Excuse me," said the woman.

"A hundredth of a percent of all potassium."

"Could I..." The mother tried to get some salt.

"And if it builds up in the cells..."

"Please, I'm in a rush."

"...then of course it erupts!" Stacy grabbed the salt substitute and sped away, leaving her cart behind. The wrong direction. She spun around toward the checkout lanes.

The mother glared, laid a tissue on the handle of Stacy's cart, and rolled it aside.

✿ ✿ ✿

In Stacy's laboratory, Aatos alternated between paper notebook and computer screen. He dragged his chair to another computer and typed; a complex spherical protein appeared. A pause, then more typing. A spot in the middle glowed purple.

Aatos mumbled to himself. "Interesting, but no trace metal." Notebook, monitor, notebook. He flicked to another screen, and another, studying images.

Stacy rammed open the door.

Mr. Praline squawked and fluttered to another perch. "Warning. Hull breach."

"Sorry," said Stacy. "Hey, I thought I was a pretty bird." She went red when Aatos grinned. "Don't say a thing. What kind of parrot is he, anyway?"

"Norwegian Blue."

Stacy looked from Aatos to Mr. Praline to Aatos. "You *are* aware that Scandinavia has a remarkable paucity of native tropical birds?"

Aatos laughed so hard he belched. "You have got to be the only person who would think of that first." An odd realization struck him. "And the only person who talks like me." He managed to shift his attention from Stacy to Mr. Praline, pointing at the lustrous green, red, and yellow plumage. Something in diet or environment was agreeing with the bird. "Most people point out he's not blue."

"Oh." Stacy regarded the parrot. "Yeah."

"So why'd you come charging in?" said Aatos.

"What? Oh." Stacy slammed the salt substitute on the bench in front of Aatos. "Find any of that?"

"Potassium chloride? Chlorine? No."

"No potassium?"

"Oh, that. Yeah. It's kind of curious." Aatos pulled up the screen with the purple spot in the center of a protein. He poked a pencil at it. "See, proteins don't have much ionic stuff. Mostly covalent. And if I expected something, it'd be sodium."

Stacy drew over a stool. "Sodium."

"But this isn't. It's a potassium atom. And it has to be. See how these hydroxyls curve around?"

"I don't have your 3-D."

"Trust me," said Aatos. "If this puppy took a sodium atom, it'd be too small to stick. When the protein's in the process of synthesization, it's gonna wait for the bigger potassium. Then it gets much better bonding."

"I never heard of potassium in the middle of protein production."

"Nope. It balances sodium in some reactions, but proteins are generally out of its realm."

Stacy nodded. "Good. The stranger, the better."

"It's worse than that."

"Yes?"

"This bugger doesn't do anything."

Stacy rolled her open hand: 'come on, come on.'

"Stable," said Aatos. "Round and smooth. No sites for things to attach, like an enzyme. It just sits there." The image occupied the screen, pulsating idly. Smug, if he wanted to anthropomorphize.

"Really…"

☼ ☼ ☼

Ngono lay in a hospital bed surrounded by a plastic tent. Grimm gave him a little salute, exited the room, and ran into Valerie.

"Good man. Smart," he said.

Valerie stepped around him. Ngono's machines were off. The mass of blood on the bandages around his head was all brown.

Grimm waited, uncertain if he was welcome, or if there was anything he could do.

Valerie didn't seem to realize tears were slipping down her cheeks, or that her cell phone case had cracked in her fist. "The one you know is worse than the million you don't."

Grimm nodded.

She sucked her lip. "Does that make me a bad person?"

"It makes you human."

Valerie appeared to consider the thought. Her face twisted. "I can't afford that. I'm supposed to help everyone." She took a step back. "Not mourn the ones I know." She hurried away, brushing at her cheek.

Grimm returned to Ngono's tent. There were things said by tyrants that were not only horrible, but more so for being true. Like Stalin's famous quote: "One death is a tragedy. A million is a statistic."

Grimm wondered how soon Valerie's work could help all the many, many ones.

☼ ☼ ☼

Aatos and Stacy sat at the computer he'd appropriated in her lab. The smooth, potassium-containing molecule floated on the screen before them. Mr. Praline fluffed his feathers and settled down for a nap.

"What's going on?" said Aatos.

"Rotate that, if you can." Stacy spread her hand. "Open it up a little."

Aatos' fingers blurred across the keyboard. The image revolved and enlarged.

"And the potassium can't get out?"

"Not once the protein is complete." He snagged a French fry off the desk.

Stacy sat back. Aatos chewed, then made a face at the pile of fries.

Stacy put her palms together and rubbed them up and down in front of her nose. She tapped her fingers against her chin. "This computational chemistry thing simulates all the chemical bonding forces, so it shows how things behave in isotonic solution? In a cell?"

"That's how I designed it." He stirred through the fries but didn't find another he was willing to try.

Stacy took a deep breath and picked up a bottle of water. "Last question."

"Yes?"

"Can you replace that potassium with calcium, and see what happens?"

Aatos considered the protein. "Calcium?"

"Calcium."

"I don't follow."

Stacy opened the bottle. "Potassium-40."

"Still in the woods. Maybe deeper."

Stacy smiled. "It decays to stable calcium-40." She took a sip.

Aatos' brow furrowed. "You mean this whole thing is a new form of radiation sickness?"

Stacy choked on her water, spraying like a champagne bottle. Aatos snatched up the keyboard, flipped it upside down, and dried it with some tissues. Stacy coughed a few times and caught her breath. "You can't... you're serious?"

Aatos shrugged. On the monitor, the spherical molecule bounced off the edges of the screen.

"Good grief, how can a brilliant scientist know so little about radioactivity?"

Aatos grinned. "I'm—"

"Three hundred millirem a year natural background radiation, twenty of that from potassium in your own body."

"I'm—"

"This virus adds like ten to the minus gazillionth extra potassium atoms."

The molecule on the screen started making chirping and bleeping noises when it bounced. Aatos set down the keyboard. "I'm—"

"And you think radiation, the most overhyped phenomenon in history, could possibly have anything to do with it?"

"I'm brilliant?"

"Oh, stifle it," said Stacy. "You think so too."

Aatos laughed.

"And could you possibly have a nerdier screen saver?"

Aatos kept laughing and slapped the space bar. The molecule deformed as it scooted to center screen and took its proper place. "Well," he said, catching his breath, "if this thing retains so little potassium, how can decay do anything?"

"Replace it with calcium and let's see. With a plus-two ionic charge instead of potassium's plus-one, calcium should alter your bonding. Maybe the whole thing breaks into pieces."

"Ah, so." Aatos spun around and typed. He glanced at Stacy, tapped a few more keys, and hit Enter.

The image on the screen bulged, twisted, distorted. Sections of the protein flipped around like a deranged amoeba, until it settled into a drastically new shape with a large peninsula sticking out the top.

Stacy and Aatos reared back on their stools.

"What's that?" said Stacy.

"No idea."

"I've never seen anything like it. What's it do?"

"Not a clue."

"It's not an enzyme?" said Stacy. "And when's it made?"

"Again, I achieve a clue-free state."

Aatos and Stacy looked at each other. Then at the screen.

"Go back," said Stacy.

Aatos typed. The image resumed its original spherical shape.

"Why doesn't the immune system respond?" said Stacy.

Valerie slammed a hand on the bench in her CDC laboratory. Glassware rattled and a stainless steel spatula *donged* onto the floor. Another researcher leaned over Valerie's shoulder to see her computer screen.

"It's a plastic bug!" said Valerie.

"Plastic?" said her coworker.

"Nonreactive, like swallowing polyethylene." Valerie pointed. A spiky, convoluted mass twined around. She hit a key. A smooth, spherical molecule appeared beside it. "Normal virus. And the stuff our virus makes."

The researcher frowned. "No spikes. Nothing to key immune receptors."

"Not in phase one. And phase two moves too fast."

☼ ☼ ☼

Aatos plunked down beside Stacy at her workbench in the laboratory. He lowered a printout from an online news service and pointed to an article with a picture of Valerie's two molecules side by side. "So that's why there's no immune response, according to CDC."

"Apparently."

"That's clever."

"No," said Stacy. "That's diabolical. The cells keep building up higher concentrations."

"So when phase two hits—"

"Boom."

CHAPTER TWENTY-SIX

Spring, Year 3

Valerie sorted the last of Ngono's pictures and personal effects between two cardboard boxes, fitting them all in. Soon she'd have to clear them through security and call his wife to pick them up. Or deliver them in person; that would be the considerate thing. But something was strange about Ngono's desk, and delaying to investigate seemed an acceptable way to put off the sad task.

The right middle drawer was too shallow. It didn't match the one on the left, and when she emptied it out and put one hand underneath, and her other hand inside, at least an inch was unaccounted for.

She pried at the bottom of the drawer, presumably a false floor, and got a splinter in her little finger for the effort. Be smarter. If Ngono had hidden something, there must be a simple way to access it. Or he knew nothing about it, but whoever had used this desk before him had reason to be secretive. Maybe it was empty. But there had to be a logical way to get in.

Valerie felt all around the inside surface, pressing and releasing, searching for a catch mechanism. Then she probed underneath with a finger and found a sticky spot. She smelled her finger. Strawberry jelly. One of Ngono's favorites, and still fresh, so definitely his stash. She probed again, pushing around the sticky area, and heard a click. The floor of the drawer popped up.

She chuckled. Tricky old guy. She lifted out the loose panel.

The cavity held three memory sticks, each in loose bubble-wrap, and a debit card from the local credit union. What had that man been up to?

Three hours later, she knew. Ngono hadn't put anything in code; cryptography and computer savvy were not in his resume. Paranoia was, and all three memory sticks held identical information. Plain text, references, and contact information to a high-tech firm outside the Atlanta beltway. A company specializing in microrobotics.

Valerie soaked it up. Not her forte, robotics, but this business had made a fortune over the years. Microbots for scouring arteries and cleaning them out, preventing heart attacks. Or for chopping up chunks of blood clots and lasering them to extinction to avoid strokes. Even better, they'd finally licked the problem of containing cells while attacking cancer tissue—in the early days, trying to cut out cells led to cell damage, which led to accidentally releasing chemicals into the blood stream, and the cancer had metastasized all through their research animals. A spectacular failure until they'd gotten a handle on it.

But those were microrobots, with propellers and cutters and tiny ovens. Nanobots would be needed for fighting infections. Nanometer-sized miniaturization, a thousand times smaller, was beyond the current technology, she'd thought.

Until she saw these notes.

On she read. Receptors able to identify a variety of chemical groups, from hydroxyls to amines to carboxylic acids. Controlled static charges over the surface of semiconductor coatings, able to bond to different chemicals. Like throwing a cape over the enemy molecules, and preferentially charging each pixel of the cape, plus or minus, to make it stick. To prevent the molecule from functioning.

Transport the coating on a microscopic skeleton of titanium, able to support a whole range of different attachments.

Pieces of a jigsaw puzzle. And no progress at all, putting those pieces together. Someone was hoping to construct artificial antibodies, targeted for specific antigens. Like, maybe, for the RIAS virus. But she saw no signs of blueprints, no signs they'd made real headway.

Valerie pulled out her phone, checked the number of the robotics company, and punched it in.

CHAPTER TWENTY-SEVEN

Spring, Year 3

A pallet of crates boomed as it landed on a debris-strewn quay. Twenty FBI and Homeland Security agents swarmed over a small freighter of Panamanian registry. An assortment of Sea-Land containers sat beside it, and a sprawl of pallets lay scattered around the pier. Nadya and half a dozen agents hauled forward three Latinos from the direction of the freighter. Chou Lee stepped out of the shadows and studied the Latinos. They sneered.

"Two Columbians, one indeterminate mercenary, and six bodies belowdecks," said Nadya.

"And not a drug among 'em, I bet," said Chou Lee.

Agents lugged over open crates. Chou Lee peered in one. A mass of hand grenades and AK-47 assault rifles, still the weapons of choice after all these years.

"They seem upset with the competition," said Chou Lee.

"Business is war?" said Nadya.

Chou Lee fingered one of the spare magazines. "Could be."

Nadya put on a plastic glove and picked up a grenade. She inspected the pin. "You need a mustache, sir."

"It's Chou Lee Lin, not Charlie Chan." Chou Lee took the grenade, hefted it, and set it down.

"A Fu Manchu would be very impressive."

"Don't come on to me, Agent. I'm old enough to fall for it."

Nadya grinned and tried on an assault rifle. It fit perfectly.

☼　☼　☼

Aatos entered Stacy's lab with a thick file and a large bag. "Red alert," said Mr. Praline.

Stacy jerked awake and almost fell off the laboratory bench she was lying on. She craned her neck and checked the parrot. He stretched his claws and didn't appear particularly concerned. Then she saw Aatos, checked her watch, and swung her legs over the side of the bench. She rubbed her face with a Kimwipe, unfolded the white cashmere sweater she'd been using as a pillow, and spread it over a stool.

"Got food?"

Aatos waved the file. "Got the full breakdown of everything made when the virus starts out, and everything blocked till it goes to phase two."

Stacy's voice got raspy. "Did you get food?" She stuffed her hair behind her ears.

"Huh?" He spotted the bag in his hand. "Yeah, here."

Stacy grabbed the bag. She sniffed, smelled the opening, then aimed her nose at Aatos and took a whiff. "Time for another shower."

Aatos went over to the emergency wash-down station—a rusty oversized shower nozzle barely head-height, with a floor drain below, intended for removing the results of chemical spills or minor experiments gone awry, but rarely needed. They'd rigged a plastic sheet around it to contain splashing and provide a modicum of privacy.

He made a face. "We never figured how to heat the water."

"Wuss."

"Wait'll it's your turn."

"You forget I still have an apartment."

"Which you could let me use."

"Not a chance," said Stacy. "No one notices your stupid hat and beard around here..."

"*My* hat?"

"...and the campus rent-a-cops don't pay attention to much of anything. But out in the real world?" She shook her head.

Aatos put a fist on a hip and thrust out his lower lip. "You never take me anywhere."

"Yes, dear."

Aatos choked.

"Stand over there so I can eat my sandwich."

The choke morphed into a chuckle. Aatos moved away, waved his file again, and tossed it down. "Anywho, you won't believe how fast they post this stuff." He pulled a bag of parrot food from a drawer.

Stacy ignored him and tore into her huge salami and Swiss submarine. She closed her eyes in contentment.

"Talk about opening doors. Every agency in the world is helping the other." Aatos opened Mr. Praline's cage and topped off a cup with pellets.

"Feed me," said Mr. Praline. "Feed me."

Stacy chewed slowly, sensually.

Aatos eased down on a stool and scratched the parrot's head through the bars. "If you're gonna fight a plague, that's the key."

Stacy's eyes flew open. She stopped chewing.

✿ ✿ ✿

Late at night, alone on his cot in the deserted laboratory, Aatos wondered about that word, 'dear.' Was there any way it could have meant something? Anything? He tried to remember all the times he'd heard it in his life, and the most he could read into it was a nice, round, juicy zero. Women said it all the time, to friends and for jokes.

Dreams were all well and good, but they never amounted to anything. Not that you could count on.

He ground his teeth, telling his gray cells to stop peddling overpriced, pointless optimism, and let him get some sleep. He had way too much work tomorrow. He had way too much work every day. And his gonad-driven cortex had better shut the frog up and get with the program.

Three hours later, he gave up and turned on the lights. Mr. Praline stirred, making unhappy noises. Aatos fired up his computer and filled the screen with data, none of which made the least bit of sense.

Until something stood out in the lower right corner of the screen. An insert with new data from CDC. He pulled it up and compared it to something he'd seen from Germany the day before. Within two seconds he was lost in the details.

✧ ✧ ✧

In the dark pre-dawn of Stacy's townhouse, she huddled in the middle of her bed.

Dear.

Sweet mother of infidelities, how in the seven corners of eternity had that word scraped through the censors and snuck its way to her tongue? There was no way she would ever give that cocky, genius, non-Romani, sweet, annoying, wonderful man the legs off a squashed mosquito, much less encourage him to think she thought about him thinking about her.

Dear heaven, what did *he* think the word meant?

Outside the window, the night was black and starless. Sleep. That's what was supposed to happen after dark, especially when you were lying around accomplishing nothing whatsoever. Sleep. Hear that, brain? What was it Aatos liked to say? Get with the program.

Okay, that didn't work. The feeble ticking from the

clock in the kitchen permeated every room in her townhouse. If there were only a simple way to deactivate the mind. A key to switch.

Right, keys. She'd been thinking about them before the lights went out. But keys to what, exactly? Where would they fit? And how would they work? Stacy clicked on the bedside lamp, picked up her pocket recorder, and leaned on the pillows, eyes glazing into the distance.

"It couldn't be as simple as I'm hoping, could it?"

✿ ✿ ✿

Outside CDC headquarters, trees swayed in the late spring breeze, pale green buds bursting open all around, turning the world into fluffy pink and white. A lone news van sat in front of the building. Grimm sat in the grass playing gin rummy with his cameraman, wondering if he should have thrown a towel on the ground first, or if it was easier to ignore the damp, or if this hand of cards was truly so hopeless he couldn't come up with anything better to think about.

Farther back, a tall, temporary fence kept away protesters. Three security guards patrolled inside the perimeter, chasing away agitators when they shook the fencing. As far as Grimm could tell, the protesters were yelling something about government cover-ups, lazy workers, and illegal delays in getting out a cure. Rumors they'd heard, or stuff they'd made up. Why they thought standing around out here would speed up the research was beyond him.

Valerie came out of the building alone, one hand over her belly. It was way too early for the baby to show, but Grimm noticed she held herself there pretty frequently. She shook her head at him and continued toward the parking lot.

A few of the braver demonstrators rushed the fence.

Metal squealed and a section around one pole sagged nearly horizontal. The guards pulled out billy clubs and chased over to stop people from pouring through. Two men attacked the guards with their signs. Grimm stood.

"Gin. Pay up," said the cameraman.

"Move it," said Grimm, jabbing a finger at the camera, then at Valerie. "Run."

Valerie raced for her car, Grimm hurried near the fence. The cameraman struggled with his gear.

Guards took down the first two people over the fence, clubs breaking signs and a couple of bones. Blood spattered across their clothes, but more protesters climbed the fence.

A bespectacled protester in the rear pulled a dark elongated object from a pocket and thrust it over his head. One guard drew his pistol. Six more guards charged out the front door, two with riot guns.

"My name is Legion," yelled the bespectacled man in a booming voice, "and I am here to stop the cure." He thumbed a cigarette lighter, lit a fuse, and drew back his arm.

"Traitor," screamed a woman, throwing herself at the man. "Cultist!"

"Bomb!" The guard with the pistol fired at the man. The woman lurched and crashed into the cultist. The pipe bomb spurted to the side. "Down!"

The guards and half the protesters hit the dirt. The rest stood in shock, watching the terrorist wrestle toward the homemade grenade. Grimm skidded to a stop. His assistant had stabilized the camera thirty feet behind, using a telephoto to capture the scene.

The bomb exploded. The cultist expanded, a red cloud blasting past him to splatter the crowd. Shrapnel shredded half a dozen people, including the woman who had tried to stop him. The shock knocked Grimm on his back.

He rolled over and pushed himself up, watching guards

crawl over the fence to give first aid to wounded protesters.

The cameraman came up beside Grimm, still recording. "Holy crap."

Grimm guided him around debris as they headed for the mess, to review, record, and report.

"Keep shooting. Damn, I hate breaking news."

CHAPTER TWENTY-EIGHT

Stacy cleared a bench in one corner of her laboratory, relocating all the analytical balances, steam baths, and Bunsen burners. Aatos helped her set up a new big-screen TV, running cables to a computer server with its cover removed. He plugged a card into the server's motherboard.

Stacy double-checked the cable connections, threw the TV's power cord over the bench, and crawled underneath to plug it in. "Now we got enough memory?"

Aatos slipped a cover over the server. "Should do." He turned on the server, went over to the fridge, and leaned inside.

Professor Sturdevan opened the door and walked in.

"Integer alert," said Mr. Praline.

Sturdevan came to a halt when he saw the parrot and TV.

"That's 'intruder alert,'" said Aatos, straightening up with a bottle of fruit juice. "Intruder." He saw the professor and went rigid.

"What on earth?" Sturdevan focused on Aatos. "What are you doing here?"

Stacy scurried backward from under the bench.

"Oh," said Aatos. "Um. Just visiting."

"Haven't seen you in years. Or have I? I'm sure I... no, that's..."

Stacy rose to her knees, lifted a finger, and snared his attention. "Hi, Prof. He's, uh, my date."

"Your date?" said Sturdevan.

"Your date?" said Aatos.

"And all this..." She indicated the TV and new computers.

"You have a date?" said Sturdevan.

"New grant money. I'll tell you about it when I get a chance." She got up and herded the old man toward the door. "Thanks for stopping by."

"Since when do you date?"

Stacy got him out and shut the door. "Damn, he's the one person who could spot you."

Aatos didn't react to that. Instead, he gaped at her in awe. "My God," he said. "Someone with less social life than me."

Stacy didn't know whether to laugh, cry, or bash him over the head and risk damaging the smattering of brain cells that were still functioning. She pointed to the computer. "Saddle up."

Aatos got this inane, hopeful expression. "Really?"

She rolled her eyes and pointed at the computer. Aatos quit pretending to be enamored, laughed, and went to work.

"Eventually, he'll remember the cops are flashing your face," said Stacy.

"Understood."

They worked through the night. Once, they disassembled all the connections and started from scratch, testing each one as they went along. Aatos held up a wire with a kink in it.

"Well, that's sub-optimal."

He rooted around for a replacement.

At some point, dawn broke over the deserted campus and they took a breather. Wisps of fog wove through the bushes. A remarkably obese field mouse waddled across the sidewalk and onto a quadrangle covered with dew-bedazzled grass and tiny white flowers.

Aatos sipped coffee by one of the second-story windows with a view of the mouse. "*Peromyscus* among the clover. That dude can't believe its luck."

Stacy munched a cookie beside the other window. A hawk swept down on the fat rodent. She grimaced. "That hawk can't believe its luck."

Aatos watched the hawk fly away. "Nature is cruel." He took another sip.

"No. Nature just *is*. Gotta have controls. Feedback." She cocked her head. "Of course, in this case, feedback is rather literal."

Aatos choked a laugh, jetting coffee. "On that happy note, shall we try again?"

✿ ✿ ✿

A beautiful young Egyptian reporter fondled her microphone, flirting with the camera while the Nile River flowed under the Imbaba Bridge behind her. "Welcome back. Once again, we're outside the Arkadia Mall in sunny Cairo. So far today we have heard man-on-the-street opinions ranging from soccer to proper child-rearing to the alleged virtues of religious intolerance. The arguments have been fast and furious, with soccer getting loudest."

She moved along the walk toward a man in a turban. "Excuse me, sir, we have a few minutes left in our program. I wondered if you had an opinion on the plague currently ravishing our planet."

The man glared from the woman to the camera. "Only Americans would dream that a small group of fanatics should impose their will on the whole world." He stomped off.

"But sir," said the woman. She gave up when it became obvious he wouldn't stick around for a response, and turned to the camera. "I guess we had to expect that from someone. Never mind that extremists have been doing this for thousands of years, and I really don't think the United States is quite that old."

A frame surrounded the image, and a Mexican news anchor appeared as the Egyptian report faded out. "And there you have it. Rationality in the face of fear. I hate to tell you how long we searched to find this clip."

✿ ✿ ✿

Stacy and Aatos bent over the new server and TV combo, hair and clothes more disheveled than Stacy would have believed possible until she caught a reflection off a shiny surface. Aatos shuffled through a raft of papers and pointed. Stacy typed a password and ran another diagnostic.

This time, the TV flickered to life. Long, winding, complex molecules grew to stuff the screen—the viral RNA and its protector protein, identical to what Valerie had shown Chou Lee months before.

Aatos raised football arms. "Transcendent!"

Stacy abandoned the keyboard. "Your turn. Now, strip off all the protector protein from phase one."

Aatos typed. Along half the length of the convoluted image, the thick outer coating of material evaporated. A slender band of simpler, colorful chemical slowly rotated.

"The phase one RNA is revealed."

"Wonderful," said Stacy. "Get rid of it."

Aatos pounded the keys. The slender band disappeared. He typed some more, and the remaining portion of thick, winding molecule expanded to fill the screen.

"Okay, this makes phase two happen," said Stacy.

"Seems so."

"And what opens it up? What strips off that coat, so the RNA can be transcribed?"

"Well, Dr. Watson, I deduce we need a key."

"You're Watson," said Stacy. "I'm Holmes."

"Can't be. You're too short."

"You're too fat."

They laughed, sharp little yips.

Aatos held a finger over the keyboard. "We're delaying, aren't we?"

"Fine," said Stacy. "Go ahead."

Aatos punched a sequence of letters. On screen grew the small, mysterious spherical protein with the purple dot for potassium. "We now know this is made in phase one."

"Right. Trade the potassium for calcium."

Aatos typed. The small, round protein twisted and deformed as before, creating a distinct protuberance. "Okay, now we let the simulation go, and see if this beasty fits in anywhere."

Stacy held her breath. Aatos hit Enter and leaned back. On the huge TV screen, the now-misshapen little protein hovered around the larger mass, bouncing off it here and there, hitting and spinning away.

Aatos bit his lip and tried a little body English. It didn't help the little protein do anything.

After another minute, Stacy let out her breath. "Nothing, huh?"

The protuberance on the small protein slid into a perfectly matching indentation on the side of the large mass.

The screen went black.

"What happened?"

"It went in," said Aatos. "I'm sure it went in."

"It crashed the program. Thought we had adequate memory?"

"We should. It—"

The viral image flared to life. Letters flashed on the bottom of the screen.

"It's sticking!" said Aatos. "Hydrogen bonding, van der

Waals."

A section of the protective coating around the large mass twisted to the side, exposing the colorful RNA inside.

"It *is* a key." Stacy gripped the edge of the bench.

The section of twisting, unwinding cover material grew, unzipping itself until the whole protector protein ripped off and drifted aside. Once free, it folded upon itself, reshaping and forcing the smaller protein, the key, to pop free. The key floated away.

"And it's a catalyst, off to do it again," said Aatos.

"Won't the original—"

"No," said Aatos. "The coating is off for good. The RNA gets used. At most, there'd be something less sticky for temporary RNA protection."

They watched the spinning molecules on the screen.

"What do you want to bet phase two makes more of those keys?" said Stacy. "Pre-built with calcium."

"Bet against that? Thought you said I was brilliant?"

"Yeah, yeah." Stacy let go of the bench. "So phase two is a go."

"Maybe."

"And that altered little baby with calcium is the key."

"Perhaps."

"Which makes your spherical form with potassium the protokey."

"That is conceivable."

Stacy went askance.

"Hey," Aatos said, "you're the one who bawled me out for conclusion jumping, remember?"

"Okay, okay," said Stacy. "We can't afford dead-end research. What's your point?"

"What's the half-life of potassium-40?"

"Um..."

"Over a billion years. I looked it up."

"Oh. So it'll never happen?"

"Seems improbable."

"But it fits so well. What're the odds it'd open up the RNA like that?"

"Less than one in a billion." Aatos scratched the inside of his ear.

Stacy drummed a pencil.

Aatos leaned far back, feet on the edge of the desk. His eyes went hazy.

Stacy stopped drumming her pencil. She tensed her fingers and it flew across the room, clattering off cabinets and chairs. She kept watching the molecules spin.

"I've got it," said Aatos. He slammed his feet to the floor.

"What?" Stacy snapped on her recorder.

"Let's get a beer."

Stacy hesitated, switching gears from screen to Aatos to recorder. Her shoulders either relaxed or slumped; she didn't want to figure out which. "An admirable suggestion, my dear Watson." She turned off the recorder.

Aatos chuckled. He filled Mr. Praline's water cup while Stacy fiddled with her bright red plastic pencil box.

"Eau de fjord," said Mr. Praline. "Pining fjord."

"At least he quit talking about cars," said Aatos.

Stacy raised an eyebrow, but he didn't elaborate. She put away her box and tossed Aatos his stocking cap. "Fluff out your beard. Remember, you're in disguise."

Five minutes later, they emerged from their building and squinted against the sun. The quadrangle was still deserted, the post-dawn shadows long. Stacy looked at the clock in a tower. Aatos looked at his watch.

"Shit," said Stacy.

"What?"

"We can't have beer in the morning."

Aatos shrugged. "Must be a girl thing."

Stacy gave him a shove.

"Fine," said Aatos, recovering his balance with a generous dose of exaggerated arm flailing. "Breakfast."

Stacy pointed across the quad, and they ambled toward the student cafeteria.

She didn't make it. That janitor, Akeem, was sitting on the library steps, shoulders quivering. She sent Aatos ahead and joined Akeem, taking his hand, saying nothing.

After a while, Akeem spoke. "Three."

Stacy waited.

"Three of my children, and I think my wife has symptoms."

"Too many," said Stacy. "One family. No one should suffer such loss."

Akeem withdrew his hand and blew his nose. "How could Allah let this happen?"

"You're thinking like a Westerner. Allah didn't do this. People did. And others need to fix it."

Akeem stuffed a handkerchief in a pocket. "People like you?"

"I don't know. Yes. Maybe."

He rose, slowly, like a man far older than he was. "There is no more time for 'maybe.'"

CHAPTER TWENTY-NINE

Spring, Year 3

"Ah, Ms. Slotowski, welcome."

"Please, call me Valerie." This was the guy Ngono had been working with at TimmyTim Microprocessing? He looked like he used the same hair stylist as Einstein, on one of his worst days. And geeks in wide glasses, with one lens way thicker than the other, should never wear camo and combat boots. It was just wrong.

"And I'm Timmy. Tim. Both, actually. I work alone, except for the staff. They're technicians. And a secretary. You mentioned Ngono?"

Less than two seconds to spit that out. Valerie spent longer absorbing it than Timmy had spent saying it. "He passed away. The plague."

Timmy scratched an ear, backed a step, and collapsed onto a folding chair in front of his desk. He glanced through a plate-glass window behind him into an electronics laboratory stuffed with instruments and a rats-nest of wiring. "Then it's over. Too late."

"What is over?"

"No more funding. No more hope. Over."

Valerie grabbed his arm and hauled him to his feet. "What's over?"

"Can't say. Doctor Ngono made me promise. No guarantees, just a plan. A dream, maybe. It was going so well. We had— No, can't say. Made me promise."

"Ngono's dead, and I found his notes. Robotics. You were developing nanorobots for him, weren't you? Something to fight the plague?"

"How did you— No. He said secret. Because it might not work. Not get everyone's hopes up."

"And what's so wrong with a little hope?"

"Uh, don't know. What he said." He rubbed his other ear and inspected his finger.

Valerie paused. Maybe stress wasn't how this guy performed best. She could push her staff at CDC, yell when she had to, but that didn't work for everyone. Ngono always said a good manager had to know their people. So time for a different tactic.

She led him over to a beat-up love seat against the wall, covered in blankets and a ratty pillow. The poor guy must sleep here often, but his office wasn't big enough for a real sofa.

"Okay, sit. Relax. Let's think this through, shall we?"

Timmy shuddered once, then settled into a corner, hugging his pillow.

"Doctor Ngono hired you."

"Yes."

"To design a specific nanorobot."

"Can't say."

"Timmy, he's dead. Whatever agreements you had are void. He can't pay you anymore, but I can."

"I... you can?"

"It was to fight the plague, wasn't it?"

Timmy scraped fingers through his hair, sending it floating. "Need cash for salaries. Lost two, so death benefits. Short on supplies. Hospitals aren't buying, don't need microbots, too much plague, nobody cares about kidney stones. So no income."

"I can help."

"Ngono lifeline, but he said don't talk. No publicity."

"Because of hope?"

"Partly. I remember, premature too. May be setbacks. Outside pressure if they hear. Screw up progress." He went back to pawing an ear.

"Maybe. Anyway, I'll be your lifeline. Tell me what you're working on."

Valerie waited. For a sharp inventive genius, this guy was sure slow to accept a change in course.

"All right. Immunoglobulin. Artificial and targeted, that was our plan."

"And how far have you gotten? We're having zero luck with biochemistry. Do you think you can design a structure that will recognize and destroy RIAS without killing off the cell?"

"Tough. Tough task. Recognize, yes, got that down, mostly. But unreliable. The agents that work best get all corroded. Body chemistry, you know. Still testing."

"And after recognition?"

Timmy gazed off in the distance. Valerie waited, trying to keep her knee from bouncing. The guy's nervous tics were contagious. Or she was in a hurry to get back to her own work.

"Semiconductor growth. That's the key, I think. Probably. Pack raw materials inside a casing, to sense the virion. Attach. Ah, there's the rub." He rubbed both ears at once. "Make it grow around the virus. The semiconductor material would strangle it. But how to attach? Tough."

"Okay, you have a plan, then. An expectation of success?"

"Someday, yes. But how long? In time? We need more tests with logical choices. Trial and error too slow." He checked his finger. "Oh my God, blood. I'm sick!"

Valerie pulled his hand down and inspected his ears. "Stop scratching. Of course there's blood. You're not sick."

"No? Oh, okay. Hmm, trial and error could be fast if unlimited funds. Lots of trial devices. Need more RNA, though."

"Viral RNA?"

"Yes, to test on."

"We can provide that," said Valerie. "Get me numbers. Whatever you need. And do it fast." Damn, the guy had her talking in sound bites too. Why did people mimic each other?

"Fast, yes. Work quick. No time to waste."

Timmy popped off the love seat and scooted over to his desk. His fingers sailed across the keys of his laptop. Valerie nodded and headed for the door.

"E-mail."

"Oh, right." Valerie took a card from her purse and laid it on the corner of his desk. "I'll hear from you soon?"

No answer. Just tapping. Valerie nodded again. Timmy had his priorities straight.

CHAPTER THIRTY

Spring, Year 3

Shadows were much shorter by the time Aatos collected Stacy from the library steps and they finished their greasy, high-cholesterol breakfast. Next, a wasted morning in the lab, reviewing data reports from other research facilities. At one point, Stacy saw Aatos checking an online newsfeed from Ohio. Right, he grew up there. Probably still had family and wanted to check the casualty lists. He didn't say anything, so she didn't pry.

A quick stop at the cafeteria for takeout lunch—reduced price leftovers from breakfast. Food in hand, Stacy dragged Aatos to the tiny park Professor Sturdevan had once shown her, hidden between rival apartment complexes a few blocks off campus. It wasn't as pleasant as Stacy recalled. No children, no families today. Not surprising. She and Aatos straddled a bench, facing each other. They plunked down drinks, steno pads, and calculators.

Stacy brushed hair from her eyes. "Okay, when all else fails..."

"...read the directions."

"Or, in our case..."

"...do the math. How many times can you roll billion-sided dice and not have your number come up?"

"Not exactly an accurate analogy," said Stacy, "but close enough for government work."

"I hope you know that's not a comforting expression."

Aatos thumbed through his pad and folded over a couple of pages. He flipped between them.

Stacy pulled out her recorder and turned it on. "Ten trillion cells in a human body."

"I got ten to the fourteenth."

"Ten times higher. Go with that." She pulled crumbs off her muffin and tossed them aside.

Aatos scribbled. "How many badass molecules per cell?"

"It's called a protokey."

He stuffed a piece of sausage in his mouth. "Like my name better."

"Who knows? Call it ten."

Stacy tapped her calculator with one hand, eating with the other.

Aatos shredded his biscuit. "E to the minus lambda tee. Try a year."

"With lambda at lon-two over the one point two seven billion year half-life of potassium-40."

Silence reigned while Stacy and Aatos punched numbers, chewed, sipped, and punched some more. Pigeons landed and pecked at bread crumbs, contesting the bigger pieces.

Aatos stopped and stared at his calculator.

Stacy frowned and typed some more. "Math error. Wild answer."

"Did you get 164 billion?"

Stacy swallowed. "Everyone in the world dead in under a year?"

Aatos leapt up and stalked across the park. Pigeons squawked and scattered to the trees. "Too many people." He spun and headed the other way. "Too many cells. Too many protokeys."

Stacy angled away, pacing at a ninety-degree angle. "So much for a long half-life."

"It's not spreading that fast," said Aatos. "It's not real. Try fewer cells. Not every kind may be affected."

"Not yet, anyway. Ten to the twelfth. And only one protokey per cell."

A half hour later, they lay on their backs beside the fountain, head to head, calculators held above them.

"You know," said Stacy, "if you lost ten pounds, got laser surgery, and learned to dress, you'd be out of my league."

"How about now?"

"I'm out of yours."

Aatos snickered.

✧ ✧ ✧

Stacy watched the shadows lengthen, spreading across the university quadrangle. Aatos came out of her lab carrying a satchel over one shoulder. Their data. Their conclusions.

He joined Stacy on the bench. She chewed a pencil. The shadows swelled.

"Caught the news," said Aatos. "Could be as high as fifteen million dead."

"Our lower estimate is holding."

"For now. Six percent per year. How fast will it increase?" The sky drifted toward orange.

"Who the hell knows?" said Stacy. "That's like four hundred million people."

"More. Phase one keeps multiplying. We're at the bottom edge of an exponential curve."

She nodded. The sky added several shades of red, mingled with yellows.

Stacy got up and marched back and forth. She opened her mouth a couple of times before her vocal cords got the message. "It's time we fix it." She kept walking the same direction for a change, passing between a couple of buildings.

Aatos got up and followed. "Destroying the protokey is the key. So to speak."

"We need a special immunoglobulin to attack that stupid sphere."

"Which means a whole slew of enzymes to build it. Then reverse code the DNA."

"And add all our stuff to the immune system database of 'safe proteins.'"

"You can do that?"

"Yeah. My latest hit." Stacy sat on another bench.

"*Tres fantastique*. So then, a virus to get it in the cell?"

"Which we expose people to."

"Well, someone does. When we give them the data, videos, calculations." He plopped down beside her and patted his satchel.

Stacy thought another moment, contemplating something far in the distance. And remembering what Akeem had said. No more time for maybe. "Ready to tell CDC? You agree with me now?"

"Of course. We've done all we can."

Hummingbirds chased each other around their noses. A freshman ran past, and the birds darted off toward some fragrant azaleas. Chimes in the administration building bell tower donged the hour, startling a row of pigeons off the eaves. Students disappeared into the few evening classes, and the campus grew still. The sky deepened to purple. Lamps popped on here and there as sensors responded to the fading light.

Stacy looked at the satchel, then Aatos. "One problem. I don't agree with me."

"You don't agree with you?"

"Not anymore." Stacy clutched the hair above her ears. There was a series of cracks in the pavement that required a detailed survey just then. Or so her fractating brain told her.

"Stacy?"

"Track me on this, right?" She slowly unclenched her hair and cupped her face with open hands. "Other labs don't know your equipment, hospitals don't have anyone who could use it." She slapped her cheeks a couple of times. "Trinity's hardly an option, even if she wasn't injured. Who else can design stuff?"

"You could. I'm sure they've got—"

Stacy stood up. "I couldn't. Too steep a learning curve. No experience. CDC?"

"Not likely. Not if you can't. I could, if they'd trust me."

Stacy walked away. Aatos hopped up and followed. She studied the trees as they paced along. And the bushes. And more trees. And once again, the cracks in the sidewalk.

"Okay, so here's the scenario," she said at last. "We give the data to the police, and you're arrested, to convince them it's not junk from crackpots. That gets the info to CDC."

Aatos stopped. "Man, this sucks. I only ran away to work on this stuff."

"Cops are funny that way."

"You have a warped sense of humor." He caught up to Stacy.

"Cops won't let you help," said Stacy. "You're tainted."

"They might."

"So CDC takes ten times longer designing a cure than you would. Then triple that to over-check it, get peer review, and get it past the FDA. Maybe longer."

"They can't. Normal protocols wouldn't apply."

"Then it's tied up in court by Luddites and maybe half a dozen religions."

"You've got to be kidding."

Stacy picked up the pace. Aatos matched it.

"Then," said Stacy, "when only a few people are still alive, the ones who are desperate try it. Others figure if they've lived that long, they're immune, so they don't bother and die later."

"Fools get a Darwin Award."

Stacy glared at him.

"Sorry. Poor taste."

"And those too hard up, without insurance, or in remote areas, never see the cure."

Aatos pulled her to a halt and turned her around.

Stacy could tell. It was sinking in.

Professor Sturdevan appeared from around a corner. He stopped when he saw Aatos. "Ah, I remember."

Stacy and Aatos took off running.

✿ ✿ ✿

Outside the FBI office, cultists on the sidewalk shook their signs: Avenge Trinity, Persecution Lives, and Mother Earth Thanks You. A couple of city police kept a close eye on them, a double-duty job watching for anything they might do beyond protesting, while also protecting them from some pretty irate citizens. Nadya flashed her Homeland Security badge and shoved through.

Inside, she barged into Chou Lee's office. The phone rang. Chou Lee snatched it up and listened.

"Time to lock up those protesters, Charlie."

Chou Lee waved her to silence. "Chou Lee. Schultz senior?"

"They're all accessories." Nadya unfolded a multipage legal-sized document and flipped it onto his desk.

Chou Lee put a finger in his ear. "Older stuff? Who'd they sell it to?"

Nadya picked up an extension phone and punched a couple of buttons, but couldn't find the same line Chou Lee was on. "You heard about the second bomb at CDC, yes? The dud?"

Chou Lee scribbled a note. "Isn't that interesting?"

He hung up. So did Nadya.

Chou Lee picked at a fingernail a couple of times. "A burned-out delicatessen is legally the proud owner of some of the world's most sophisticated biogenetics equipment."

Nadya leaned forward, fingertips on the desk.

"Of course," he said, "it doesn't seem to be there at the moment."

"Someone else made the virus?"

Chou Lee folded his note. "Plague started when the older machines were still at Schultz's. But now?"

"Why would they need more production? Isn't it everywhere?"

Chou Lee started reading the forms Nadya had thrown down and didn't answer. After a moment, he said, "All of them?"

"All the pre-plague cultists. The conspirators."

"Roger that," said Chou Lee. "The whole thing has mushroomed since the news hit. We could never find all the latest members."

"And they're not likely involved," said Nadya. "Meanwhile, the reverend has evaporated. We don't even have his real name. Damn retrobate."

"You mean reprobate?"

"That, plus ultra back-to-nature freak. His retrobate followers must know something. It's more than one or two inspired fanatics. Multiple strikes make it collusion."

"Right." He picked up the phone. "I don't suppose Homeland Security is going to reimburse us for all this."

Nadya chuckled like he was a stand-up comic.

✿　✿　✿

In her small townhouse bedroom, Stacy threw clothes from closet and dresser drawers into a suitcase. How quickly would Sturdevan get around to calling the cops? Probably done already. He wasn't very absentminded when he didn't want to be, and they'd already delayed to get some of Aatos' stuff from the lab. How soon would the police be here? No way to guess.

Aatos stayed out of her way. She'd closed the door on her spare room, and he didn't seem disposed to explore the house, thank goodness. Be kind of embarrassing if he found what she had in that other room.

Aatos turned on the TV and scanned the stations. "So what's the alternative?" he said. "If CDC and FDA won't bend their rules, I mean. We can't make people work faster."

Stacy kept packing. "I don't know."

Mr. Praline hopped from perch to perch every time Stacy dashed past. "Urgent, urgent."

"Just give CDC the info. See how they do." Aatos sat down and put the cage on his lap.

"Fine," Stacy said. "A copy. But do other countries have your apparatus? Fewer rules, using you, they'd have a cure out faster."

"No one but Schultz has that kind of facility. No one else could design new chemicals, model and test them, then manufacture on an industrial scale."

Stacy stopped packing. She clasped the sides of her suitcase. "Schultz. No one else has the equipment."

"No. I invented it," said Aatos. "One of a kind."

"And you need industrial production."

"The only way to make a cure that matters."

"And a worldwide distribution network." Stacy picked up her red pencil case.

"Obviously."

"And money. Security. Loyal workforce."

"I guess," said Aatos. "So only governments could do it."

Stacy turned and sat on the bed. She missed and slid to the floor. She never noticed.

"Stacy?"

It hurt, deep down. Something inside told her she'd known this was coming. A roiling, burning feeling, presaging the ultimate sin. The crime some part of her must have been foreseeing since she'd first realized what a cure might entail. Her own, personal, one-woman conspiracy. The deception and ruination of family for the sake of outsiders. The one unforgivable act in her culture.

News came on the TV, an anchor's voice over the pictures. "In plague-related news, the FBI says more than Schultz Pharmaceuticals was involved. Older design instruments were sold to the former Dynamore Delicatessen in New York City. Any suspicious activity around Dynamore in the past several months should be reported to the police."

Aatos' head whipped around. "She said she scrapped it."

Stacy's face went vacant. "Uncle Billy."

CHAPTER THIRTY-ONE

Spring, Year 3

An enormous trench ate into the edge of a jungle outside a town in eastern India. Twenty feet deep and forty feet across, it stretched for hundreds of yards, lined with sticky clay. Pre-monsoon rains had taken a break, and a thousand narrow trickles of runoff washed in from the trees beyond. Bulldozers roared and churned the mud. The remaining light drizzle did nothing to muffle the sound. One bulldozer dug in its tracks and pushed. A hundred human bodies flopped into the hole.

To either side, long lines of bulldozers plowed into pile upon pile of twisted bodies, shoving them into the trench. Every driver wore a face mask.

One driver stood up and peered over the blade at the bloated face of one particular corpse. He ripped off his mask, leaned over a tread, and vomited. A news crew swung over and got a close-up. The evening news replayed the scene in every time zone from Delhi to Madrid to Chicago to Tokyo.

✿ ✿ ✿

Grimm stood outside Cranbrook's empty office. A tiny woman, with bones as delicate as a bird's, chirped around the room.

"That's right, I am Ms. Rinaldi. I heard you wanted background material on that Aatos Pires boy."

"You knew him? In what capacity?"

"He came to my day care center to teach."

"A teacher? I doubt we're talking about the same guy."

"Don't be foolish. How many Aatos Pires can there be? And I know he attended that university that's been all over the news. He visited my kids to talk about animals."

Grimm took a breath. "Animals. Very well, what do you know?"

"Oh, it was a delight to watch him. You just knew he was having a blast."

☼ ☼ ☼

Aatos sprang onto a wobbly, child-sized school desk and dropped one foot to the attached chair to stabilize himself. "And all those eggs your mother cooks with? Pigs lay them."

"*Noooo!*" cried twenty-seven preschoolers. "Chickens!"

"Pigs go *oink*."

"Really?" Aatos slapped his five-foot stick against a chart on the wall. "And chickens go *moo*."

"*Noooo!*" "They go *cluck!*" "Cows go *moo*."

"And bacon comes from sheep. And sheep go *caw, caw*."

"*No!*" "That's pigs." "You're messing it up." "Crows go *caw*." "You're silly!"

Aatos scowled at the laughing faces. "So you think you know all about farms now, do you? Want to see one?"

"Yeah." "Yay!" "Field trip!"

Aatos caught the eye of Ms. Rinaldi along the side of the room. She nodded.

"Okay then, I'll make some arrangements, and let your teacher know what I can line up. Won't be my farm, though. That's a couple of really big states off that-away." He pointed west.

Ms. Rinaldi came forward. "All right, class, let's thank Mr. Pires for another wonderful talk."

A cacophony of high-pitched voices hurled appreciation at Aatos. "See you next time," he said.

Ms. Rinaldi escorted him into the hallway, patting down a wisp of thin, white fly-away hair. "Thank you again for coming. The children so enjoy your animal stories."

"It's fun," said Aatos. "And good for them. City kids have no notion of farm life."

"True. Next week, yes?"

"Sure thing. But not the week after. Got a conference."

"I'll mark my calendar." The old woman nodded, and Aatos headed for the entrance of the day care center.

✿ ✿ ✿

"Halfway down the steps," said Ms. Rinaldi, "he paused when a pretty girl looked at him. Gorgeous auburn hair. But she went the other way and he left alone. Too bad. He deserved to find someone."

"How often did he come?" said Grimm.

"Off and on the better part of two years. But then he finished graduate school."

"So this was all before his time at Schultz. Before he went bad."

Ms. Rinaldi took a step back. "My point is that he was not the type to do what you news services claim he did. I came to set the record straight."

Grimm raised a hand, palm out. "Sorry, I don't mean to offend. We just don't know much about him. Trying to learn all we can."

Ms. Rinaldi studied him a moment. "No, you're just trying to sell stories. Make sensations. I don't know why I bothered."

Grimm apologized again and asked if she knew anything else, but the woman bustled down the hall and wouldn't say another word.

CHAPTER THIRTY-TWO

Spring, Year 3

Stacy waited for Aatos by the alley gate behind her townhouse. She set down the blanket-covered birdcage and shifted her suitcase to her other hand.

Aatos opened the door, wiggling the picture of his parents. "Almost forgot." He stuffed the picture in his satchel, flung it over his shoulder, and lifted another bag.

A crash came behind him, from the front of the apartment. Aatos hurdled off the steps toward Stacy. She picked up his birdcage, and they raced into the alley.

"Near miss," Aatos said.

"We still have to get away."

"Oh, yeah, that."

They snuck between a fence and some trash bins.

Chou Lee and a junior FBI agent came around the side of the townhouse. Lights and noises continued inside. Chou Lee pointed up the alley and nudged the other FBI agent. "This is where you were supposed to be."

The junior agent bobbed his head. "Sorry, sir. End unit. No one was covering the side door, and I thought it was the back." He hurried down the dingy lane, either searching for signs of Stacy or trying to appear busy.

The door opened, and Agent Nadya came out. "Clear. But you are not going to believe what she has in there."

"Oh?"

"A spare bedroom stuffed with wedding gowns. Wall-to-wall store-type racks. White satin, colorful oriental, even a sari or two."

"A dress collection?" said Chou Lee. "Interesting."

"It's pathetic." Nadya came down the stairs. "Must fit a profile of some kind."

"The old prof said Aatos Pires and Stacy Romani were doing pretty heavy research. If Pires worked with Trinity Schultz, then got help here..."

Nadya glanced at the townhouse. "I'll bet she's the female equivalent of the unibomber."

Chou Lee's cell phone rang. He sent it to voicemail, and he and Nadya went back in the townhouse. Time for the detailed search. Why did he have so little confidence they'd find anything? Other than clothes...

✿ ✿ ✿

Stacy's old rattletrap rumbled down the dark city street. She was impressed with how long she'd kept it running, mostly because she didn't mind leaving it in the shop half the time. She slowed until an even more ancient vehicle, a lavender Volkswagen Beetle covered in flower decals, disappeared down a side road. At that point, nothing else was moving. Stacy parked midway between streetlamps, as far from light as possible. She and Aatos got out, Stacy lugging suitcase and birdcage, Aatos toting his satchel and a bag.

"It's not that I don't appreciate having somewhere to go," said Aatos, "but you're actually suggesting we do this? Make our own cure?"

"Life ain't easy." She had to stay focused. Stay upbeat. She had to sell her plan. No one could know what it would really cost them all, or she'd never get the help that was so essential. From Aatos. From her clan. She must act the Stacy of old and make them believe they would get through this with money in their pockets and a grateful world at their feet.

"I still say CDC is competent," said Aatos.

"They are. But the world will die before the law lets them do anything."

They entered a dark building.

Some time later, they came out of a different building, of crumbling red brick. Stacy led Aatos down a murky alley, her draggling, wheelless suitcase collecting more debris than a broom. She shook it off, and they zipped across a side street.

Aatos dodged a trash can. "You look like you know what you're doing."

"Yeah."

"That's a little scary."

"Yeah."

They disappeared into yet another dark building and came out in an alley with two or three more light bulbs per block. This time, Aatos had the suitcase and birdcage, Stacy the bag and satchel. They ducked into a shadow as a fourteen-foot cargo van pulled up. The side read Ace & Ace Pet Supplies.

The back door of the truck rolled upward. Stacy darted out, flipped in the satchel, and hoisted up the bag. Aatos trailed behind.

"Thanks for coming, Uncle Billy." Stacy grabbed the suitcase from Aatos and heaved it into the windowless van.

Uncle Billy took the birdcage and jutted his chin at Aatos. "Who's he?"

"Brains. Under my protection."

"Huh. Wait, he's that Evil Designer they talk about."

"Trinity Schultz calls him that. He invented those machines you bought."

"Not evil?"

"She wants him stopped before he crafts a cure for her

virus. That would be evil. She thinks."

Aatos had about fifty lines etched into his forehead. Stacy didn't think he could show more worry if he tried. If there had ever been the slightest trace of a chance of impressing Aatos, of coming on to him someday if she ever dared—which she wouldn't, of course—she'd blown it all to hell. She'd let him see her relatives.

Hands reached down and helped Aatos and Stacy into the van. The door rolled down, and Mr. Praline squawked as they moved off.

In the roomy, dim, empty cargo area, two guards with shotguns relaxed near the front. Uncle Billy joined them. The vehicle rattled and shook.

The blanket on the cage slipped aside. The parrot clung to the bars, tugging the cloth with his beak. Stacy pulled it the rest of the way off, reached through, and stroked his breast. "Pretty bird?" she asked.

"Pretty bird," mumbled Mr. Praline, not sounding convinced.

Aatos shifted on his bottom, ignoring the parrot. "Who are you?"

"Never mind," said Stacy. "Are you in?"

"You want us to infect the world again, with our private little virus? That's what Trinity did."

"We've been over this. Fifteen million dead and counting."

Aatos slid against a wall, as far away as he could get.

Stacy wedged the cage between bag and suitcase, and looked at Uncle Billy. "I'm taking over. We're shutting down."

"What?"

Aatos crossed his arms. "We're talking about changing the genetic structure of every human being on this planet."

"Without asking," said Stacy. "And regardless of religious beliefs. They'll hate us."

The guards sat mute, but Uncle Billy's eyebrows shot up. "There is no way—"

"I own the place. I sign the checks. Now I need it."

"And you think this is right?" said Aatos.

Stacy volleyed attention between her uncle and Aatos. "I didn't say it was right. I said it was the only way to save people."

"We've got obligations," said Uncle Billy. "A customer base."

"If we don't stop the plague, you won't have a customer base."

Aatos chewed his lip. "I don't like it."

"Nobody will," said Stacy. "Not the point."

"The fanatics will have your hide."

"When we're done, they're welcome to it."

"You expecting trouble?" said Uncle Billy.

"Good question." Stacy scooped some hair behind her ear, pulled it free, and shoved it back again. "Siege mentality. Pull in favors. Stockpile raw materials, close down nonessential communications."

Uncle Billy shook his head. But after a long pause, he nodded once.

"Farewell, free will," said Aatos.

"First survive. Then condemn." Stacy fought down sentiments she had no time to identify, much less deal with.

"Hell of an agenda." Aatos picked at a splinter in the floor of the truck. And another one.

Uncle Billy said, "He's—"

Stacy glared at him and held up a hand. Uncle Billy shrugged.

✧　✧　✧

Aatos kept picking at splinters. And splitting them in pieces. Then he slammed his fist into the side of the van. He rubbed the red weeping from his knuckles. There was another time he had blood on his hands, wasn't there? Just before the first time he'd met Stacy.

He thought about it for over an hour, while the driver sought out every pothole on every road leading toward wherever they were going.

Playing God. Of course, if people were made in God's image, that was sort of expected. Especially if there wasn't a choice. And if you weren't into theology, the issue was moot.

Stacy. It would have to be her who cooked up such a harebrained, risky, high-stakes, and possibly necessary plan. Plan? More like plot, or shady scheme. And necessary?

Aatos ripped off a loose piece of skin. Shit, if he wanted to be honest with himself, it wasn't necessary. It was crucial. Or vital. Or grab a thesaurus.

Crash it all, if it hadn't been Stacy who proposed it, he'd not have given it enough consideration to ever realize that. But... but frag it, he'd be damned if he'd make it easy on her.

"Okay," he said, still rubbing his hand. "So I help you, get some exercise, fix my eyes, and let you choose my clothes. Anything else?" He looked at Stacy.

Stacy burst out laughing. And gasping. And trying to speak. "You'll save the world for a date?"

The van jerked to a stop. Everyone tumbled.

✧ ✧ ✧

Chou Lee's patience, or impatience if he wanted to be honest, had finally been rewarded. His latest oil had arrived, by the greatest Rembrandt imitator in the world. Nadya held the ornate, gold-leaf frame against the wall of his office while he balanced on a stool and stuck tape alongside, marking where he wanted the supports. "Up a bit," he said.

"That's not what you said when you saw it from down here."

"Well, Nadya, maybe I'm changing my mind." He

rubbed another piece of tape on the wall and stepped down.

"Gonna change your mind about buying me coffee?"

"You only want to go out with me because of the dangerous, imminent death scenario."

"In this business, that's our whole lives. Guess again."

"Because I'm rich?" He selected a pair of screws and got up on the stool.

Nadya handed him the drill with a screwdriver bit inserted. "A better guess. But with your alimony, not likely."

"How do you know about that?" Chou Lee drove in the first of the screws. "Never mind. Common knowledge. Hmmm. Maybe you've got a thing for Chinese men, sort of like guys who chase blondes." He put in the second screw.

Nadya took the drill, set it down, and handed him the painting. "Three strikes, and this ain't bowling."

Chou Lee mounted the painting on the wall. He got down and admired it for a moment. Nadya pulled a folder from her briefcase and gave it to him.

"When they assigned me this case, I read your file," she said. "So here's a copy of mine. Fair's fair."

Chou Lee held the file. It wasn't clear which was prettier, Nadya or *The Abduction of Europa* adorning his wall. He had a bad feeling he knew the answer. He sank into his chair and rested the folder on the corner of his desk. "It's just not..."

Nadya turned away and studied a different picture.

The phone rang. Chou Lee answered and listened, jaw sagging open. He clenched the receiver, joints gone white. "Her collegiate home of record was the same burned-out delicatessen?"

Nadya snapped her head around.

Chou Lee smashed down the phone. It shattered. "Trinity Schultz worked with Aatos Pires. Pires is working with Stacy Romani. Romani's fake home is where the old Schultz production equipment ended up."

Nadya took a step toward him. "Two plus two plus two."

Chou Lee erupted from his chair. It crashed into a bookcase. He flew out of his office, stabbing a finger at the first subordinate he saw. "Find out who owns that delicatessen. Find out who used to own it. Find out who brokered the deal to sell it. Hell, find every son-of-a-bitch who ever bought a goddamned sandwich!"

He charged down the hall, Nadya close behind.

✧ ✧ ✧

Dawn broke over the Romani gas production facility as dust settled around the cargo van. The side of the truck now read Multi-Purpose Gas, Inc. Stacy soared out the back in a nonstop torrent of laughter. Aatos jumped down with a reddish cast to his face and trailed her toward a warehouse. Uncle Billy and the guards followed.

"Right, then," Stacy said, coming up for air. "A date."

She couldn't have stopped laughing if she'd tried. She kind of hoped some of it was relief that Aatos had agreed to help, not merely a reaction to his request. Granted, she had the relationship skills of one of the less experienced juniors to ever emerge from the high school pupating stage, but really, *now* Aatos asked her out? Now, after all those years of knowing him and shutting him down if he so much as sneezed in her direction? And after, for heaven's sake, he'd seen Uncle Billy?

Quite the challenge, guessing which was more weird—that Aatos had an interest in her after all, that he got up the nerve to ask her out at the most unlikely and worst possible time, or that Uncle Billy hadn't played tyrant-parent games the moment he tried, threatening him with annihilation for coming on to a clan member. Her family was supposed to hate outsiders. What was Uncle Billy thinking, grinning like a toad and giving Aatos that dinky little thumbs-up he didn't expect her to see?

Stacy crooked her finger in a 'come-hither' curl she expected would give Aatos all sorts of nightmares. Aatos grimaced and followed. Behind them, Uncle Billy maintained his ludicrous and thoroughly inappropriate smirk, toting the birdcage and one of their bags.

CHAPTER THIRTY-THREE

Summary, Year 3

As days passed, the Romani plant went into major construction mode under Stacy's heavy-handed guidance. At least, it must feel rather heavy-handed. Uncle Billy had trained everyone well, though, and the work was all in the family. They'd have no personnel problems.

Stacy watched a trio of her larger distant-cousins wheel a huge piece of equipment down a passageway. Nearby, two workers directed an overhead crane lowering a metal monstrosity onto a steel foundation. Stacy jogged over to the foreman and showed him a blueprint, jabbing her finger from paper to overhead crane. He nodded and got on a walkie-talkie to the crane operator. Stacy handed him the blueprint and left for another warehouse. She paused in the open space to watch a pair of forklifts negotiate a corner with their oversized loads. Further off, Uncle Billy pointed at guards; they slung rifles and helped workers manhandle a crate into position.

One morning after another got dedicated to meetings with their two engineers, their chemist, and multiple technicians, sketching out the design changes needed for the production Stacy envisioned. Then reviewing the engineers' detailed plans and explaining all the modifications and improvements necessary to ensure everyone's different concepts meshed. They were, alas, constrained by Euclidean space, the plain old-fashioned three dimensions, and Tanya's transformer panel simply could not occupy the same spot as Clarence's compressor. Configuration control got harder every day, and the number of changes needed to perfectly good plans, to accommodate someone else's idea for a different device, became insane, a never-ending battle between good enough and better, with judgment calls guaranteed to leave everyone on edge.

Fortunately, Uncle Billy took on more and more of the design and construction oversight once Stacy's intentions were clear, and after she understood there were some rather good reasons why certain of her desires were impractical. Work-arounds and alternatives abounded, thank goodness. And when it came time to oversee ordering new parts—piles of piping, tons of tubing, new barrels, additional forklifts, etc. ad nauseam—there was Uncle Billy again. Good thing too. Stacy desperately needed to get on with the immunological work.

Then she tried to get the engineers to write clear, detailed operating instructions for their personal pieces of the pie. Good grief, she should have been a dentist. Yanking out their teeth sans anesthetic would have been easier. No wonder she'd wanted to be a research scientist, pulling her own hours and, most of the time, being her own boss. Management stank.

Once, when Stacy couldn't take it anymore, she stole a break to check on Aatos' progress. She found Mr. Praline roosting high above Aatos in a closed-in section of a warehouse, freed of his cage at last and flitting about wherever he wanted. Aatos bent over a keyboard, surrounded by other keyboards and computer screens. Differently-shaped, colorful molecules gyrated leisurely on each screen. In one image, a long, spiky protein failed to grapple the protokey sphere.

"Goddamn slippery snake-in-the-grass." Aatos moved to another keyboard.

Stacy lowered the hand she had almost put on his shoulder. She set down the cupcake she had brought to celebrate her birthday. No interruptions. Nothing mattered but the work. Aatos never surfaced as she backed away and stole from the room.

✿ ✿ ✿

Talking heads flickered on a huge television high in the corner of a tavern. Not sports. Four customers were a luxury these days, and the bartender tuned in what interested them most.

The picture switched to the interior of a Turkish museum. Blood streamed from the ears of a fifteen-year-old girl shuddering on the floor. She quivered like an epileptic until a guard ripped a spear from a display and rammed it into her chest, sliding her across the polished marble surface, pinning her to a blossom-bedecked urn. He yelled to the side. A translation scrolled along the bottom of the screen: 'Bring containment.'

The image broadened, revealing a news anchorman beside a screen showing the museum. "Forty million dead," said the anchor. "When are those ivory tower academics going to find a cure? We've been feeding them tax dollars for decades, but when we really need them, who's going to step up and deliver? Is anyone even trying anymore? Is anyone left?"

"Turn it off, please," said a voice from the back of the bar.

Joshua Grimm swiveled on his bar stool. A rival news service had set up in the corner and started recording before Grimm realized who they were.

"You, sir," said a smoothly-groomed hunk of a man, aiming a microphone at Grimm. "What do you think of the authorities' slow response to the epidemic?"

Exactly the kind of showcase reporter Grimm hated.

"Pandemic, you illiterate. It's international."

Grimm stormed out before they could snag him for a follow-up. He'd be damned if he'd be questioned for a competitor's broadcast. It was absurd, anyway. Who seriously thought random civilians had anything meaningful to contribute?

It gave him an idea, though. No one had yet pulled together the whole story of the plague. They nibbled around the edges, reacting to each dribble of news. He was in a position to do more, to turn all his own articles, images, and interviews—and if he was lucky, one key diary the police had found—into a documentary. Not that there would necessarily be anyone to see it. Not that he would survive himself, long enough to finish it. But it was something he could try. The culmination of a second-rate journalistic career.

Well, if he was going to do this thing, he should do it right. Start with patient zero. No, that term didn't apply in this case. Find out something about the culprits, then. The day care teacher, Ms. Rinaldi, had been a start, but no one had landed an interview with that Sturdevan fellow yet. He brushed off reporters like so much lint. There had to be a way to crack that facade.

CHAPTER THIRTY-FOUR

Summer, Year 3

Four retro-punk teen boys sat around a card table, grinning, posturing, trying to out-macho each other.

One reached out and spun a revolver in the middle of the table.

Along the wall, three of their girlfriends smoked and talked among themselves. A fourth trembled, fingers and legs twitching nonstop. She rubbed a spastic hand against her bloody right ear.

"It's not fair," said the trembling girl. "I haven't done anything."

"I know," said one of the other girls. "You don't deserve this."

The revolver came to rest. The boy it pointed toward grinned, picked it up, and spun the cylinder. He aimed it at the side of his head.

Click.

He set down the revolver and twirled it.

"No," said the infected girl, "I mean I haven't accomplished anything. Write a song. Climb a mountain. Have a child." Blood ran from her left ear, worse than the right.

The revolver came to rest, pointing at a different boy. He reached for it.

The trembling girl leapt toward the table and snatched the gun. She fumbled it, dove away from the boys, and stuck the barrel in her mouth.

"Susie!" yelled a boy.

She jammed her finger twice before she got it through the trigger guard.

Click. Click.

A blast took off the top of her head. The remaining retro-punkers pancaked the far wall, brushing at blood and specks of flesh, unable to close their eyes.

☼ ☼ ☼

The next issue of Uncle Billy's favorite news magazine held a color picture of the dead retro-punker, neon-purple hair in a pool of red. The headline read Despair Running Wild, with the subheading, Suicide Pacts Spreading. Below the picture ran an article: 'Police say the death toll among infected and healthy alike is...'

Aatos couldn't see the rest. It was buried under computer printouts and blueprints spread across a large worktable in one of the gas production facility warehouses. At the next table over, Stacy flipped from one document to another, fingers splayed across graphs and data charts, concentration darting from one to another. Aatos marveled at how she juggled a zillion details all at once. That lasted several minutes. He decided to try pacing and guzzling his Coke, instead. This was his last chance for exercise until his next stopping point. Was she really going to go out with him someday? She'd promised, so she must want to. Then again, he'd blackmailed her, so who knew?

"We need more," said Stacy, when she reached the last page. "It's got to affect germ cells."

Aatos stopped pacing and lowered his hand. "That's new. Makes it permanent."

"The human race changes. Every kid has got to be immune."

Aatos put down the bottle. "You want our work to

perdure."

"Okay, even I haven't heard that one. Perdure?"

"Endure to the endureth power."

"Right," said Stacy. "Leave it to you."

"Why use a word everybody understands when there's a perfectly good obscure one?"

Stacy gave him a look that might be amusement, locking him eye to eye. He rather hoped it would perdure.

She pulled up another paper, breaking the moment. "Fifty million. It was twenty when I said fifteen. Information not real-time."

"Accelerating," Aatos said. "Of course. Cells keep making more protokeys."

Stacy nodded.

"I was hoping we might have time for a movie," said Aatos, "but—"

"Three-hour delay," said Stacy. "And worst of all, it isn't how fast people are dying right now."

"I know. What matters is the rate they'll be dying near the end, just before the cure. Three hours, even three minutes..."

Stacy nodded again. "And did you ever think what would happen if one of *us* goes down?"

Aatos shuddered. "I'm in denial on that one."

"Great plan." Stacy tossed down her pen. "Neither of us could finish this alone."

"Scary."

"Scary for you and me. What about the rest of the world?"

She was right, of course. That was the issue. The angle. The perspective. He bolted for the door, leaving behind his Coke.

☼ ☼ ☼

"Forty-three," said Nadya.

Chou Lee watched the camera for interrogation room two. A skittish young man in rumpled, nerdish clothes, thick glasses, and mussed hair played chopsticks on the table with his forefingers, humming the tune and throwing short, desperate peeps at the camera now and then. His fingers weren't coordinated enough to make the song work on a piano.

"Forty-three what?" said Chou Lee.

"Names for the reverend who inspired Trinity. Alleged names."

"And how many protesters have we picked up?"

"Forty-three," said Nadya.

Chou Lee tapped a matching version of chopsticks. "And how many different plots do we have so far?"

"Forty-three, not counting Trinity's. Everything from some idiot who thought she could torch an SUV dealership with eighty-proof bourbon, to this boy's plan, smashing Boulder Dam."

"Smashing it? You mean blowing it up?"

"No," said Nadya, "smashing it. With boulders. Somehow. The details weren't clear, but he thought it would be poetic."

"Poetic." Chou Lee made his hands stop beating on the table. "Terrorism is now poetic." He pulled out the bowl end of a broken pipe and wiped the inside with his thumb. He watched the young suspect switch over to a more elaborate keyboard rendition of something not meant for human fingers. The tape recorder dutifully recorded every pitter-pat he pounded out.

"Let's be thankful no one told him it was renamed Hoover Dam several decades ago," said Nadya. "He'd probably have tried to vacuum it up."

"Right. Let's go. We're late." Chou Lee stalked out the door.

An hour later, Chou Lee and Nadya were admitted to

the chambers of Judge Archibald Goldbloom, a heavyset man in a yarmulke, who liked to remind everyone he was a childhood friend of the President.

"Special Agent-in-Charge Lin, I wanted to speak with you personally regarding this request for a search warrant." The judge thumbed through a thick sheaf of papers. "Despite the fact that Trinity Schultz claimed to have created the RIAS virus, you want to raid every home in the country with the family name of Romani. Because you think this Stacy person helped."

"I don't see we have any choice at this point, your honor. I've asked the Canadians to do the same."

"Have you, now? It's not that rare a name. And it's Italian."

"As the warrant states, we are limiting the search to where it refers to Roma."

"And why target them?"

"Italians have big families and are proud of them. Stacy hid her background. That's suspicious."

"I see. And when you find nothing, will you extend your raid to every person having Gypsy background?"

"That would be next, yes."

The judge leaned back and steepled his fingers. "So essentially you wish me to authorize a witch hunt."

"I wouldn't call it that. But I see no other way to find Stacy. And Pires."

The judge contemplated Chou Lee so long that Nadya put a hand on his shoulder in support.

"Would you ask me to do this if the person in question had claimed to be Hispanic, or Irish, or Japanese?"

"That would not be practical, your honor."

"You find it acceptable to follow a racist policy if it's practical?"

"I'm trying to find the makers of the pandemic. The only way we have a chance."

"Will finding them in any way slow down the disease?"

"It might provide information leading to a cure."

"It might. If we speculate. If we disbelieve Trinity Schultz's claim that no such cure exists. If we disbelieve her mother that Trinity never developed a cure for anything in her life. If I allow you to insult an entire culture for no better reason than to shut a barn door when the cows are dead and gone."

"Your honor—"

"No, I've read this thing in detail. I had someone call that professor fellow she worked with. What you want is to break every civil liberty the Roma have because a woman who lied about her home address, fabricated high school credentials from a non-existent town in Utah to get into college, invented all her contact information, and provided a fake social security number, is suddenly going to be believed about a last name she laid claim to, and a potentially implied ethnicity. Did she ever show the slightest sign she was a Gypsy? Did she wear traditional clothes? Was she known to play Gypsy dance tunes in her laboratory? No, and no. You have not the slightest evidence that this one single piece of information you wish to act on, her stated name of Romani, has any validity."

"That may be true, your honor, but it's all we have to go on. We need to track the only lead we have left."

"Not at the cost of alienating every minority in the country who will see a precedent that could be used against them someday. Not when you have no real basis to believe your actions would result in a better or faster remedy than CDC and every other health agency in the world are working to find. When your actions would serve only to perhaps find a terrorist. And as admirable as it is to apprehend criminals, that alone cannot justify such a wide-ranging infringement of people's rights."

Chou Lee thought about arguing. Or approaching

another judge. Once you had a 'no,' though, the old 'asked and answered,' that could be a career-ending move. Acceptable, if it would work in the short term and he could find the bastards responsible. But Goldbloom was likely to hear about any such attempt, and his points might be repeated by another judge, anyway.

But what was his next step now?

"Understood, your honor."

Nadya preceded him out the door. Behind them came the sound of papers ripping in half.

CHAPTER THIRTY-FIVE

Summer, Year 3

Valerie trudged up to a bank of microphones outside CDC headquarters. She wrapped her fingers around the edges of the podium, forcing them to remain still. She'd been doing all these press briefings alone since Ngono passed away. Reporters and camera people clustered before her. Behind them, summer green adorned the trees. Farther off, a trickle of concerned citizens and a beefed-up security force eyed each other through the fence in the background. No one wanted to be called a protester anymore, and all seemed well-behaved.

Valerie had hoped to have news on the robotics project by now. Something positive. But Timmy was still flailing with platform stability, sensor issues, and finding a suitable agent to attack the virus when it was identified. Progress everywhere, he said, but nothing solidified yet. She didn't know if he was telling the truth or painting roses to keep the money flowing, but she dared not take a chance, so she wasn't about to cut him off.

She scanned the reporters' faces, wondering how they'd take the news she did have to release.

"I have something new. You know we're trading information with agencies around the world. But we also received data from the FBI, captured from the creators of the disease, identifying the key that sets off phase two of the virus."

The reporters shouted questions about how or when a cure would be available. Valerie held up a hand.

"I'll continue these updates, but even knowing the key, finding a drug that won't kill the cell is tricky. I'm still crossing fingers for—" She took a breath. No, stick to her prior decision. No robotics info until it really stood a chance. "Just crossing my fingers."

More pointless questions. More pointless pressure.

"Think about it. We're cramming years of research into weeks. Or trying to. I imagine by now, we've all lost someone. Push all you like, I can't stop you. But we're moving as fast as we can."

☼ ☼ ☼

In the gas production facility warehouse, Stacy watched a television on the wall, where Valerie turned away from the microphone and went inside CDC.

"Captured? From the creators?"

Aatos studied his computer screen and kept typing. "Who else could they think we are?"

"And thus endeth the spoon-feeding." Stacy reached over Aatos' shoulder and pointed to twisting, intertwining molecules on his computer screen. He leaned in and smelled her hair. Stacy smiled briefly and taped a piece of paper to the monitor. "This will regulate production of the sensor chemicals."

"Feedback for the feedback."

"Right."

"Is this an infinite regression?"

"That's it for this part of the problem."

"This part."

Stacy shrugged.

Aatos grabbed the sheet. "Life is too bloody complicated."

☼ ☼ ☼

A trackhoe operator twisted his machine around, digging a short, narrow trench in a rolling, grassy cemetery. His boss lumbered over and swiped a finger across his throat. The operator centered a couple of control levers and shut off the machine.

"New law," said his boss. "They're cremating all plague victims."

They were in a graveyard so vast it disappeared over low hills in every direction. The trackhoe was surrounded by forty fresh, empty graves. In the distance, other workers dug more holes, a raucous maelstrom of activity.

"What earthly good will that do?" said the operator. "You've heard the news."

"You know politicians. Gotta show they're doing something."

"Right. What about Muslims?"

"Huh?" The boss scratched an ear. "Oh, there's some special containment rules if you've got religious prohibitions. Not cheap. Doesn't much apply around here."

"No, of course not. Merely another opportunity for us to look like a bunch of bigots." The worker spat tobacco juice at the graves. "So what do I do with these?"

CHAPTER THIRTY-SIX

Summary

Summer, Year 3

There was a technical term for the lighting in Professor Sturdevan's office, Grimm thought. He was pretty sure it 'sucked.' The wooden ladder-back chair for visitors filled almost all the floor space between the door and the desk where Sturdevan sat, backed by a large window full of afternoon sun.

"Could you close the shade, perhaps?" said Grimm. "That glare is a killer, and I doubt we could move one of your bookcases to get a better camera angle."

"Haven't used that shade in twenty years," said Sturdevan. "Doubt I want to release whatever's living in it."

Grimm squinted at the professor. Behind him, the cameraman banged the legs of his tripod off the door.

"Besides, glare is useful," Sturdevan said. "Especially on undergraduates who need a kick in the ass."

Grimm snorted. He should have brought a barrel or two of salt to leaven the old man's words. "I don't suppose you'd change your mind about moving outside."

"What's on your mind, Mr. Grimm?"

"We wanted your personal take on certain prior students, sir. Specifically, Trinity Schultz, Aatos Pires, and Stacy Romani." Grimm tried to get comfortable in the chair. "Now that they're accused of the largest mass-murder in history, is there anything you recall, anything in how they acted when you knew them that, in hindsight, could serve as a warning for the future?"

"Do I have a psychology degree now?"

"Just asking your opinion, sir."

"So you can scare people about introverted, friendless geniuses?"

"That's not my intent."

Sturdevan scoffed. "Since when does a reporter's intent mean anything? Anyway, forget the molds. Nobody fits them."

"I—"

"What's this really about, Mr. Grimm?"

Grimm coughed a couple of times and shut his notebook. "You're filler material, sir."

"*Filler* material?"

"Yes, sir. People want to believe in progress, so we have to keep talking about the problem. Doesn't matter what we say. Personal interest stories are always welcome. If the subject stays on page one, they'll believe we're doing all we can."

"All you can," said Sturdevan. "What is it a news service does to fix problems?"

"Keep the public off the back of those doing the real work."

Sturdevan went blank, then broke up laughing. "My God," he said, "a reporter with a magnanimous mission." He came out from behind his desk, took Grimm by the arm, and led him outside to continue the interview. The cameraman struggled along in their wake.

"Let me tell you about my students," Sturdevan said, still laughing. "Schultz is totally believable. Pires wouldn't hurt a fly; he'd put a splint on it and give it a transfusion. But once he got hooked on Romani... ah, romance can twist your soul..."

Grimm recorded everything. It was amazing how long Sturdevan could talk. It shouldn't have been; he was a professor, after all. But he was also Sturdevan, when all was said and done. Grimm wasn't sure he'd print a single word of it. Most everything he got seemed to be either libel or science fiction. Or worse, romantic comedy.

"Let's see," said Sturdevan, launching into another tale. "I recall ethics was always an issue with those two."

☼ ☼ ☼

Aatos entered the professor's office and sat in the one free chair. "You wanted to see me, sir?"

"I drag all my undergraduates in here for counseling now and then," said Professor Sturdevan. "Don't look so nervous. Hmm, says here you rejected veterinary medicine."

"Correct, sir," said Aatos. "Only heal one animal at a time?"

Professor Sturdevan nodded. "I see. You're one of those."

"A big picture guy."

"A big ego guy." The professor chuckled. "No insult. I'm one myself. We do the technical stuff while the meek inherit the earth we build. And generally speaking, outvote us."

Aatos fidgeted in his chair. He could never get comfortable around such an august figure, particularly since you could never take anything he said at face value.

Sturdevan leaned back and propped one heel on the corner of his desk. His office would have been generous for two or even three people to share, if it had about ninety-five percent fewer overstuffed bookshelves. Aatos wanted a room just like it someday. Unless he could get a bigger one. Dreaming wasn't greed, was it?

"I'm hearing all kinds of good feedback on your tutoring," said Sturdevan. "They tell me you help half the students in your class. Perdition, boy, you got that Simmons girl through chem lab."

"Thank you."

"Surprised me. All things shall pass, but not all people do."

"Uh..."

"You dating her?"

Aatos blushed. He wished to hell he would outgrow that. "A sorority princess? Not likely."

"Ah. Don't worry, your ego will continue to expand."

Aatos decided not to respond.

"Still a sophomore, and tutoring upper level classes already, yes?"

"Um, yeah. I read ahead a lot."

"I see," said the professor. "So you're smart, you want the rigors of research, and you're a good teacher. As your college advisor, I think I know where those line up."

"Yes, sir."

Sturdevan put his other foot on the desk and spread his arms. "And what could be better than the generous salary of a professor in a state university?"

"Especially when the state is on a tight budget."

Sturdevan laughed out loud. "Goodness, you *are* well informed."

☼ ☼ ☼

"Um, sir, are you sure that was accurate?"

"That's how I remember it," said Sturdevan. "I may have put a few thoughts in his head, but I doubt it. Aatos would make a terrible poker player. You could read him like a freshman's first computer code."

Grimm checked his cameraman. Way too much memory in digital media these days. He couldn't use the 'out of film' excuse to get away from the professor.

"And then there's Stacy. Caught her in the hall one day in graduate school and hauled her off to give her a teaching assignment. I swear I'll only embellish with what I learned later."

☼ ☼ ☼

"There you are."

"Professor Sturdevan, hi," said Stacy. "Isn't our next session on Thursday?"

"Waste of time. Cancel it. You don't need course advice. Or career advice, for that matter. Got something else for you."

Stacy followed the venerable geezer, as she liked to think of him. By the time they went up a flight of stairs and circled the building to his cluttered, absentminded-professor office, she was pretty much back to normal after her disastrous luncheon with Aatos. She hoped.

Stacy slowed as she entered, like she did every time she came here. Anybody who could cram this limited space with that volume of books, no pun intended, was an absolute hero.

"Here," the professor said, tossing her a folder. "Next semester's teaching load."

She opened the folder and read a line. "This is ethics."

"Then I didn't give you the wrong one."

"But Professor, I was worst in that class. Too pragmatic, you said."

"Hence the assignment."

Stacy started to say something, then swallowed it. A thought hit her. "Aatos Pires used to help you with that."

Sturdevan sat down. "Verily so. Had hopes for that boy. Ended up seduced by gold."

"Gold?"

"Camille Schultz. In fact, there was another failure. Hanging out with wanna-be eco-extremists."

"Camille appeared very professional. Aatos was—"

"Not Camille. Daughter Trinity. Had her teach ethics too." He got a distant look. "She outgrew the rebel stage, but still went to work for her mother. Maybe this isn't working.

Gimme that."

"But—"

Sturdevan leaned over the desk and grabbed the folder. "I'll get someone else. Don't want to screw you up too."

Stacy raised her hands in surrender. "I'll do whatever you like."

"Yeah? Then you've got freshman chem. Again. That'll teach you to be accommodating."

Stacy let out a breath, barely able to suppress a laugh. "Yes, sir."

"What are you standing around for?" Sturdevan swept out his arm, pointing at the hall behind her. "Back to work."

Stacy saluted, did an about-face, and marched away to carry out her master's commands. She had to dodge a rubber band on her way to the door.

☼ ☼ ☼

Grimm signaled the cameraman to pack up his gear. Enough was enough. Sturdevan told vignettes like an actor, adopting the role of every character in sight. Insanity. Grimm needed confirmation from elsewhere before he could print this stuff. Like from that diary the cops snagged, should he ever be granted access.

"Thank you for your time, sir. We have deadlines to meet."

"Really?" said Sturdevan. "I was just warming up."

Grimm towed the cameraman down the sidewalk as fast as he could go.

"Wait. You're supposed to be pitching those two as evil masterminds. I've got more dirt on them."

Grimm shoved the cameraman into their van, got in the driver's side, and slammed the door.

CHAPTER THIRTY-SEVEN

Summer, Year 3

Aatos plunked down in a chair near Stacy. The warehouse banged and squealed around them as workers installed equipment and rerouted piping. Stacy had a cubbyhole carved out amidst monolithic gray machines where three new computers were her sole domain. Aatos' 'office' was far across the bay, in another convenient nook. Stacy hunched over one computer, typing, banging a heel off a chair leg, over and over.

Aatos massaged a wrist and waited, eyelids drooping, until her fingers paused. "Does your database modification include suppression of allergic reactions?"

"No immune response will be sufficient, I hope."

"What?" said Aatos. "Cutting corners?"

Stacy drew back. "A hundred million dead."

"Yeah. By the way, I designed a key to unlock the protector coating on our DNA."

Stacy stopped typing and closed her eyes. "Thank you."

"Always a problem, going fast. Miss things."

She cracked her lids. "You know the answer to that."

Aatos rubbed the other wrist, then nodded. "Exception to every rule. That's us." He leaned over the desk and pushed himself to his feet. "Get some rest."

"That's likely. Every time I nap, twenty thousand die."

"And how many will if you don't?"

Stacy seemed befuddled, like it was a trick question.

She shook herself and resumed typing. "All right," she said. "Soon." Her fingers stumbled across the keys.

It was the best Aatos could hope for. He couldn't convince her of anything when his own brain was limp as a... well, the fact he couldn't think what, said it all. Stick with limp. He limped down the aisle toward his bunk.

CHAPTER THIRTY-EIGHT

Summer, Year 3

Grimm loomed over Chou Lee and pounded the mahogany. "In the middle of all this, with everyone looking over everyone else's shoulder, how could anyone break into Schultz Pharmaceuticals and haul off eight tons of gear?"

"Far too easily, it turns out." Chou Lee threw papers into a tooled leather briefcase on his desk. "Twenty-five heavily armed men. Big truck. No regard for the guards."

"Dead?"

"One in intensive care. The rest are fine."

"Police?"

"Their own guard force. No one figured they had much worth stealing. Or nothing small enough to steal." He grabbed a pipe, a shamefully battered meerschaum today, and tore off down the hall, Grimm hot on his heels. "What are we up to now?"

The classic question, the one on everyone's lips each day. Grimm tried to keep up with the numbers, but their accuracy fluctuated from country to country and agency to agency. "Something in the neighborhood of two hundred million, I think," he said. "Plus or minus."

Chou Lee hit the stairwell and bounded down two steps at a time, muttering under his breath. "Should have kept smoking. Could have done it for years if I'd known a plague was coming."

Grimm kept silent. He wasn't meant to have heard. Everyone was allowed their moments of angst, and in the case of Chou Lee, it wouldn't last long.

✧ ✧ ✧

Stacy spread oversized sheets of paper across a picnic table in the rocky area between warehouses. Aatos helped her hold them down with ketchup, mustard, and a bottle of rather dubious, purplish salad dressing. She'd checked a calendar that morning. Days slipping away she could understand, but they'd been working so long the weeks had turned into oil. And fast approaching the point where she'd have to think in terms of months.

Damn it, concentrate.

"This is what I want," Stacy said, pointing from page to page.

Aatos studied the papers, then nudged her out of the way and dug in more deeply. Stacy combed wind-tossed hair out of her eyes while Aatos flipped from one sheet to another, backed up, then went to the end.

It was a beautiful day. When was the last time she noticed?

After the better part of an hour, Aatos shook his head. "People are dying. We don't need this."

"We have to."

Aatos rearranged two pages. "I've got the immunoglobulin. Every enzyme it takes to build the thing."

"And what happens when the virus mutates?" said Stacy. "It will. The key will change."

Aatos kept shaking his head.

She pointed from interconnected tables of data to a long equation to a complex chemical formula. "This reacts to change, adapts, revises enzymes to revise the immunoglobulin."

"You're talking weeks. You will personally kill fifty

million people if you make them wait for this."

"We've got one chance," said Stacy. "One. Once this cure is released, they'll track us down. You think they'll ever let another virus infect the world, to fix our mistakes?"

Aatos turned away.

"Everything evolves," she said. "We release this thing prematurely, we release a one shot deal, then after the plague mutates, everybody dies."

"You don't know that!"

She had no comeback. The truth was there, when he chose to see it.

Aatos took a shaky breath. He studied the papers some more. "Weeks," he said, turning another page. "At least."

Stacy watched him. After several more minutes, this time filled with silence, Aatos swept up the papers and stormed away.

He hadn't even bothered to flirt.

✿ ✿ ✿

Chou Lee raced out the front door of his office building, Grimm still hot on his heels. Chou Lee spotted a black car with Nadya leaning on the hood and headed for it.

Grimm couldn't let go of the Schultz equipment theft. The reporter part of his brain wouldn't let him. "You can't hide eight tons of delicate high-tech metal," he said. "Weren't there witnesses?"

Nadya barked a laugh.

"We're still rounding up Trinity protesters," said Chou Lee. "Still interrogating. They're all playing dumb, but one of them may know something."

"You're sure they took it?" said Grimm.

Nadya cocked her head. "It had to be someone helping Aatos Pires. Who else knows how to use that stuff?"

Chou Lee and Nadya got in the car.

Chou Lee scowled at Grimm. "Eco-religious doomsday

cult. Pires and Romani. Got over twice the production capacity now." As the car pulled away, Chou Lee shouted out the window. "Print it!"

Grimm watched the car drive off. He stood in the middle of the sidewalk, blocking the flow of pedestrians, flicking his notepad open and shut.

Why would they need more plague?

☼　☼　☼

A truck-mounted crane lifted the massive new DNA/RNA transcripter from Schultz Pharmaceuticals off a flat-bed truck and set it on the floor in one of the Multi-Purpose Gas warehouses. Stacy led Uncle Billy out the twelve-foot door of the warehouse, heading for the algae ponds.

"You've got fresh algae?" said Stacy. "All the old production plants dead?"

Uncle Billy gave a thumbs-up. "Every pond purged, regrown, and tested, like you wanted. Redid one pond twice."

"Feeder lines to gas cylinders purged, bled, and repurged?"

"Yup. Even cleaned the fire suppression system to ensure no cross-contamination."

Stacy grinned at him. "Good thought. How about QC?"

"Quality control labs up, running, and tested on blanks."

They walked along the rows of algae ponds, inspecting all the preparations.

"Smudge pots," said Stacy.

"What?"

"Those things they use in Florida to keep the orange groves from freezing. It's gonna get cold up here before we're done. We need a couple hundred, so the algae ponds don't freeze and stop producing."

"I'll get on it," said Uncle Billy. "We only used a few ponds last winter, and steam heating wasn't efficient. Smudge pots, that's an idea, but won't be enough when it gets bitter."

"Buy plastic? Make a giant tent?"

"Maybe, if we need to. And kerosene heaters. I'll see."

They kept pacing and checking around. Stacy figured there were likely tons of ways to make the whole thing more efficient if you were investing for a production run of years, but long-range planning was hardly the point.

"Whatever happened to Theresa?" said Stacy. "I haven't seen her since I got back. Or Rudy."

"Theresa married into our sister clan. We sent Rudy away the moment you turned up with Aatos."

"What? Why?"

Uncle Billy looked at her through his eyebrows, the way he did when she was small and he thought she was being obtuse. "We're bringing them both in, though. Need experienced people. All we can get, especially with our losses."

"Oh. Right." How thoughtless of her. They'd lost more people. Franky was only the first. And she hadn't even considered it.

A relief valve lifted, hissed, and reseated, dragging her back to business. "What else?" she said. "What are we forgetting?"

"Well, we could give the crews a little time off. They're exhausted."

Of course they were. Something else she'd ignored. "They've broken routine, haven't they?"

"I'll say."

"Local bars will be curious." She rubbed her elbows. "You know them. Give 'em a cover story—discrete, believable—and let 'em go."

"They're used to that. And you can relax with your

boyfriend."

Her breath caught.

Strange. How could one simple word put an ache in her chest? And no, she couldn't relax. Neither could Aatos. Not yet.

CHAPTER THIRTY-NINE

Late Summer, Year 3

Valerie approached the bank of microphones in front of CDC headquarters and twisted them around, so she'd not have to stare into the setting sun. Pretty oranges and lavenders around the clouds, but too much glare for a press conference.

She smiled at several of the reporters, faces she recognized from all her time out here. Smiled because today, months after she first met Timmy, she'd decided she'd heard enough about his latest developments, his tiny robot designs, that optimism could finally be justified. And hope released to the public.

"At long last, I have some good news. Not with chemical agents, as I'd expected. Something else. I'd like to announce that our esteemed late Doctor Ngono began a project that may lead to a cure."

She parsed out the nanorobotics information, watching the reporters scribble notes, type on phones, or mumble into recorders. Some of the oldest veterans had the newest toys, oddly enough. It was actually fun watching them scramble to jot down thoughts for later. They weren't about to miss anything—they were recording her every word—yet still they acted panicked, like a rival might beat them to something.

She didn't identify the company working on it; these vultures would inundate the place, and poor Timmy would never get a lick of work done.

"We're after the very enzymes the virus uses to attack the immune system. And the virus can't fight back. It has no mechanism to identify or damage the semiconductor coating on our nanobots. Gallium arsenide may do the trick, if they can lick the poisonous issue. I suspect they'll need to identify other coatings, capable of both protecting the robot and attacking the virus with fewer side effects. And they still need a functioning platform to enter the body, to uniquely home in on the virus, and to remain stable for the weeks necessary to complete the process."

This time, Valerie didn't mind the barrage of questions. She had a whole slew of notes to refer to, and for the first time, she could grin at one of these events. For the first time, a ray of light could enter the arena, and cut through the miasma of despair sweeping across the world.

When it was over, when the interrogation had degenerated into repetition, she wound it up and closed her folder. She didn't go back inside, though. This time, she deserved a break, and she wasn't about to let anyone intercept her. She headed for the parking lot, turning off her cell phone as she went.

Sleep. Get off her feet, ease her aching back, have dinner with her husband, and then more sleep. She'd earned it, and no one was going to stop her.

✡ ✡ ✡

"Chad, get your productive little ass over here."

"Sure thing, reverend." Chad ditched the last bite of his veggie-burger. Couldn't stay thin if he kept eating when no longer hungry. "What's up?"

"Did you catch the news? Do you ever watch the news? Never mind, why do I ask? Just hurry."

Chad made it to the reverend's latest hideout in record time. He'd repainted his old van four times so far and made new realistic-looking fake license plates every few weeks. Pretty clever, if he said so himself. The reverend had his own notions of security, as well, and they seemed to be working. He and Chad were two of the few originals still free.

He drove behind the reverend's latest shack, crunching across the gravel into the shade of an ancient hemlock. Plenty of rocks from road to abode, the reverend advised. Best way to avoid tire tracks. And never leave your vehicle where drones or satellites could find it. Never leave it where sunlight could reflect, signaling its presence to those far away. Little things like that were the reverend's mantra, and Chad had no problem lapping them up.

The reverend came outside as Chad slammed his door. "Hush. Get in the habit. Do things quietly, so it becomes an instinct. In case it matters someday."

Chad nodded. The old guy was getting more and more paranoid, probably with good reason. "What's up?"

The reverend pulled four sets of three sticks of dynamite from his deep pockets and handed them to Chad. "Hide these, then follow me."

Inside the shack, the reverend pointed to half a dozen five-gallon gasoline containers.

Chad grinned. "You finally found me a target?"

"Not quite. Put those in the van. Drive around, fill them at different places. No more than one per station to avoid suspicion. I'll call you soon with a location."

"What kind? Power plant? Dam again?"

"Nothing so mundane." The reverend was grim, not at all his usual confident self. "That genius recruit of yours may have created the solution we always craved. But—"

"Boy, did she."

"Listen. They may have found a way to stop it."

"Shit."

"For sure. Just announced it. That irresponsible pencil-pusher from CDC spouts out news about a potential cure in the offing, without a trace of security, then a camera catches her leaving the facility. The way she was talking, meeting with the folks involved, I figure it's gotta be somewhere close."

"What a moron. They think we have no teeth left?"

"Exactly. Even worse, it's a desecration. A violation of God's grand design. They want to fill us with robots."

"What? Turn us into automatons?"

"It's the first step. A slippery slope. I'll find her address, then you have to persuade her to tell you who's doing the work. If I'm right, if it's some nearby factory or laboratory, you need to be ready to take them out. Fast. Before anyone wises up."

Chad tossed the last of the empty gas cans in the back of the van, checked the battery on his cell, and took off. At last, a worthy mission. Admit it, he'd been jealous when Trinity's bug had proven to be the salvation of planet earth. There'd not been a single thing he could do, or that the reverend would let him do, to sow havoc as other believers had done. The reverend wanted him in reserve, 'just in case.'

What do you know, the reverend had been right all along. They did need a reserve. And now it was time to deploy it. Deploy *him*. He gunned the engine, plotting out the best sequence of gas stations for filling the containers, positioning himself after the last one near a major intersection for when the reverend identified his objective. And he'd better have one more smoke, while he could. He'd have to knock off the cigarettes once he loaded up on gas.

✧ ✧ ✧

Nadya finished marking a report and passed it to Chou Lee. He added it to a pile without letting it distract him from a different one.

"Don't you think you should find out what that guy

wants?" Nadya pointed to the junior agent tapping on the glass of Chou Lee's door. His hand inched toward the knob, then jerked back, like he'd been burned one too many times bursting in uninvited.

"Screw him. He thinks it's time for my annual sensitivity training. Like that matters when the world's coming to an end."

Nadya chuckled. "Ah, take mercy on the poor kid." She opened the door and said, "What is it, agent?"

The young man held out a flash drive. "Latest CDC press release. It's got something new. Think Doctor Lin should know about it. You too."

"Thanks. I'll give it to him."

Chou Lee looked up. "I was wrong?"

"Had to happen sometime." Nadya slipped the drive into her computer.

Two minutes later, she swore.

"What's up?" Chou Lee came over behind her and Nadya replayed Valerie's press briefing. "Holy shit."

"Damn right. Who's she talking about? What company? Where? And do they have any more security than that Schultz factory?"

"Cursed fools." Chou Lee swept up his suit coat and herded Nadya out the door. "After hours. Call CDC. Find out where she is. Where she lives. I don't know if that doomsday cult has any fanatics still active, but the reverend is out there. God, I hope he's not heard yet."

Nadya punched her cell as they chased down the hall.

✡ ✡ ✡

Twilight lingered, reluctant to bid adieu to the day. Chad crept to the back door of the Slotowski residence. The reverend swore it was the right place. He'd heard Valerie's husband was a fireman, and this was the only Slotowski that fit.

Chad listened a moment. No sounds but the murmur of a television, and not even a good show if it was that quiet. He pulled out his Glock 20, magazine stuffed with ten-millimeter, hollow-point shells, and caressed the barrel. He'd not been able to shoot anything in years. The reverend wouldn't allow it. He figured shooting ranges would be staked out, watching for potential terrorists, and target shooting in the woods tended to get the neighbors calling the sheriff. Low profile, that's what the reverend wanted, and Chad would be loyal. Obedient. It was the one thing he could claim set him apart from so many others.

Was the door locked? Should he break a window? Be subtle?

Screw it. He lifted a foot and smashed the handle. The door flew inward. Chad barreled inside, waving his gun. He caromed off the kitchen table and into the next room. Valerie and her husband were rising from a dinner table, reacting to his noise.

"On the floor. Now!"

He didn't have time for pleasantries. The husband was slow, so Chad fired a round at his feet. Valerie screamed, grabbed his hand, and they both dove flat, facedown.

"Where's that place you were talking about?" Chad poked Valerie in the back. "That robot factory. Where?"

"Don't tell him." The husband. The target. Valerie's weak point.

Crack! One bullet, one toe gone. The man screamed, the same pitch as his wife.

"Where?"

"Don't—" Another toe.

"Damn it, stop. I'll tell you."

"No, Valerie, too many lives—"

Crack! His right hand this time.

"I got spare magazines. How much more I gotta do?"

"Don't—"

Crack!

"I'll tell you!" Valerie spilled it all. Name, address, even directions. Chad crushed their phones and raced out the back.

"Thank you, Valerie. But you shouldn't have told him."

"I couldn't help it."

"We could be dead any day. We should have let him kill us."

"That place has locks. Steel doors. And nobody will be there."

The argument faded behind Chad. He grinned. If he'd given them time to think, they might have been heroic. They might have denied him what he needed. But shock had ruled the day, as so often proved the case. He could have killed the pair, but witnesses were irrelevant.

Why did Valerie talk, though, really? Why did anyone talk in such a situation? It was so cockamamie. Ninety-nine point nine percent of the time, anyone doing what he'd been doing was going to waste them no matter what they said. Why not put up with a little pain and deny their tormenters? Yet another reason to wipe out the illogical human race.

Ah, well, the plague would finish them off, soon enough. As long as he stopped the robotics guy.

Chad fired up the van and took off. The feds knew what was in the CDC briefing, and would be worried about security soon enough. He didn't have much lead time, if any at all. He could reach the robotics lab and find it crawling with cops, already in place to protect it. But there was a chance they'd be too slow. A chance to head off this threat to all Trinity had accomplished. A narrow window, at best.

And if it was there, if he found the slimmest crack, he'd blow that window wide open.

☼ ☼ ☼

The van motor faded away. Valerie leapt up and raced

to the upstairs bathroom, grabbing gauze and tape. Back downstairs, she made stop-gap bandages for her husband and bundled him out to the car. Hospital, fast, was all she could think. He'd stopped berating her for talking to the doomsday cultist, stopped talking altogether, and she feared he might pass out. Shock. That wouldn't be good.

She floored it, tearing around the corner. The emergency room had damn well better take him, stat. Unlike plague victims, this was something they could fix.

✿ ✿ ✿

Nadya and Chou Lee screeched to a halt in front of Valerie's house. A second car passed them and pulled into the driveway on the right. Nadya ran to the door, three steps ahead of Chou Lee, and began pounding. Agents from the other car headed around the house to check the back.

"No answer," Nadya said. Chou Lee peered in a window.

An agent behind the house shouted. Nadya stayed where she was, covering the front. Chou Lee headed left, checking out the remaining side of the building.

A few minutes later, the agents from the second car opened the front door from inside, beckoning Nadya to enter. "Clear. No one home. Back door's shattered."

Blood on the dining room floor, scattered dishes. Nadya went back out and met Chou Lee as he completed a circuit of the house.

"No car," he said. "Kidnapped."

"Maybe," said Nadya.

Chou Lee shouted orders to the junior agents. "Alert police. BOLO on their car. Check hospitals. We'll get CDC staff to rifle her notes. We need to find that robotics place. Move!"

✿ ✿ ✿

Chad cruised along the edge of the light-industrial park.

Dark as shit, tight as a virgin's ass. The cheapskates owning all the little shops didn't bother with nightlights. They think they didn't have anything to steal? Or their locks would keep everyone out? Chad checked the side streets, but they were equally deserted. Alleys, really. Not a soul around. Scattered streetlights farther off, but enough of a glow he could navigate with the van's headlights turned off. He couldn't have done it in a modern vehicle, with auto-on lights. Yet another government conspiracy to keep track of people.

Same thing with sticking GPS everywhere. Watching, watching. And connecting every speck of data to the grid. Whose idiotic notion was it to connect power stations or even street lights to the Internet? Things should be free-standing. The benefits of universal control were far outweighed by the risk of hacking, which was more than bad enough, but the real risk always came from government. Messing with everyone, screwing things up, blaming it on terrorists, all for the sake of keeping the public in line.

People sucked.

Come on, back on track. Chad released an airy laugh. The reverend was right, as usual. He always said Chad's mind wandered too far, too fast.

So, a black, locked up research lab. Or factory. Or combination. Whatever. At least the cops weren't here yet, unless they were hiding, ready to jump out when he got close. No, that was paranoia; security never tried to hide. They'd advertise if they were here.

Safe, then. Time to approach.

He pulled up to a point a block away, on the uphill side, killed the engine, and coasted down to rest with the rear of the van even with the front door. No reason to carry stuff farther than necessary. He got out, opened up the back, and slid out a crowbar. The grill over the main entrance may look tight, but he knew how to lever it out of the latch.

Noisy. Several squeals, a loud snap, and the metal mesh

outer door popped open.

A light clicked on inside. Another light outside.

"Shit." So much for subtlety. Chad rammed the crowbar into the gap by the inner door latch. He grabbed the bar with both hands, ready to heave.

The door swung open, the crowbar fell, and Chad stumbled back.

"Who's there? What are you... hey!"

Chad shoved the guy inside. He sprawled across the floor. Chad pulled out his Glock and aimed it at the belly.

"Wait! There's money here. A little. Okay, not much. You don't need to—"

Chad shot him. Belly, chest, then closer up, head. Whoever this man was, it didn't matter. Chad wasn't here for negotiation.

He clicked off the outside light and went to work. The glow from the desk lamp was all he needed.

First things first. He went to the van and dragged out his favorite toy, an oversized electromagnet. He set it on the desk, plugged it in, and fired it up. Then he went to work on every computer, terminal, or flash drive he could find, from the office to the shop floor beyond. Erase a computer file, and it could still be retrieved. Overwrite a disk a few times, and experts could still sort through residual magnetic signatures and find what used to be there. Chad would have none of it. Whatever information these people had come up with, threatening the sweet accomplishments of Trinity's virus, he would put an end to it. A super-powerful magnetic field didn't leave a single speck of data alive.

It was taking too long. He searched out all he could, destroyed it all, but there was still a small iron safe in the corner. What might be in there? Maybe he'd shot the guy too quick. Maybe he could have gotten the combination out of him.

Tough. The safe was metal. If there was any more data

storage secreted inside, it could still be fried. Chad set the electromagnet on top of the safe, made sure it was at its highest setting, and turned it back on. And left it there. Maybe it would take a while, and he had other things to do.

Still no sign of police. Lucky, that.

Dynamite first. He only had the four sets. He put three of them in likely-looking locations across the shop floor. What he wanted to do was take the time to manually smash every piece of gear he could manage, but he didn't dare. If he messed this up, if he disappointed the reverend and failed his mission, failed to utterly destroy this place... well, it didn't bear thinking about.

Back outside, get the gasoline. One container after another, sloshed around, pooled under key equipment, ran across the shop floor, and one whole can saved for the office itself. Desk, walls, that ratty love seat. He got a little on himself, but no matter. He'd be careful. He pulled out his lighter, flicked it on, and held up the final sticks of dynamite.

Flood lights lit up the front of the building, pouring inside and glowing through the office. Chad froze, lighter next to the fuse.

"You inside. Come out with your hands up."

Crap. They'd come in silent, lights out, same as him. He hadn't given the authorities credit for sneakiness. He should have. He was always accusing them of it. And they'd clearly seen the door off its hinges, so they knew things weren't kosher. Crap, crap.

"Out. Now. In five seconds, we're coming it."

Screw it. The mission was everything. And maybe they hadn't covered the back. He might be able to sneak out after all. Time for ignition, time for liftoff.

He lit the fuse and flung the sticks down.

He barely had time to register his mistake. The fuse lit the gasoline. The gasoline spread the fire immediately.

Including along the whole length of the fuse. Clear up to the dynamite. He didn't have seconds to run away. He had no time at all.

☼ ☼ ☼

The blast threw Nadya back into Chou Lee. They sprawled between two SUVs. Four other agents fared no better. She covered her ears. Too little, too late, but Nadya figured it was an instinct and didn't feel too foolish.

The building contained most of the destruction. A solid structure, and civilian-grade dynamite was nowhere near as powerful as military-grade explosives. A flame-fest raged inside, however, and they hadn't thought to bring the fire department. Not that there would be anything to save.

Three more detonations ripped the night. Everyone backed away, just in case, but that seemed to be the end of it. Now it was just the roaring of fire.

Chou Lee put a hand on her shoulder. "You all right?"

"Yeah. Oh, yeah. Peachy. We failed to save the only cure CDC had on tap, but I'm just fine."

Chou Lee didn't respond. Maybe he figured a bit of sarcasm was warranted.

☼ ☼ ☼

News services dribbled in. Grimm was among the first. The regular police held them back. Chou Lee and Nadya headed away with other federal agents, and Grimm decided to abuse his privileges with Chou Lee to find out what had happened.

Chou Lee made him pay for the favor. He made Grimm leave his camera toter at the scene and go to the hospital to find Valerie and fill her in. They'd located her there with her husband.

The worst task Grimm got stuck with in decades.

Valerie didn't take it well. She led her husband outside and Grimm offered to drive them home. They could pick up her car later.

"Why are you the one telling me this?" she said. "Why aren't the police here? Or Chou Lee?"

That was something else Grimm didn't want to reveal. But he had no choice.

"Chou Lee is furious. He wants to arrest you. That Nadya with Homeland Security stopped him. But you need to avoid them both for a while."

Valerie nodded. "I see."

Grimm was sure she did. Leaking info before TimmyTim could be properly secured, presuming the cult had shot their wad and would do nothing more. "Naivety bordering on criminal negligence. An Armageddon cult. What was she thinking?" Or so Chou Lee had ranted. Nadya had taken him aside, calmed him a little, and sent Grimm on his way.

And Grimm wasn't about to pass that along to Valerie. She was hurting enough.

✧ ✧ ✧

Deep in the Romani warehouse housing Aatos' office, Stacy shook her head at the reports coming over the computer screen.

"They actually had a plan," said Aatos. "They actually had a backup for us."

"They'll pass the idea to all the robotics companies. No reason to keep it secret. But others have only the concept, none of what was in that designer's head."

"And not likely a clue how to use the information. That guy was years ahead of everyone on the technology, apparently."

"So the plague rages on, and they don't have a prayer of catching up." Stacy shook her head. "Even if this hadn't happened, you think that robotics stuff stood a chance?"

Aatos shrugged. "Call me old-fashioned. I can't imagine

any computer code, much less a new-design mechanical device, working right the first time out of the box. Those things iterate for years before they get it right."

"And we'd all be long dead. Or infected with faulty nanobugs, with side effects, then dead."

Aatos laughed. "We're a real pair of hypocrites, you know?"

"Why? Just because we're rolling in ego for us, and drowning in skepticism for anyone else?"

"Yahtzee." Aatos chuckled again. "I suppose it's not really funny."

"No," said Stacy. "No, it's really not."

CHAPTER FORTY

Late Summer, Year 3

Two police women, one uniformed and the other plainclothes, escorted Camille Schultz down the austere hallway of a federal penitentiary, through a metal detector, and into a further series of corridors with their own checkpoints. Chou Lee had pulled some strings with a couple of judges and gotten Trinity confined there, despite not having been tried or convicted yet. 'Extraordinary circumstances,' the order read. Officially, the reason was to provide decent medical care within a secure facility, for protective custody. In reality, Chou Lee was concerned some crazy might try to break her out. Who knew who might be a supporter, these days? The FBI could hardly keep up with all the weirdo websites popping out on the Internet, pushing suicide or some other brand of ecological purification. Even one of the guards could be a cultist. Or they could develop symptoms or become one of the bereaved, either way eager for revenge. So they doubled the personnel responsible for Trinity, with extra layers of security before anyone could see her.

And all the effort was turning out to be nothing but wishful thinking. Chou Lee had hoped that if they kept Trinity alive, she'd break down and give them something toward a cure. Today, that hope was gushing down the sewer. Trinity had never gotten off the critical list from the gunshot, and this morning, the bleeding wasn't just inside her chest. It was coming out her ears.

When the guards reached the infirmary cell, the uniformed cop stayed in the hall and the plainclothes woman led Camille inside, where a prison nurse doubled as care provider and extra guard.

"The Evil Designer must be stopped," Trinity said to the nurse. She coughed, nearly choking. "He has the equipment. You have to find him."

The nurse ignored Trinity and injected her with something that stilled most of the spasming in her hands and legs. When Trinity settled down, the nurse put bandages on her ears.

Camille stepped up to Trinity but didn't touch her. After a moment, Camille said, "Getting your own disease is a rather obvious piece of justice, don't you think?"

Trinity's upper lip curled. "It's about time. I'm the first one I infected. Guess where that puts you in line."

Camille's forehead twitched. She watched the nurse finish her ministrations and step aside. "I did love you, in my own way."

"Mother, Mother," said Trinity, "don't you realize you've admitted you don't anymore?"

Camille took a deep breath. "Isn't there anything you can give us? Something that could help?"

Trinity shook her head a fraction of an inch, all she could move it. "You know I don't do cures."

Camille let out her breath. After a moment, she faced Trinity again and reached out. She took a pair of Trinity's fingers.

Trinity's hand jittered, clutching at Camille.

"I'm sorry," said Camille.

A faint smile wavered on Trinity's lips, then faded. "It's strange," she said. "I think I'm getting a little scared."

Camille sucked in a tiny gasp. She dropped onto the edge of the bed, bowing her head over Trinity's hand.

✿ ✿ ✿

In a room fifty feet away from Trinity and Camille, Nadya and Chou Lee kept their eyes on a video screen. Camille didn't move for a very long time, even after Trinity's monitoring equipment went silent.

"Was that remorse, after all this time?" said Nadya. "Maybe Trinity thought Aatos would speed up the plague."

"It *is* speeding up." Chou Lee rubbed the side of his nose, scratched for a second, and shut down the video. "And that's all we'll ever get. Another finger pointing at Pires."

Nadya squeezed Chou Lee's arm.

CHAPTER FORTY-ONE

Late Summer, Year 3

Stacy paged through papers as she neared a distinctly thinner Aatos in his makeshift warehouse office. He'd been right about one thing; it had been weeks. A lot of them. Fast approaching sweater weather.

His parrot clung to his wrist. Aatos stroked feathers, occasionally breaking off to tap his main keyboard. Molecules twisted on the monitor; two aligned and merged, splitting one in half.

Stacy bumped into a stool. It barely entered her perception. She pulled it to the side and sat, still reading.

Mr. Praline nibbled Aatos' shirt. "Feed me."

Aatos shushed him. He picked up one of Uncle Billy's clay figurines and played with it while Stacy kept flipping around, studying his report.

She turned another page. "My God, this is elegant. You've got a recognition sequence that'll improve the whole immune system. For everyone. Forever."

Aatos shrugged. "That's the point. Don't want you coming up with another idea delaying things. Especially with CDC and World Health at a standstill."

Stacy reached the last page and put a fist over her heart. "I'm actually glad I yelled at you."

"Yeah," said Aatos. "Natural-born boss."

"Pretty awful, huh?"

Aatos grinned a little. He set down the figurine and

tapped it. "Nice elf."

"Pfff!" Stacy dropped her hand. "It's an ogre baby." Then she blinked at the statue. This one looked like it might be an elf, after all. That it might make something people needed.

Aatos hit a key. "Now what?"

She tore her contemplation from the elf. "We've got the protokey digester."

"Check."

"Feedback on immunoglobulin production."

"Yes, the cell won't go crazy." Aatos moved the bird to his other wrist.

"We've got feedback on the feedback."

"On the feedback. Nothing else to do."

Stacy flipped through the pages again. "Okay. I agree."

"Can we start production now? Let's get this elixir out there."

"No. We test it first."

"What?" said Aatos. "How? On who?"

Stacy shied at her own words. "I don't know. Anyone."

Aatos jerked his arm. Mr. Praline squawked a complaint and flew to an overhead beam. "You are *not* doing involuntary human testing! Not on top of everything else."

"Why not? You were going to release it to the world. You think it's safe."

"There's a difference. Either you believe it's ready, or you don't."

"Ah, democracy," said Stacy. "Kill everyone or no one, but never a shade of gray."

Aatos shoved his chair away. "Every time!" He stalked across the room. "I get used to one thing, and you pop off something worse."

Stacy said nothing. Who was the ogre now? Not that little hunk of clay.

"Look, it's good to go. Let's—"

"No," said Stacy. "Too likely we missed something."

Aatos stared at her. "Do you always have to get your way?"

"Only when I'm right."

"And who decides that?"

Stacy took a breath. She was the monarch for this project. She had to be. In fact, she was the monarch for this whole facility, ruler by right of birth, whether she liked it or not. But she could never tell him how scared she was, crossing one line after another, going way too far to find her way back. Caterpillar, butterfly. What was she now? There was nothing pretty about her anymore.

She let out the breath. "When this is over, and they come hunting for a ringleader, you'll all know where to point."

Aatos wasn't staring at her anymore. She knew why. He couldn't stand the sight.

Stacy rubbed her wrist, then her palms, massaging scrapes and calluses she'd accumulated over the past few months. Killing time. How much she treasured having someone around who wanted to agree with her but argued anyway because he couldn't. Honesty, when she had so little herself.

"I'm sorry I lied," she said at last.

Aatos furrowed his brow.

"I can't go on that date. When this is over, I'm afraid we'll all be tied up for a great many years."

Aatos turned to Stacy and let out an aborted laugh. "Yeah. That's the real reason I was rushing production."

A minuscule twinge caught the edge of Stacy's mouth, and died. "If the cure has no side effects, it won't delay release very long. And people we test won't be any worse off than if we did things your way."

"I get it, I get it," he said. "I wasn't being logical. Only moral. Something we've all forsworn for the duration."

A sad smile tore at Stacy's face.

CHAPTER FORTY-TWO

Fall, Year 3

Dull brown leaves whisked by in the wind outside a large high school a few blocks from the hospital where Dr. Nielsen had first suspected a new disease. Cars, vans, and pickups covered pavement, grass, and squashed bushes around one end of the school. An ambulance threaded up the drive, siren blaring, inching its way between people too numb to notice. It stopped and a pair of EMTs jumped out.

Inside the school's gymnasium, bleachers held several dozen sobbing people. Parents with children, an old man alone in the top row, a young man twisting a woman's scarf. The young man didn't seem to have any idea he was talking. "Shelby. Shelby. Shelby. Shelby."

Rows of cots and gurneys clogged the floor from one basketball hoop to the other. Nurses and aides dodged around them, changing IVs and bloody bandages, and checking charts.

Dr. Nielsen pointed. "How long since you replaced that dressing?"

"Hours," said a nurse. "CDC's push-packs ran out ages ago, and there's precious little we're not short on."

Nielsen slipped on a spot of blood near another bed, caught himself, and tapped the patient's shin. "This one too. Keep this room for those we can help."

An aide wheeled the comatose patient toward an exit in

the far corner, leading to a hallway full of classrooms. "Shelby!" said the young man. He clattered down the bleachers, scarf trailing from one hand, and hurried after the aide.

The EMTs entered from a side door, pushing another gurney.

Nielsen collapsed between a pair of cots. A nurse knelt beside him, but Nielsen hauled himself to his feet. "Leave off. I just need sleep." He ignored his own advice and faltered toward another bed.

☼ ☼ ☼

Chou Lee always had too many files on his desk, and today was no different. They hadn't sent him out in the field for a while; there was too much happening locally, and working in the elegant surroundings of his own office was definitely more pleasant. He rubbed a stiff place on his neck with one hand, and a sore spot on his back with the other. Okay, if this was pleasant, how taut would he be if he were somewhere else? Not good. Maybe some of those touchy-feely relaxation techniques might actually work. He opened another file, read briefly, and tossed it in the out-basket.

Nadya came in with more folders. "I can't believe there's no trace." She eyed his in-box and set her folders on a chair, instead. "Catch the news? Interviews with Pires' and Romani's old college mates? Apparently, they're nasty, helpful, gay, straight, sleazy, honest, tall, short, fat, thin—you name it."

"Typical."

"Not a whiff of Romani's real past."

The phone rang. Chou Lee raised a finger to Nadya, picked up the receiver, and listened. "No, I've got a medical mystery. I don't have time for—"

He listened some more, then sat up straight.

"When did they get in the country? And who the hell's

tracking them?"

Nadya opened a file stuffed with photos of Stacy's lab. Chou Lee hung up.

"Columbians again?"

"Three cartels," said Chou Lee. He glared out the window. His pipe beat staccato on the table. "I don't need this."

✿ ✿ ✿

Uncle Billy walked along sidewalks decorated with Indian corn, pumpkins, and a wide variety of witches, zombies, spider webs, and the odd skeleton. Colorful leaves fluttered down the streets of the small town. He paused frequently, directing his chest at pedestrians, at traffic and drivers, and through store windows at shoppers and clerks. He reached up and adjusted the lapel of his suit, panning a tiny pin along the street.

Back in the gas production warehouse, Stacy watched Aatos manipulate a joystick, controlling the image of the town on a computer screen.

She stood behind him and murmured into a microphone. "Leave it steady, Uncle Billy. Aatos is aiming from here."

Uncle Billy's voice came through the computer speaker. "Damn technology. Takes all the fun out."

Stacy smiled slightly. This was the same guy who wanted every new technological toy he could get his hands on, if it helped the factory. The picture of the town stabilized.

"Okay, this time I don't see any effects," Aatos said.

"Me neither. Oh, check that kid."

Aatos panned the shot to a mother and boy. "He's just clowning around."

They watched a moment longer. Stacy murmured again. "Come on back. I think we're ready."

"'Bout time," said Uncle Billy.

Aatos clicked off the screen and spun around. "Don't say it."

"You know, the puking and diarrhea weren't fatal."

"I said you were right."

"Though after several years of allergic reaction, they might have wished it was."

The glint in Stacy's eye must have ruined her attempt at pensive. Aatos leapt up in mock attack. She cringed, laughing, and Aatos retreated.

"I suppose I should admit you asked me about allergies way back when," she said.

"What?" said Aatos. "You mean the time you blew me off?"

"That's not very specific. I blow you off all the time."

Aatos lolled in his chair. "Alas, 'tis true."

Stacy's laugh drained away. She sighed at the blank screen. "We don't actually know it will do the trick. Only that it seems benign."

"If nothing happens, we study it to death and try again."

"Not enough resources," said Stacy. "More expensive than I expected. One production run."

"Okay, understood. So what do you want to do?"

Stacy drummed her fingers a couple of times. "I can't think of anything else. The chemicals demonstrably work. We've watched them on screen, we've tried *in vitro* and *in vivo*."

"You've analyzed blanks and tissue samples. The damn protokey always disappears when we dose it."

Stacy picked at a cuticle. "Every time anyone thought of anything, we added it to the checklist."

A warehouse foreman behind them tossed a clipboard with the latest equipment logs on the desk. "I can't believe you made us start over every time we dry-ran the production and something needed tweaking."

"Too much interrelation of variables," said Aatos. "If you change anything, gotta repeat from the top."

"But our last run was perfect," Stacy said. She raked both hands through her hair, fingers grabbing handfuls, tugging. Aatos waved off the foreman and sat mute, letting Stacy think. She closed her eyes, gnawing at her lips, tugging bigger globs of hair.

And then she let go and lowered her hands. "Okay. Sleep. In the morning we decide."

As Stacy went to her own cubbyhole, she let herself indulge in a moment of regret. Whatever feelings she may once have sparked in Aatos had to have burned out over the summer. She'd shown a side she never knew she had. The bitch was outed, while Aatos kept an even keel, his genius shining in every gene he fashioned. They had worked so well together, in the sense of getting a job done, but not hardly, not in the slightest way, had she preserved a prayer of a future relationship.

She stuffed the thought in a deep, dark hole. The job was all that mattered. What else did they need to do before morning? What could they possibly have forgotten?

✧ ✧ ✧

People in funeral attire, some neat and some ragged, clogged steps, sidewalks, and all but one lane of the avenue in front of an impressively-refurbished old cathedral. Some people kept a little space around themselves. Other people hugged. A dozen clergy worked their way among them, trying to console those who most needed it. Police cleared a pathway from the entrance to the street and set up a rope barrier.

A television frame surrounded the scene. An anchor's voice rode over the background sounds. "Some people have given up avoiding each other. We're all infected, and the need for comfort outweighs fear."

A parade of hearses pulled up to the front of the cathedral, edging aside the few people still in their lane. Ten, twenty, forty vehicles... the line disappeared in the distance.

"In the largest funeral in history, churches, mosques, and temples of all kinds are holding simultaneous services around the world. And it doesn't begin to convey the enormity of the loss."

Pall bearers emerged from the cathedral, carting one cremation urn after another. They reached the first hearse and packed the urns inside, front to back and door to door. Other bearers attended the second hearse. As each person released their burden, they headed back for more.

"Three hundred ten million to date. With a major fraction of the world's population affected, world leaders are meeting this week in Rome to deliberate options for a post-plague world."

✧　✧　✧

Inside a cavernous warehouse, Uncle Billy stood at the head of two lines of Schultz production equipment. Workers stationed themselves along the lines, fiddling with papers and tools, killing time until told what to do.

Aatos met Stacy at the door and walked in with her, at a loss for what she might still think of him. All summer long he'd resisted her plans, yet every step of the way he'd realized the benefits of what she wanted. He no longer believed any of it was overkill. Every delay? Justified. And now she must think him an obstructionist, incompetent without adult supervision. She was the brilliant one, not him, and he'd blown any chance to impress her.

They'd nearly reached the equipment before Aatos stuffed his defunct hopes where they belonged, up high on the unreachable shelf of daydreams. Only today mattered.

He took a quick side-trip to check gauges on the side of the Synthesizer 1000 and hopped back beside Stacy.

Uncle Billy rubbed his hands together. "Sure is weird. Algae producing a virus that helps people."

"And doing it faster than machines, to boot," said Stacy, eyeing the workers.

A cloud halved the sunshine in the wide doorway. "Hope it doesn't rain," said Aatos.

Uncle Billy gloated. "Won't stop my little pets."

Stacy picked up the laminated status sheet on the nearest mechanism and checked some numbers. "Did you get any sleep last night, Aatos?"

"Nope. But neither did you. Saw you bouncing around the warehouse."

She turned the sheet over, saw nothing out of order, and put it on its hook. "Came up with eighty-seven things we meant to do but might have missed."

"I win," said Aatos, not sure why he was acting competitive. "I had ninety-one."

"And?"

"All covered."

"Yeah," said Stacy. "Same here."

She looked at him. She didn't say anything else, her silence inviting his opinion. He nodded. Stacy turned to Uncle Billy.

It had to be a momentous occasion. Something famous ought to be orated for posterity. The moment dragged on, unfilled.

"All right," Stacy said. "Do it."

Uncle Billy gestured. Workers flipped switches. One bank of machines after another hummed to life.

Aatos got out of the way.

CHAPTER FORTY-THREE

Fall, Year 3

Atos, Stacy, and Uncle Billy scrutinized and rechecked every inch of the facility during the next several hours, the next several days. They marched up and down the algae ponds, watching workers adjust valves, skim goo off the top of the ponds, and collect it in fifty-five-gallon drums strapped two to a forklift.

The forklifts met another device that emptied the drums into vats at the start of a processing line in a separate warehouse. Farther down the line, a dozen different machines whirred, popped, or blinked lights.

Workers logged readings from dials on electronic clipboards that sent the information to a central computer, monitoring trends and operating parameters. It hadn't been worth fully automating the data system, another example where 'good enough' was faster and cheaper for what they had to do. Stacy pointed at one dial; a worker nodded and adjusted a valve.

Near the end of the production line, a dozen sets of plastic tubing fed from the last piece of equipment to a board mounted with a hundred more snaking lines, color-coded and tagged. All of the tubing was high-performance engineered plastic free of plasticizers. Tiny valves covered the board, each with a minuscule label plate. Stacy inspected the board, watching the flow through the various lines. A worker nudged her aside, leaned close to listen, then tightened one connection.

At one point, Aatos checked outside. A flat-bed truck filled with vertical gas cylinders of different colors pulled away from the loading dock, and an empty one took its place. In the distance, three more laden trucks rumbled down the road. It was a case of the old army joke, 'hurry up and wait.' Now he was into the waiting part, and oddly, inactivity was more nerve-wracking than what had gone before. Sort of a helpless, useless feeling.

Another day, Uncle Billy spied them at the main entrance, where Stacy and Aatos watched the road. He waved, and Stacy waved back. Aatos thought she'd relaxed, at least for now, reflecting on the results of their labors. Would the anxiety kick in for her, or had it already, and she was better at hiding it? Another truck finished loading and rumbled up the drive. Those already on the road faded in the distance.

Aatos and Stacy stood there, watching. Light dimmed as truck after truck after truck loaded up and drove off, and empty ones came to replace them.

✧   ✧   ✧

Days turned into weeks, and still the warehouse churned. Stacy and Aatos strolled along the production line several times each morning, each afternoon, each dead of night. When Stacy frowned, a worker dashed over to adjust a pair of valves. When she pointed at a gauge, a worker rushed to check it. Overall, though, Stacy knew there was little more they could do. The product was designed, the system built, and it was too late for anything but worries. And the raging desire that operations would continue smoothly, and something would come of it all.

And, oh yes, the trivial little wish that Aatos would stop fidgeting, biting his fingernails, and trying to get Mr. Praline to memorize pi to a gazillion digits.

☼ ☼ ☼

A smattering of people wandered down a city sidewalk lined with barren trees. No one jostled or pushed. Cars took care to yield to each other. Everything felt fragile.

A TV anchor's voice said, "We all expected looting. Fires. General chaos. Troops deployed months ago." The view swung over to a corner with a couple of bored National Guard soldiers. "But the mood is more like nine-eleven. A catastrophe that brings people together."

The camera swiveled again, pointing toward an empty park. "The World Health Organization puts the official count at three hundred sixty million, but other sources claim the toll could be much higher. Communications in some parts of the world are very sporadic. There is still no word on either a cure or any survivors."

The framed view cut to a graph, an exponentially rising curve bearing the title Deaths. The lower left was blue, nearly flat, gently rising. The rest of the curve sloped up steeply in red.

"We're well into the red. Every country is facing a breakdown in medical services. Since losses are random, some places are hit harder than others."

The view expanded, blowing up the steep right-hand part of the curve, highlighting a small white X. "We're talking millions of people a day at this point. And still rising. If key industries lose too many workers, they won't be able to get out a cure when they find one."

CHAPTER FORTY-FOUR

Fall, Year 3

Nadya led the handcuffed Reverend Whatever-His-Real-Name-Was through two halls in the FBI building and across a room full of agents doing paperwork. She'd had not one iota of trouble arresting him and bringing him in. The guy was all angles and bones, without enough muscle to fight a cricket.

"Hello," said the reverend, nodding to everyone they passed. "Have a nice day. Hope you're well. I like your poster. Those are lovely flowers, miss."

Nadya threw a 'what can I do about it?' look at the other agents and got the reverend seated in an interrogation room.

Chou Lee arrived a second later. "You're sure?"

"He ran the website we found, and he claims he's the one," said Nadya. "Inspiration for the Life Cycle Revolutionaries. I still think 'retrobates' fits them better."

"Confirmation?"

"ID'd by two cultists we picked him up with and matches video of the Schultz protesters. We saw him ourselves, once, briefly. So yeah, pretty sure."

Chou Lee nodded. "What's your name?"

The reverend smiled at Chou Lee and repeated the litany of aliases he'd gone by over the years, same as he'd given Nadya. The list included quite a few they'd not heard before from his followers. Must be one helluva memory to keep them straight, Nadya thought.

"Never mind," said Chou Lee. "It'll take days to track those down, and likely none are real."

"Exactly," said Nadya. "But he's open about everything else."

"I opened that website this morning," said the reverend. "Fast work. I am impressed. Yet our fundamental beliefs and the reasons for our actions have already spread around the world. The ultimate phase is under way and the so-called Evil Designer shall founder in the moment of climax. Purification is holy. People will accept their extinction, now they know why it is necessary."

"Accept their…"

"Yup," said Nadya. "Doing us all a favor. Ask God if you don't believe him."

Chou Lee glared at the reverend. "How do we stop it? Who was Trinity working with? Is Aatos Pires making more? What other schemes you got planned?"

The reverend clapped his fingertips together. "Oh, this is truly delicious. Revolution 101. Use society's strengths against itself. Philosophical judo."

"What is he talking about?" said Chou Lee.

"Anything at all. He never shuts up," said Nadya.

"Mob psychology against tyrannies, where people are lemmings," said the reverend. "But not here. Oh, no, not in America, land of the cowboy. Here we believe in independence, and individualism. Every disciple goes their own way. And with enough devotees designing destiny, crafting cataclysmic conceptions, enlisting aid and spreading the word and growing ever stronger, one of them has stricken gold."

"Do you follow any of this?" said Chou Lee.

"I fear I do," said Nadya. "Except for the 'stricken' part. I thought it was 'struck.' And I'm afraid if I can understand him, I may need therapy. Aatos Pires is the Evil Designer and Trinity Schultz created the plague. Otherwise, from what I've been able to gather over the past three hours bringing him in, he doesn't know a blessed thing."

"Blessed news, yes," said the reverend. "You have it exactly."

Chou Lee ignored him. "Meaning?"

"He preaches, he recruits, and he sends every fanatic he finds off to do their own thing. All in the name of eliminating man's impact on the world."

"And woman's," said the reverend. "We are equal opportunity abusers of God's gift. But now we shall cease our depredations, and the Almighty may begin anew."

"That much we've heard before," said Chou Lee.

"He thinks Trinity was the mother lode. He has no idea how many others she got to help her, or where they are, or what they're up to now. The good news is, no other disasters are in the offing. Most of his people are about as competent as the Boulder Dam Kid."

"Not all, my dear, not all." The reverend squealed in glee. "One other came through. One other, indeed."

"The robotics plant," said Nadya. "He thinks one of his people was involved. But he won't provide a single detail to back up the claim."

Chou Lee patted his pockets. He seemed at a loss when none of them turned up a pipe. He pointed at the door, and he and Nadya left. "You don't think we'll get anything more out of him?"

"Blood and turnips. Like I said, been questioning him for hours." Nadya kicked a dollop of mud off her shoe and nudged it to the side of the hallway. "I wish to hell the FBI hadn't figured out pleasant conversation was a better interrogation technique than torture."

"I'm with you. I'd really like to hurt that guy." Chou Lee gave up on his pockets. "Lord save us from people who know they're right."

"Doesn't everyone think that?"

"Not think. Know. People without doubt shudder my rudder."

"Ah," said Nadya. "You like doubt."

"Great stuff," said Chou Lee. "There's nothing more dangerous than moral certainty."

"I'm not sure I agree with that."

"Good. You're learning."

Nadya made a fist and aimed it at his triceps. Chou Lee sidestepped.

☼ ☼ ☼

"Why not let me try?" said Grimm. "You've been interrogating the guy for over a week, right? You got nothing."

Nadya pulled off a shoe and rubbed her foot. "I hate to say it, but where's the harm at this point? You've given up yourself, right?"

Chou Lee muttered around his pipe stem. "Not per procedure."

"The world's falling apart, and you're worried about procedure?"

"Shut up, Grimm," said Nadya. "You're not helping your case."

Chou Lee spat the pipe into his hand. "I suppose, with all the cameras rolling, we could give it a go. Waste of time, though. Waste of film."

"You've long since gone digital. I'll spot you a few electrons."

"Shut up, Grimm." Nadya stopped rubbing her foot and stuck it toward Chou Lee. "Here, you wanta do this for me?"

Chou Lee backed like it was a snake. "If I ever do that, it wouldn't be in public."

Nadya flashed a smile of triumph at Grimm. "He said 'if.' That's progress."

Chou Lee twirled his pipe on the desk. "Okay, fine. Take your best shot. Put me down for a fiver on failure."

Grimm grinned. "Cheapest interview I ever paid for. And that's only if I lose."

Nadya slipped her shoe on and rose. "Follow me."

✿ ✿ ✿

The reverend chittered like a three-year-old overdosing on sugar. All right, it wasn't appropriate behavior for an adult, especially one in his calling, but he couldn't help himself. This Grimm character was so amusing.

"You believe a reporter can make a better interrogator than the FBI?"

"I have no idea. Just thought you might open up in a less stressful environment."

The reverend looked from his shackled wrists to the overhead cameras to the locked door. "Less stressful?"

Grimm leaned back and flipped open a notepad. "Point taken. But why not let your story out? Might interest your followers to learn a bit about you."

The reverend stretched his chains, pulling his hands as close together as possible. He tried twiddling his thumbs, but they didn't quite reach each other.

"What do you have to lose?"

The reverend relaxed his fingers. He had nothing to lose, but so what? Why indulge the authorities? Whatever he said wouldn't make it out of the building, and his disciples had done their duty in a most splendiferous manner with no further information, so why cater to those who had never embraced his vision?

He leaned back, studying the ceiling. No, he would not provide these people with ammunition to psycho-babblize him. To attempt to make him feel guilty about his decisions, his actions. He knew he was doing right by the Lord. These people had no need to hear about his mother, starving her thirteen-year-old son to force him into sex with her friends, then spending the money he earned on her own sex addiction. She could have used drugs like a normal junkie. She could have let him steal like others did, to support her habit. But no, she had to be unique. And she didn't filter his 'clients' with even the coarsest kind of sieve. Female, male, old, sick, or riddled with deviant desires—all were sent his way.

And then he learned how common 'uniqueness' was. His mother's actions paled against what his paramours whispered in the night. Bragging. Thinking to impress him with their cleverness, their inventive innovations in ignominious acts. Every one of them had discovered a singular way to defraud, debase, or desecrate some person, some institution, some aspect of life. For money, for power, for fame.

Why was he thinking these things? He'd promised himself never to dwell on the past. Damn these—no, no, be fair. He mustn't blame his thoughts on the police, or this reporter. He must accept responsibility for his own mind.

But if he was already swimming in this polluted memory stream, may as well finish the lap. Those people his mother knew, the people she forced on him, their ego was what did it. What gave him the impetus to flee, no matter how hungry, cold, or bruised his body. What gave him the courage to realize that several hundred warped souls, one hundred percent of those he had ever known in his run-down warehouse of a life, constituted enough of a data set to condemn the entire species. To inspire him to dedicate what remained of his existence to being, himself, unique. To fixing the race that had spawned him. Or rather, to realizing it could no longer be fixed, and doing something about it.

Ah, Trinity, ah, Chad, the world should honor your sacrifices forever. And in a way, it would, if 'forever' was defined as the duration of humanity.

My, my, that Grimm fellow was leaving. Slamming the door behind him. He'd only been sitting there, what, an hour or so?

Some people had no patience.

CHAPTER FORTY-FIVE

Fall, Year 3

After several weeks of nonstop effort at Stacy's factory, with nothing to show for it, the occasional temper flared, like the trace discoloration of incipient corrosion. One dreary, drizzly morning, the kind of weather renowned for breeding rust, Uncle Billy raced down to stop a dispute between two truck drivers near the loading dock. He chopped his hand to the side. The empty truck backed and the full one pulled away, past a tarpaulin-covered pile of shrouds. The Romani factory's recent losses. The crematoriums were overtaxed, and Uncle Billy couldn't spare the labor for burials.

Stacy came out of a side door, scribbling reminders to herself on a small memo pad. She caught the scene and approached. "Trouble?"

"No." He booted a rock after the trucks. "Got the last of the contracts. Hope you know what you're doing."

Stacy watched the empty truck take its place at the dock and another batch of freshly-painted gas cylinders get placed onboard. "We had to get this everywhere."

Uncle Billy scratched his head. "Yeah. But undercutting prices in Kenya was the last popsicle. That, and the overtime and bonuses we're paying to keep up delivery rates, what with all the people our subcontractors have lost. We're hemorrhaging so badly, we'll shoot through our reserves in a month."

A worker chained the last of the cylinders in place and the truck pulled away, smoothly replaced by the next in line. Most of the trucks were a bit worse for wear, overdue for tune-ups or new tires. But they were running. That's all that mattered.

"In a month," said Stacy, "you'll have saved humanity." She jotted a note and turned away.

Uncle Billy took a theatrical pose. "Always wanted to be a hero."

Stacy froze, and something inside her twisted. She couldn't imagine what her face must look like, and her words... her words had the inescapability of a tar pit.

"I said you'd save the world."

The pen in her hand snapped. Ink oozed out like blood.

"I never said you'd be a hero."

CHAPTER FORTY-SIX

Late Fall, Year 3

From high above, the Eiffel Tower and the Arc de Triomphe shone in all their glory, rivaled by the rest of the moonlit city.

Today, the anchor's voice held a different timbre. "Although the toll continues to rise unabated overall, there has been a surprising development in a few isolated areas. Medical personnel tracking onset of phase two have identified six areas around Paris that have statistically lower rates than elsewhere."

Aatos listened to the newscast on his computer monitor, feeding broccoli to Mr. Praline. He dropped the stalk and pumped a fist. "Yes!"

"*Ja, aye, oui,*" said Mr. Praline.

Across the room, Stacy watched her own computer, sliding the cover open and shut on her red pencil box. "God, did we miss something?"

"Stacy, try channel four."

Her hand shot out to the remote on a nearby television.

✧ ✧ ✧

A few days later, masses of people crowded the base of a British cathedral, waiting to enter. The wider spacing between people was long forgotten. Indigent and middle-class mingled without distinction.

A reporter shifted his position a few inches closer to the camera, straightened his tie, and adjusted his microphone.

Someone snapped their fingers. "Oh, already? Great. Um, as you are aware, both of our usual reporters have recently passed away. The plague, of course. But I am here to tell you, all that may be changing."

A priest came out and blessed the multitude. People knelt.

"The Vatican has no comment, but two, uh, three other Christian denominations and one Muslim imam are taking credit for stopping the plague. Even though it's not yet stopped."

Limousines pulled up. The crowd grew lively and parted for them.

"However, in the wake of French reports, other agencies have studied recent data, and thousands of pockets of resistance are springing up in the most unlikely places."

Tennis stars emerged from the limousines, dressed well but carrying tennis rackets they lofted in victory. Fans and sports-haters alike roared their admiration and tried to catch the rackets.

"A bizarre correlation springs from an Internet site that claims an inordinate number of these safe pockets are centered around tennis courts."

☼ ☼ ☼

In their warehouse, Stacy and Aatos gaped at a computer screen showing the news report.

Aatos turned up the sound. "Tennis courts?"

Uncle Billy appeared behind them, Mr. Praline perched on his shoulder. He cleared his throat. "Yeah, um, it seems some manufacturers favor our gases for their upscale tennis ball cans."

"What?" said Stacy. "Isn't that just air?"

"Usually, sure. But we came out with a line of scented gases that enhance sales, for some reason."

Stacy pushed away from the desk and stood up. "You

are *not* using—"

"No, no, none of that. This is actually legit."

"Legit," said Mr. Praline. "Let's have none of that."

Stacy sank down.

Aatos watched Uncle Billy leave. "What did he mean, actually legit?"

Stacy gave him a haunted, sideways look. Before she could think what she could possibly say, Uncle Billy's voice roared from outside.

"How can you call another surprise inspection?"

Stacy tore across the floor of the warehouse. This was either a very welcome diversion or a disaster.

"You've been here six times in the past two years."

"That's because you take me to dinner," said a woman, nearly as loud as Uncle Billy. "I thought you wanted to see me."

Stacy skidded to a halt inside the doorway and pulled her head back before the woman could see her. Damn, where was her mind? The TV had painted her picture as often as Aatos' the last few months. She was lucky she'd changed so much, including her name, that none of the old high school crowd ever realized who she was. But if this outsider got a solid gander, you could write off the entire population of every country they hadn't gotten the virus to yet. She reached out and scraped some grease off a bearing, rubbed it on half her forehead and one cheek, then stuffed her hair into a hard hat. She used her clean hand for that; good, her brain was working again.

Outside, Uncle Billy and a rotund middle-aged woman faced off, arms akimbo.

"What are all those trucks?" said the woman.

"Our products."

"You never ship this much. The county got complaints from half a dozen neighbors about traffic, and when they saw erosion damage, they called us."

"Highway maintenance isn't our problem. We pay taxes."

"Noise and road congestion get people upset. Calls hit the state, and we all catch heck for not knowing what's going on."

"Frog farts."

"It's true, Uncle Billy," said Stacy, coming up behind him. "You didn't notify everyone we had a new product line? Big introductory ship-out?"

Uncle Billy hemmed. "Uh. No."

The woman broke into a grin. "William, do I get to meet that niece of yours?"

"William?" said Stacy.

"Oh, er…"

"So introduce us already," said the woman.

"Um…"

"Hi," said Stacy, sticking out her grease-ridden hand, "I'm Anastasia."

The woman's grin broadened. "Pleased to meet you. I'm Greenfield, NYSDEC." She shook Stacy's hand like a truck driver, no hint of reaction to all the grease.

"Greenfield?"

"I know. Call me Gladys, dear. I met a Mr. Steele who was a materials scientist, a Forest who worked for the Park Service. Maybe my name did get me into the environmental business."

"Cool," said Stacy, letting go of her hand. "Oh, sorry."

"No problem," said Ms. Greenfield, rubbing off the grease on her jeans. "And I want to thank you for turning around this old curmudgeon and making him see the light. Not many companies do voluntary sampling and remediation programs."

"My pleasure," said Stacy.

They chatted about regulations and weather for a while, steering clear of Greenfield's curiosity about their new shipments, and Uncle Billy agreed to hire off-duty police to help control trucks out at the end of their access road, where they had to enter highway traffic. Then Ms. Greenfield decided to call off her inspection, so she could go home and change in time to meet Uncle Billy at the local steakhouse.

As the NYSDEC representative drove off, Stacy rounded on Uncle Billy. "You're dating a regulator?"

"Once every few months isn't exactly dating."

"An outsider?"

"Though it is getting more frequent."

"After all your lectures about clan loyalty?"

Uncle Billy squirmed. "You had good arguments yourself. Maybe it *is* time for a little trust."

Stacy gave him a quick hug and stepped back. "Any chance she might have recognized me? What did you tell her my name was?"

"Oh, damn. Good question," said Uncle Billy. "Hmmm. Don't think I ever did. And you're ugly as piss in that helmet."

"Thanks. Your call on Greenfield, then," said Stacy. "Maybe you... could shack up with her until we finish getting out the product."

Uncle Billy blustered a bit at her choice of words, but the bluster quickly blurred into speculation. Stacy left him watching the trail of dust from Ms. Greenfield's car.

Trust, and change. Well, maybe. But it had to sprout from centuries of family paranoia. Salty soil, indeed. Meanwhile, Stacy had something else to think about.

She went to her room and spent an hour staring at the wall. She had barely used the words 'shack up' to Uncle Billy. What almost popped out of her mouth was 'lock her up.' She had actually, if only momentarily, contemplated kidnapping to keep their work a secret. Never mind it would have been stupid. NYSDEC had to know where Greenfield had gone. The point was, the thought had entered her mind. A thought the like of which had never before appeared.

Stacy kept staring as another hour crawled by. Ends and means. Once you opened the floodgate, the justifications came spurting out. How far would she be swept along in the current she had unleashed?

✿　✿　✿

Grimm and CDC's very pregnant Valerie fought past other reporters to reach the parking lot. Grimm helped Valerie into his car, pushed the journalist competition away, and got behind the wheel.

Valerie pressed against the far door as they drove off. Grimm plowed on with a pitch he was already well into.

"Think about it, Valerie. The designer drugs were a damn sight purer and safer than anything else on the street. Freaked out the police pathologist. No side effects, no dependency."

"I don't have time for this."

"The new drugs take over the market, the Columbians get pissed, then the glut dries up. No more designer shit."

"So what?" said Valerie.

"The glut started right after the old Schultz equipment was sold."

"Right after."

"Tons of different chemicals," said Grimm. "Mass production. After the Schultz purchase."

"But if they were making drugs, they weren't making..."

"Plague."

Valerie twisted in her seat. "So the plague all came from Schultz?"

"That's the only pattern they ever found. All over the world, it started where Schultz sold hogs."

"True. Pig and human chemistry."

"'Ultra-healthy breeding stock.' Rather sardonic, don't

you think?"

"But then…" Valerie rubbed her belly. "What are Pires and Romani up to now? With two sets of equipment?"

"The drug supply dried up sometime after Pires and Romani disappeared," said Grimm. "But the key fact is this: Schultz people said it was Trinity's job to make animals sick. Aatos Pires was the genius who made them well."

Valerie drummed her fingers on the door handle, so hard she broke a nail. "Stacy Romani," she said. "World-class immunologist."

Grimm jerked his head forward and swerved to avoid something.

Valerie flicked the lock up and down, up and down. She picked at her broken nail. "Maybe," she said after a while. "Makes more sense than several thousand pockets of spontaneous, simultaneous, natural resistance."

"Or a sudden outburst of miracles."

Valerie bit off the nail. "Why not come to us? Why go it alone?"

"Who'd believe them?"

Valerie shook her head. "We could have helped them. We could have tested to avoid adverse reactions. We could have tried alternatives."

Grimm glanced at her, letting it linger.

Valerie clenched her hands. "We could have slowed them down for months. Years."

They drove along in silence for another mile.

"Tell the FBI," said Grimm. "They trust you. Before they find that place and kill them all."

"They still made drugs," said Valerie. "Same people."

Grimm considered that for all of a heartbeat. "Yeah, you're right. Who cares if cops shut down the cure?"

Valerie flinched.

CHAPTER FORTY-SEVEN

Late Fall, Year 3

Stacy settled on a stool behind Aatos' shoulder. He fingered a map of the Middle East on his computer screen, tracing the distance from one green dot to another. In the background, their production line purred along in harmony with Gypsy dance music flying from overhead speakers.

Aatos stroked the touchpad, and the view rotated across Asia Minor to Europe. "Here, for example. There's nothing in Bulgaria."

"They're not the only hole. We sell specialty mixtures to a lot of universities, precision stuff almost no one else makes, but some places don't want anything we could supply. I'm hoping the Istanbul pocket will spread there soon, and there should be spots in Bucharest and Thessalonika."

Aatos scrolled to Africa, jumped to Australia, then hit a hotkey, and the whole picture switched from the real world to the artificial terrain of a game map. "The sooner the better. Now would you please explain why my workers can't build a tunnel through these mountains?"

Stacy laughed. "I'm glad I didn't show you this until we got the virus out. Your version of relaxation looks more like monomania."

"At least I didn't watch four movies in a row."

"At least I didn't snore like a hyperventilated

hippopotamus for nineteen hours."

"Ouch." Aatos clutched his chest. "I'm hurt! Hurt, I tell you."

Stacy reached around and clicked a mouse, pulling up a rule book that explained (again) what Aatos could and couldn't do.

"If you read that," she said, "I'll go read one of those books you recommended."

"Oh, all right. But you know men and instructions."

Stacy took the short story collection he handed her. "Hard to believe we finally shifted to a lower gear."

"Watch it. Machines are masculine metaphors." Aatos scrolled through the manual.

"Feel free to use feminine fare."

"Hey. You're worse than I am. No fair."

"Fair," said Mr. Praline. "My fair lady."

Aatos' mouse clattered to the floor. "I did *not* teach him that."

Stacy leaned over and picked up the mouse. "Sorry. He was watching movies with me."

"Oh, really?" Aatos took the mouse and glared at the parrot. "What's he got that I haven't?"

Another laugh burst from Stacy. "Ah, Mr. Praline. He'd never have caught on to our little secret if production wasn't going so smoothly."

"Traitor," said Aatos, tossing the parrot a piece of apple. "I'm surprised your uncle didn't chase us out weeks ago. These guys know what they're doing."

"He should have. I think we sort of continued from momentum. Too big a fly wheel."

"There you go with the machines."

Yet one more laugh flew out as Stacy got off the stool. Strange how things worked out. She and Aatos had similar tastes even in none-too-witty witticisms. But similar or not, they were quite the pair of loners, and after all the months of intense interaction—worse for Aatos, surrounded by strangers—grabbing a bit of alone time had been stunningly welcome. Perhaps they should have expected that, when their product worked, the relief would bring not elation, but exhaustion.

She was recovering a little humanity, though. She hadn't played the bitch in weeks. Maybe Aatos would forgive her. After all, she'd read the books. They all said how little judgment men had. Thank God for hormones. If he considered her desirable, he'd forgive most anything. And he had once let slip he thought she was beautiful, at that one luncheon, eons ago.

So maybe Aatos didn't despise her and hide it well. Maybe he really did like her. Maybe they'd been alone enough. Maybe the clan could accept Aatos now, even if he could never accept the clan, once he knew everything. Maybe, for now, he was no longer a stranger. And besides, hadn't Uncle Billy set a precedent with outsiders?

Stacy lifted a hand while Aatos played his game. She hesitated another moment, then laid it on his shoulder. Aatos stopped in the middle of a keystroke and slowly turned his head.

"Stacy?"

"Maybe..." Stacy took a breath and started again. "Maybe there are other ways to relax."

"You don't..." He swallowed. "Are you sure?"

"Maybe," she said. "Maybe I'm sure."

He put his hand over hers. She took his fingers and drew him up. She cupped the side of his face, and he gave a miniature version of his silly, lopsided grin.

"Let's find out," she said.

Stacy led him through the warehouse, out the side entrance, and across the gravel to the cottage she hadn't lived in since high school. Too bad she hadn't had a chance to dress up first, for a moment like this, but she hadn't exactly planned it, and she didn't have anything nice here anyway.

Aatos never said a word. He watched her face and quivered now and then, like a half-trained dog straining on a leash. Stacy had a feeling once she got the door closed, it wouldn't take much to break that leash.

She wondered if he'd notice he was her first.

☼ ☼ ☼

Rudy put down his wrench and straightened up. Stacy sashayed past with Aatos, heading for the cottage. Once again she ignored him, as she'd done so often before, even when he went out of his way to be extra friendly. She'd never acted that way with Franky or Theresa. And she was way too cozy with this outsider. He snatched up the wrench and ran into Theresa.

"Oh, sorry," he said.

Theresa studied him. "Still? After all these years?"

Rudy glowered. "She had no business bringing him here."

Theresa laughed. "You know why."

"How do we know they're even making the cure? You know what they say about this guy. Maybe somebody else fixed it. He's playing her for a dupe and making something worse."

"Give it up, Rudy."

"I can't."

Theresa blinked. "No. No, you can't, can you?" Her shoulders slumped. "I never had a chance, did I?"

Rudy couldn't figure what she meant. She pushed past him.

Rudy glared at the cottage. He thought he heard noises from inside. That was the last thing he needed.

☼ ☼ ☼

When Stacy and Aatos returned to the warehouse two

hours later, Uncle Billy descended on them. "Time to make some money."

"Now what?" said Stacy.

"Governments know the cure works," said Uncle Billy. "We close the tap, they'll pony up nice."

Aatos gasped. "What kind of a—"

"No," said Stacy. "He knows the moral argument."

Uncle Billy cocked his head.

"There's no way to extort this safely." Stacy raised three fingers, one at a time. "Communications, money drops, bank accounts. They'd find us."

"And?"

"They may not pay. We're stuffing a phage down their pharynx, after all. Meanwhile, your customer base dies. Or is that too moral?"

Uncle Billy snickered.

"We'll get donations later. People will be generous when they're sure they're safe. Churches, Red Cross—everyone will want to get on the bandwagon, showing they did their part."

"You're the one who knows outsiders." Uncle Billy set off down a passageway.

Stacy called after him. "Don't worry."

"Never do."

There was a distinct jauntiness in Uncle Billy's walk. He must have had a good time with Ms. Greenfield, but he was already back to his old way of thinking. And still believing her. Believing *in* her. Never once considering she had just uttered the biggest lie of her life.

Aatos goggled at her. "You have no concept of a normal family."

Even Aatos glossed over her outrageous prediction. He believed in her too. But not for much longer. They were running out of time.

Stacy shrugged. "I've read about them."

☼ ☼ ☼

Chou Lee and Nadya busted out the door of the FBI offices and charged down the street, nearly bowling over pedestrians.

"Why the hell didn't we hear sooner?" said Chou Lee.

"We were chasing shadows over the Schultz equipment and religious eco-fanatics."

"You ever hear of rhetorical questions?"

"No. Should I look into those?"

Chou Lee gave heaven a 'why me?' look and kept going. "Give it to me again. Details."

Nadya broke into a few steps of running to keep up. "Drug supply shot. Prices out the roof. The Afghan route is still interdicted, and there's desperation for a whiff of anything. Twenty-seven shootings last night."

"Columbians?"

"Cut smuggling when shafted on deals. Then the designer spigot shut off."

"Why?" said Chou Lee. "There's gotta be rumors."

They angled down a ramp into a parking garage and paced along a row of cars. A few lights dueled against the dark; one sputtered and hissed.

"More rumors than clerks in the Kremlin," Nadya said. "But not on that."

"So spill."

Nadya panted, expelling words without slowing down. "Every snitch is going crazy to win the lottery. There's a fortune for info on where the designer shit came from."

Chou Lee slowed, dragged a foot, and stopped. "A fortune."

"Yeah."

"And it ain't from law enforcement."

"Ha. We dream of dough like that."

Chou Lee glared. "Where are those Columbians now?"

Nadya went mute.

Chou Lee's cell phone rang. "Valerie? Oh, yeah, CDC. Look, can this wait?"

CHAPTER FORTY-EIGHT

Mid-December, Year 3

Arc lights blazed over the gas production facility at night, bright as a football game. Workers moved here and there, a never-ending stream. Aatos didn't know if their high morale was because of a little pep talk Stacy had grossly overused every chance she got, or in spite of it.

A truck pulled up to the loading dock. The purchase of oversized mufflers, a prohibition on engine braking, and a discrete gratuity to the nearby town council's parks fund a few weeks ago, which Aatos didn't think he was supposed to know about, had removed the last objection to night operations. The whole process was so smooth, the workers so well trained, they had reduced shift size and now ran around the clock, racing to use up their raw materials before the weather broke. Racing, more than anything else, because news reports kept moving that little white X further up the death curve. It'd be over ten million a day by now if they hadn't slowed it down.

He and Stacy perched atop a picnic table on a slight rise between the main offices and the *vardo*, the brightly-painted Gypsy waggon, surveying the activity while a breeze mussed their hair. Aatos had gotten rid of what he had to admit was a ridiculous beard. A trace of Portuguese Macao ancestry and a desire to emulate an ancient rogue did not make his full beard at all successful, and he was tired of the goatee he'd tried before, so he was clean-shaven for the first time in ages. He also had no glasses anymore, had shrunk to his college-era waistline, and wore nicer clothes than usual, including a black leather jacket. It took a real effort to pay attention to details like that, but he'd promised to try back when they first got here.

Stacy had on her favorite white cashmere sweater, the shoulders covered in layers of her ever-lengthening hair. Kind of ragged. She probably hadn't had it cut in months. Or trimmed, or styled, or whatever women called it.

She plunked down her latest high-tech toy, a tiny black cube, and pushed a button. Classical music wafted out, the overture to *Orpheus in Hades* by Offenbach. Uncle Billy had picked up the cube for her when he was scouting the nearby town for side effects of their virus.

Aatos had never gotten Stacy a present. Why hadn't that occurred to him? It wasn't that difficult a notion. Maybe it would have been inappropriate, or premature, before, when he could get to a store. He never had figured out the proprieties of these things.

He shook away the thought and put a hand on the bars of the birdcage beside him. "Last evening for Mr. Praline. Getting too cool."

"Cool bird," said the parrot. "Pretty cool."

"Probably so," said Stacy. "But we've been lucky all fall."

"Boy, don't I know it," Aatos said. "Warmest autumn in years. We never even lit those smudge pots you ordered."

"Yeah," said Stacy. "Almost makes you believe in divine intervention."

"Except we didn't need it. You planned ahead. That's what mattered."

Stacy tilted her head and gave a nod, accepting the compliment. She fingered her red pencil box.

Aatos watched Stacy play with the cover, open and closed, open and closed. "Been meaning to ask you for quite a while," he said. "What's that all about?"

He reached for the box. After a moment, Stacy let him take it. He slid open the cover. He opened his mouth, shut it, and leaned over the box. "You have a slug."

"Yes."

"A pet slug."

"Yes."

Aatos studied the gastropod. It didn't move. He wanted to frame his next question very, very carefully. Ah, he had it.

"Why?"

"I'm teaching it to talk."

Aatos thought a moment, putting a couple of twos together, and then a few more. His bird. The slug. Stacy. "My God," he said. "Someone else believes it physically impossible to overdo the Dead Parrot Sketch."

Stacy smiled and retrieved her pencil box.

Aatos put a hand on hers. "You never considered a parrot, did you?"

Stacy pulled her hand from under Aatos', the smile slid off her face, and she shut the lid of the box. "You mean risk losing something I got really attached to?"

Stacy delivered the line with such a light tone she probably hoped he would take it as a joke. Aatos let it ride and the peace of the moment overtook them, until the overture migrated into its next movement, popularly known as the *cancan*. It seemed an odd selection.

A guard sauntered by, rifle slung over his back, fingers thumping his belt buckle in time to the music. He touched the brim of his cap, and Stacy replied with a one-finger mini-salute.

The tune finished. The guard pointed his chin at the facility. "Reminds me of an old family yarn."

"How's that?" said Stacy.

"Some long-gone ancestor was part Sicilian. Story goes, back in World War II, the Italian Family and the FBI laid aside their differences to fight Nazis." He grinned. "I figure this is at least as good."

Stacy smiled, and the guard moseyed off.

"Family?" said Aatos. "Differences? Isn't it about time you told me what's going on?"

Stacy took a deep breath. Held it far too long. And let it out. She gazed at the stars.

✧ ✧ ✧

Chou Lee stuffed enough file folders in his out-basket to pry the in-basket off its pins. The in-basket was on top of the stack, since it generally had more things in it.

A rather meek junior agent stuck his head in the door. "Um..."

Chou Lee didn't bother to do more than stand up. It was time to go home.

"We got another piece of, I think, evidence, sir," said the young agent. He put a manila envelope in the in-basket, then picked it up and handed it to Chou Lee.

Chou Lee pulled out a handful of photographs, a series of pictures from Stacy's visit to a drug rehabilitation center many years earlier, according to dates along the bottoms of the photos. "This is timely."

"Yes, sir," said the agent. "That place is right near her university. Someone was scanning in old surveillance material. When we did another facial recognition search on the data banks, she turned up."

Chou Lee singled out one blow-up of Stacy leaving the center. He took a magnifying glass out of its case and examined her face. It held a Mona Lisa smile. "Not the appearance most addicts have after visiting that place."

The agent coughed, reached over, and picked at a piece of paper sticking out from behind the photos. Chou Lee skimmed it. Then he read it more slowly. "*That's* why she was there?"

"Apparently, sir. According to the place's records."

"Hell of a big contribution." Chou Lee rubbed a cheek. He took a breath, slid the photos and paper back in the envelope, and flung it on his desk. "And now we know where she got the money." He sent the junior agent back to work and put on his coat. He stood another minute, assessing the envelope. He scratched a mole by his ear, picked up the envelope, and weighed it in his open hand. He'd finally seen the decrypted Schultz records, and Trinity made no reference to Stacy Romani. Only rants about Aatos.

Immaterial. He dropped the envelope and killed his desk lamp.

Nadya burst in the door, waving a scrap of paper. "Found 'em, Charlie."

"Chou Lee. Found who?"

"Cartel goons. Broke cover. Heading upstate at high velocity."

"Let's all wonder why. Move it."

Grimm burst in, waving a scrap of paper. "Found them!"

Chou Lee and Nadya stopped dead.

"Probably." Grimm handed Chou Lee the paper.

Chou Lee perused it. "Survival plume?"

"Figured there'd be one wherever they made the antidote. Got a hit eighty miles upstate, near a factory held in the name of Anastasia Romani. Could be Stacy."

Chou Lee and Nadya pushed past Grimm. "Who else knows?" said Nadya. "Someone leaked this."

Chou Lee yanked out his cell phone and punched a code.

"You'll protect them, right?" said Grimm. "CDC called?"

Chou Lee snarled into his cell. "It's on." He snagged Grimm's shoulder and handed him off to Nadya. "Put him on a chopper."

Chou Lee and Nadya dashed out.

Grimm followed. "Nadya? Valerie called? You know the

truth?"

Nadya threw him a glance. "Keep up."

☼ ☼ ☼

Stacy and Aatos perched on the picnic table. The facility beyond glowed under its arc lights. Stacy gazed at the stars, as much as she could with all the glare. She took a breath.

"Tell me, is this what you planned for your life?"

Aatos got thoughtful. "It's been kind of one-dimensional. I used to play tennis. Did some volunteer work. Had a guitar."

"I played French horn for a while," said Stacy. "Never got very good."

"Then work took over. I always wanted to cure animals. But I took my job for the money."

"Why?"

"You're kidding, yes? It's money."

She said nothing.

"I like nice things. Video equipment. Vacations."

She stayed silent. Give him time. Everyone had secrets.

"All right," said Aatos. "I thought I had a good reason. My parents' livestock was dying. Some rare bug. I wanted to fix it, and Camille Schultz showed up again. Offered to replace our losses with healthier strains, gratis, if I'd work for her."

"And your family needed the help."

"Yeah, we were going broke. But didn't you hear the news? FBI broke the code on the Schultz files last week. They'd been releasing viruses to wipe out competitors' stuff. She must have done the same to us. It was all blackmail."

"You didn't know that."

Aatos shrugged. "Doesn't matter. I stayed long after I needed to. For the money. I got used to it. Wanted it."

Stacy nodded. She kept watching the stars, and nodding, and watching. Eventually, she said, "That's not bad. I always wanted... many things."

She shivered and scuffed a toe in the dirt. Aatos was awfully patient with her. It took a while, but at last she managed to continue.

"I own a drug company," she said.

"Here?" said Aatos. "They also make pharmaceuticals?"

Stacy raised her head and looked at him. And waited. What else was there to do?

It took but a second for Aatos' transformation. Confusion to shock, to horror, to fury.

☼ ☼ ☼

In the FBI parking garage beneath their building, dozens of agents in full battle gear crammed into unmarked vans. Doors slammed. The vehicles tore up the ramp, tires squealing. Chou Lee and Nadya hopped in a car and followed.

Outside the building, stubby pillars across the entrance ramp sank into the ground. Vans poured up from the garage. The lead vehicle bounced over the last half inch of the slowest pillar, and the convoy took off down the road, silent. Streetlights shimmered off their polished black finish.

Chou Lee's car fishtailed and caught up.

☼ ☼ ☼

"You're all criminals!"

Stacy and Aatos leaned on opposite sides of the picnic table, glaring at each other, yelling.

"What should I have done?" said Stacy. "Go to the cops? Turn in every person who ever loved me?"

"Not—" Misery rippled across his face.

Stacy leaned back a hair, then leaned further, looking at Aatos as if for the first time.

"Why did you bring me here?" A vein pulsed in his neck.

"Where else could we get production facilities and worldwide distribution?"

Aatos remained rigid.

"Our stuff's no worse than alcohol," Stacy said.

"Your stuff ruins people's lives."

"It's better than what they *were* using."

Aatos gave that all the value it wasn't worth.

"It's the best I could do."

That didn't change his face either. If anything, the filth kept getting deeper. She'd had the chance to act when she was fourteen, and every year since, and she hadn't done a thing. She had accepted the unacceptable. Maybe made it worse every time she helped Uncle Billy. There might be fewer addicts if the drugs were more dangerous. Well, no, that wasn't true, but so what? What else could Aatos feel except disgust, or utter revulsion? What had she ever expected, when he learned the truth? She fired her last warped, splintered, headless arrow.

"If they're going to break the law, they can damn well face the consequences." Her voice was barely a whisper.

Aatos looked at the production facility. And then, again, at Stacy.

After a moment, she wilted.

So did he.

✧　✧　✧

Valerie waddled out the front door of CDC headquarters, scanning papers in the light from both building lamps and countless television crews. She went up to a bank of microphones, mumbling. "My God, every corner, every continent."

Beyond the reporters, a gaggle of citizens yelled when they saw Valerie step up behind the microphones. Parents, children, and hugging couples smiled and waved.

"Thank you!" yelled several. "God bless the CDC!" "We

love you, Ms. Slotowski!"

The reporters all grinned at her. Valerie couldn't believe it. Where did these people come from? Didn't they know CDC had nothing to do with it?

"Uh, we didn't... I mean..." She fingered her papers, lowered one microphone, and tried to smile for the cameras.

✿ ✿ ✿

Aatos and Stacy slowly climbed back onto the picnic table. Aatos thought he should put some sting in his voice, but he had none left.

"You said you were Holmes to my Watson. I forgot Holmes was into drugs."

Stacy shuddered. "Why do you think I hid in the lab every Saturday night? I could never bring another into this life."

"You brought me. Though I suppose I started it."

Stacy let a bitter smile flicker and die. "I should never have gone to the same school as you. But I was curious. I'm sorry."

"I probably should be too. I'll work on it."

Stacy's mouth twitched again. The little black cube on the table flew into *Ride of the Valkyries*. "Still think we're doing the right thing?"

"You being repensive again? It's a little late for soul-searching."

"Repensive?"

"Well, it oughta be a word. Pensive. Repentant."

"Uh-huh. And the question?"

"The right thing?" said Aatos. "Yeah. Or I wouldn't have done it."

Stacy seemed to accept that, after a moment. "Of course, if you pick the lesser of two evils..."

"...you're still seen as choosing evil."

They grimaced and listened to the music. After a few

more bars, Aatos pointed at the cube. "You? Wagner?"

"My family won't listen. It's a racial thing."

"So I've heard."

"But it sounded fitting tonight. Genetic manipulation and all."

Aatos couldn't tell if she felt ironic, masochistic, or repentant for any of a number of things. Perhaps she didn't know herself. Perhaps it didn't matter. All he knew was that he ought to feel angry, or deceived, or something a lot less irrational than protective, toward a woman surrounded by her own guard force.

He reached over to the cube and flipped to the next track. A few bars in, he realized what it was. "Hades, Valkyries, and *Dance Macabre*?" He clicked off the music.

Stacy gave him a grateful look. They went back to studying the stars. After a while, she said, "We've changed the world."

"Yeah," said Aatos. "Modified the genetic code of every human being, forever."

"No, I mean the knowledge. How we did it. We've healed the Pandora Pandemic, and the lid is off the box."

"It's just power," said Aatos. "No worse than fire or gravity."

"There are fire and building codes. This needs control."

Aatos knew he was getting defensive. "We're being careful."

"Yes. But imagine what others might do with this ability."

"Ah. Yeah." Aatos rubbed his ear, then reached over and scratched Mr. Praline's head.

"Here we are," said Stacy, "unwatched, unregulated, doing whatever we please."

"In the end, I suppose we could be angels in Angola, and devils in, um..."

"Developing nations?"

Aatos grinned. He quickly sobered. "Okay, you've got a point. They'll hate us. Vilify our work. Lock us away."

"They have to," Stacy said. "What we do may be right. But it can never be legal."

Aatos peeled a fleck of paint off the picnic table, broke it into tiny pieces, and cast them away, one at a time. "My parents would have been pissed. They always wanted grandchildren."

Stacy nodded sadly. "Both, then. I'm sorry."

He should have known she'd pick up on his past tense.

She set down her pencil box and tapped it once. "When you—" She gripped both her elbows. Hard. "When you were a little kid, playing in the sand, did you ever think you'd grow up to be a villain?"

Aatos touched her hand. Stacy trembled, then leaned into his shoulder. And Aatos did what he had wanted to do for almost as long as he had known her. Something he should no longer feel like doing. But he couldn't help it.

He put an arm around her.

"Danger," said the parrot. "Proximity alarm."

"Relax, Mr. Praline." Stacy closed her eyes. "You, at least, have nothing to fear." A few seconds later, she spoke again. "I suppose, if we were the last two people on earth, the human race would be doomed."

"If we were the last two, we'd have this place repopulated in no time flat."

Stacy snuggled closer, and Aatos tightened his arm. He loved it when he managed to say the right thing. It came so rarely.

The chirp of the crickets went silent. It didn't taper off.

They all stopped at once.

CHAPTER FORTY-NINE

Mid-December, Year 3

An explosion shattered the ground beside Stacy and Aatos. The picnic table flung them aside. It crunched down a few feet beyond. Shards of rock tore holes through clothes and skin, streaking blood across face and arms. The birdcage tumbled into the dark. The pencil box lay crushed.

Machine gun fire ripped the air. Yells came from the trees. Guards took cover and returned fire. Workers sped inside.

More bursts ripped out whole sections of fencing and shattered piping, trucks, and the corner of a warehouse. Flame spouted from the building. Stacy and Aatos dragged each other behind a decorative boulder. Stacy clamped a hand over a cut on Aatos' arm. He pushed back, stanching blood on her thumb.

Dark shapes flitted around the bushes. Workers came back out of warehouses, armed, joining the guards. Shooting crisscrossed gravel and grass, bushes and cars. Ricochets and broken glass sprayed everywhere.

Stacy pulled Aatos lower. "Shit, not now. We're almost done."

Aatos fought her, trying to see. "Stop them! We can't shoot cops."

Uncle Billy leaned out of a warehouse nearby, firing an assault rifle. Stacy winced at the sight.

A black-clad form vaulted atop their boulder. Stacy and Aatos hid in the shadows.

Rudy charged out of the office building, shaking a wrench on high, screaming at the top of his lungs. The figure on the boulder spun around, Rudy threw, the figure leveled a rifle, and the wrench smashed his forehead as the rifle fired, one more crack amidst a million. Rudy and the black-clad figure fell together at Stacy's feet.

She pawed Rudy's still form, searching for a wound. Aatos checked the other body.

"What the…" Stacy rolled Rudy over. "He was shot in the back."

Aatos pulled open the coat on the other body. "This guy ain't Fed."

Another figure attacked from beyond the parking lot. Uncle Billy fired; the man fell. Uncle Billy broke cover and ran toward the boulder. Bullets pocked the ground like hail.

Uncle Billy faltered. Stacy raced out to him. They collapsed in plain sight, short of the rock. Stacy pressed Uncle Billy's stomach, blood welling through her fingers.

Aatos moved toward Stacy. Another shot popped the dirt in front of him. He ducked behind the boulder. "They aren't cops! Latin, I think."

A convulsion rippled through Uncle Billy. "Our competition," he said, when it ended.

Stacy's throat went tight. What secrets had Uncle Billy kept?

The deeper snap of heavy caliber shells mixed with higher pitched machine guns, shrieks, and detonations. The acrid scent of cordite filled the air.

Stacy closed her eyes. She squeezed Uncle Billy's hand, took a deep breath, and pulled off her white sweater. She leapt upward, hands held high, shaking the sweater.

"We surrender! Stop shooting! Truce!"

She stalked across the compound, dodging clouds of

smoke, waving the sweater toward her own people. Shooting near her sputtered out. Shock spread on workers and guards. Stacy kept walking a few more meters, then headed back toward Uncle Billy, this time facing outward. She yelled as loud as she could, but the smoke made her hoarse.

"We quit making drugs. You win. No competition."

A last shot came on the periphery, then several sharp commands in Spanish. Stacy hovered by Uncle Billy. Aatos crawled out and tried to stop the bleeding.

"No drugs," said Stacy. "We're making medicine. You lost anyone to the plague?" She stood there, waiting, holding the sweater. Muttering came from bushes outside the lights.

A figure rose. It leaned over another bush. After a second, the Columbian strutted toward Stacy, holding his rifle casually.

"I speak English. What you want, bitch? Why we don't wipe this place out?"

"Three reasons," said Stacy. "You don't have enough men. You heard the gunfire same as me, and I know how much we got."

The Columbian grunted.

"Second, what we're making is the cure for the plague. I know it's wiping out your country same as mine."

"Like I'm gonna believe that."

"You can inspect it later," said Stacy. "Third, you came to stop the competition. It's already stopped. Forever."

Uncle Billy made a noise.

"I'm sorry, Uncle Billy. I'm a traitor. They'll find this place soon. You'll never make anything again."

The Columbian shouted over his shoulder. A laugh came back.

"I've ruined the family. No one will ever pay us for this." She swung an arm at the algae ponds, the fleet of trucks, the sea of cylinders.

Uncle Billy raised a finger and made a weak attempt to shake it at her. He struggled to speak, barely audible. She knelt.

"You... always were... a precocious child."

Stacy couldn't help smiling, much as she resisted.

"You forget something," said the Columbian. He jutted his chin at the bodies behind the boulder, then at Uncle Billy. "We got blood feud, you and me."

Stacy climbed to her feet. "No," she said. "We just have pain. Go home. Take a couple of containers with you. Heal."

She pointed at the stockpile of gases. The Columbian bit his lip and rubbed the sight on his rifle.

Then he relaxed, leaned on the broken picnic table, and dangled the rifle from one hand. He yelled toward the bushes in Spanish. "They got an offer. Let's talk."

A massive explosion tore up the ground beside him. The remains of the table came down twenty feet away. Nothing was left of the Columbian. Another blast ripped open the *vardo,* splinters flew past their ears, and Stacy landed on her back, dazed. Uncle Billy and Aatos didn't move.

Firing erupted again, at twenty times the level before. Two helicopters appeared in the distance, closing fast, searchlights sweeping the area. Sharp military commands snapped out, ringing the complex.

Workers and guards shot blindly. One after another was hit. A grenade took out the corner of an algae pond. Water surged out below and showered from twisted piping above.

Columbians zigzagged from bush to building to parked car, firing in all directions, caught between workers and something ringing them from outside.

Stacy clawed her way to her feet, still clutching a shredded sweater. She waved it feebly, took a step, and stopped over Aatos and Uncle Billy. Both lay still, covered in blood. Aatos looked almost peaceful, but Uncle Billy's eyes were open and glazed, and blood no longer pulsed from the hole in his gut.

All around, workers and Columbians laid down arms. Swarms of armored FBI agents and other police closed in. Stacy watched, numb. It was over. Everything they'd worked for, everything she'd hoped for. Over. She'd chosen the world over family, breaking faith with a lifetime of training, hoping it was somehow right, and it was all for naught if the cure didn't spread.

More police came from every angle. Firing still crackled in the distance. Stacy contemplated the wreckage, lingering on nothing. Images fuzzed and focused at random, and the howling of a thousand hyenas built in the back of her head.

And then Theresa appeared, three feet in front of her, leveling a semiautomatic at the bridge of her nose. Why would Theresa do that? Very strange. The whole night was inexplicable.

"Yes, I shot Rudy," Theresa said.

Even Theresa had a gun. A fancy one. Did that matter? Should Stacy have a gun?

"The clan gave you everything. And I couldn't even get *him*. They shuffled me off to an overweight, overage souse."

No, she didn't need a gun. She was more effective. She killed fifty million by delaying the cure.

"Then you had to rub it in his face," said Theresa. "You and this *gorjer*."

Theresa truly hated her, didn't she? Stacy let the feeling wash over her skin. Lots of people would hate her now the secret was out.

"So I got even with you all. Our location for a pile of money. But Rudy heard me."

Was it her turn to be shot? It didn't seem important anymore.

"All he ever wanted was to protect you."

Stacy turned away. Where did Aatos go?

"Look at me, dammit! I couldn't let someone else kill him. He was mine."

No, Aatos was gone. Uncle Billy was gone.

"Look at me! We're going to stand here, until—"

Another snap, quite loud. And a thump behind her. So many strange noises tonight.

✿ ✿ ✿

Chou Lee and Nadya entered the light, carrying pistols, hulking in their body armor. They surveyed the carnage.

"Thank God for spy drones and infrared," said Nadya. "There's nothing like good intelligence."

"Shut it down," said Chou Lee. "All of it."

"But Valerie said—"

"Can't be. They're filth. If there's a cure, there's something worse hidden in it."

"We can't know that."

"This kind never does nothing for free."

Nadya still hesitated.

"Now!"

Troops sprinted toward the buildings. Other troops bound captured workers, guards, and Columbians. Nadya jogged toward Stacy.

✿ ✿ ✿

The last of the firing died out. The deep, thick felt of Stacy's mind let that speck of information trickle through.

She took one last halting step. Bodies lay everywhere. Blood, twisted limbs, and burns. The desolation of her life, and Dante's deepest hell. Circle nine, the level of treason. The road had been so very clear, so perfectly paved by her every act, from the first day she learned of her family's business. Betrayal of others for sake of clan, betrayal of clan for sake of outsiders, betrayal of proper, peer-reviewed science for sake of desperation.

For sake, forsake. And now she was utterly, irredeemably forsaken.

Stacy sank to her knees between Aatos and Uncle Billy. She dropped the sweater and put a hand on each. Blood smeared under her fingers. A single tear tracked through the dust on her cheek. Her vision lingered one last time over the devastation all around, narrowing, tunneling, drifting out toward the darkness.

She sagged back on her heels, thoughts skittering off into oblivion. Every trace of expression drained from her face, every nuance of emotion, until it was blank as a piece of virgin slate. The only sign of movement was the reflection of flames off her open, glassy eyes.

✿　✿　✿

Nadya stopped by Stacy, pointing her weapon. "On your face. Hands behind your head."

Stacy remained inert. Nadya nudged her with a toe. Stacy swayed forward, then back, balanced, impassive. Nadya toed her again.

The hum and faint whine of machinery faded away, and at long last, silence fell.

CHAPTER FIFTY

Mid-December, Year 3

Soaring low over the gas production facility, Grimm's camera recorded FBI agents, Homeland Security personnel, and state police moving around securing the site, loading prisoners in vans, and putting out fires.

Chou Lee paced in the background. Nadya stood over Stacy, pistol aimed with one hand, scratching her head with the other.

Grimm's voice overlaid the scene, the anchor for his own report. "The records were extraordinarily detailed, as if they expected to pass on their work. The World Health Organization confirmed there is no hidden agenda in the curative virus."

The helicopter circled the site, spotlight roving from craters to bodies.

"Some countries have no pockets of resistance. They demand the cure be resumed, screaming 'genocide' if they are left out. Others resist. One online news service, the Sniffer Dog, actually calls for protection from the cure, saying it's all a government conspiracy."

More vehicles showed up, including ambulances and a Homeland Security truck.

"Dr. Valerie Slotowski of CDC in Atlanta describes the sophistication of the immunization process to be..."

✿ ✿ ✿

"...far beyond Nobel quality." Valerie sat on a stool in

her laboratory, tapping a pencil on the lab bench. "But what if they'd made a mistake? Work like this needs oversight."

Grimm spoke from off camera. "And we always expect a tragic error, don't we? Too many mad scientist movies."

Valerie didn't bother to answer.

"So what if they'd come to you?" said Grimm. "Done it right?"

Valerie's pencil sped up. "We'd—" Then nothing. She closed her mouth, stopped tapping her pencil, and put a hand on her swollen belly. She looked aside at a two-by-three-foot chart. A graph, the exponentially growing death curve seen before on TV.

The small white X on the steeply rising red part of the curve was higher than ever before.

✧ ✧ ✧

The helicopter centered over Aatos and Uncle Billy. An EMT rushed over. Homeland Security agents catalogued the rubble while FBI and police concentrated on the arrests. Grimm's voice continued.

"Thirteen religious and nonsectarian groups condemn the healing virus as an 'unnecessary and unjustifiable violation of nature and God's plan,' pointing to nanorobotics and saying an alternative cure would have been found someday. Never mind two of the same organizations condemned nanobots in the brief time they were considered a viable option. Meanwhile, other religious leaders claim Aatos and Stacy were divinely inspired."

Two medics wearing Homeland Security jackets had an altercation with the EMT, after which the EMT left, and the medics put Aatos and Uncle Billy in body bags. Nadya kept watch over Stacy as the medics put the bags in their truck. Stacy never reacted.

"On the other hand, Stacy Romani's mentor, Professor Sturdevan, says—"

☼ ☼ ☼

Professor Sturdevan turned from the big-screen TV in Stacy's lab.

"Hell, yes, they did the wrong thing. They were starting a golden age in biochemistry. Who knows what else they'd've done? Provided they survived the plague, of course."

He kicked a stool to the side.

"Let politicians dither, let FDA delay. Purge population pressure."

"But sir—" said Grimm.

"Then fanatics and science haters refuse the cure. Chlorine in the gene pool. Instead, the fools saved everybody."

☼ ☼ ☼

From overhead, Grimm's camera watched the Homeland Security medics move a compliant, catatonic Stacy to a gurney, where they laid her down. Her limbs moved easily. Her view stayed forward, unseeing. Nadya put away her gun and followed Stacy toward the medics' truck. The medics put Stacy inside and Nadya sat on a bench next to her. Chou Lee came over, shook Nadya's hand, and closed the doors.

"It is possible you may not agree with Professor Sturdevan," said Grimm.

The Homeland Security truck pulled away, joining ambulances on the road to town. Grimm went on with his story.

"Aatos Pires gave his life for the cure. Is catatonia Stacy Romani's parting gift? No one has to decide whether to lock her up or canonize her. The world can think what it likes."

The vehicles faded away.

☼ ☼ ☼

A mother knelt with her boy on the edge of a large city park. She removed a breathing mask from his face and pointed at a swing set. The boy raced away, laughing.

The mother sank onto a bench. Other parents arrived, hesitated, then let their children join the boy, darting around the play equipment. An ice cream truck pulled into the parking lot, music blaring. A little girl offered her cookie to the boy. A pair of dogs dove into the fray, two blue jays scolded from the trees, and an annoyed cat scurried away from the bedlam.

✧　✧　✧

Dr. Nielsen walked down a hospital corridor crammed with gurneys, all of which were now empty. He lifted a chart from a slot outside an examination room and went inside.

Judy bobbed up and down on the exam table, holding a bloody bandage in her hand. Her mother beamed with hope.

Dr. Nielsen flipped through a few pages of the chart and peered in Judy's ear. He used a piece of gauze to wipe a spot of blood off her cheek, then grabbed the bandage and threw it in the biohazardous waste bin. He smiled at Judy and signaled her to leave.

Her mother let out a cry and hugged her.

✧　✧　✧

Outside CDC headquarters, four lab assistants gossiped past bushes covered with blinking holiday lights and surrounded Valerie's car in the parking lot. Valerie emerged, back to something approaching normal size. She opened the back door and unbuckled her gurgling baby girl.

The assistants gushed and cooed, while Valerie glowed with pride.

Grimm's voice floated through the animated babble as he came to the last section of his report.

"Perhaps, as Stacy's final recording says, it's a matter of

priorities."

✿　✿　✿

A glorious dawn broke over a large European plaza surrounded by a Gothic cathedral, cafés new and old, elaborately decorated edifices now housing apartments or offices, and a clock tower obscured by renovation scaffolding. A few people wandered into the open space, sweeping and straightening tables. The giant clock gonged the hour.

More and more people came out of the buildings, some with children. One man pushed his ancient mother in a wheelchair. They were dressed for Sunday, yet didn't head for the church. They acted hesitant, moving slowly, checking each other out.

Gradually, some of them smiled and approached each other. Whole families came out, a wide cosmopolitan mixture. A trio shook hands.

(Stacy's tape was a scratchy thing, reflecting
the old-fashioned recorder she always used.
This first time, her voice held a trace of pride and
defiance.)

"Let them live to condemn our decisions."

Braver souls in the plaza embraced. Grins broke out. Faces relaxed and people roamed as the crowd grew, ever more lively.

In a flurry, the mood shifted. People laughed. Café attendants brought out more tables and chairs and set them up any old place. People carried out food and introduced strangers to each other. Some brought out a mishmash of instruments. A clarinet, an accordion, a pair of violins, a guitar, and a French horn. They forged an impromptu band

and started tuning up.

*(The second time, Stacy showed resignation,
with a tinge of bitterness.)*

"Let them live to revile our names."

More and more people crowded into the plaza. Two men lugged out a sofa for the elderly and went inside for another. Chairs were set up for the musicians. A streamer flew out of a window, followed by a dozen more.

Two policemen at the corner of the clock tower had been watching the buildup, fingering their riot clubs. They looked at the streamers, at each other, at the faces all around. And they relaxed.

The national anthem blared out. Everyone stood for the duration. Then the band settled into a collection of classic old tunes. People talked over it, voices vying with music for supremacy. A couple danced, and when neighbors backed away to give them room, others joined in.

*(Yet all that came before meant nothing.
Stacy's final words held only anguish.)*

"But God, let them live!"

Children scampered, laughed, and splashed in a fountain. The crowd kept multiplying, the mood rising, the revelry swelling. Pets dashed around in mad confusion, one trailing a leash. A teenage girl pinched a boy and ran. He wasted no time giving chase. Pigeons scattered from the eaves, fleeing the scene of chaos.

More food, more music, more laughter filled every nook of the plaza. Along the tops of the buildings, at gargoyle level, a swarm of high school students unfurled rows of flags and banners.

The celebration burst out of the plaza, flowing through side streets, and flooding into alleys, growing, and growing, and growing.

"*Let them live to condemn our decisions.*
"*Let them live to revile our names.*
"*But God, let them live!*"

The End...

...for seven years.

CHAPTER FIFTY-ONE
Aftermath

Joshua Grimm's documentary earned him two journalism honors, an Academy Award, and excoriation from half the world for glorifying criminals. The thing that most surprised him during the research phase was the diary confiscated by the FBI. Among other things, it verified Sturdevan's extravagant yarn-spinning, his tales about Stacy and Aatos.

Seven years later, another diary surfaced, betokening a further conspiracy that began mere hours after the raid on Stacy Romani's factory. Grimm came out of retirement and, following several weeks of interviews and records searches, pieced together surprisingly consistent corroboration. Most notably, there was a dearth of information to refute the tale. Authorities denied a Freedom of Information Act request regarding the case, on the somewhat spurious grounds that the Privacy Act trumped FOIA.

Eventually, Grimm published a follow-up to his documentary, purporting to describe events a fortnight after the raid. It was prefaced with a caveat concerning his source material, yet, for all that, claiming accuracy.

Early January, Year 4

Darkness faded, with a click of metal on metal. A sound. She knew that word. Sound.

She realized she was aware. Thinking. And therefore alive.

Murmuring voices approached. "She's responding." "Same chemical that worked when she was ten?" "No, couple generations later. And double the expected dose." "Interesting. Call you-know-who. And prep the guy. He's over the concussion; they've got him sedated."

Stacy's eyelids fluttered open. Stacy. Yes. She was supposed to be dead. Everyone else was. She trembled as memory flushed away the comforting oblivion. Fire. Nothing but death. Had she hidden in another chrysalis? Withered away the butterfly and been left a raw, unformed creature, ripped untimely from the womb by these voices?

A gurney rolled closer. Creaking wheels. A technician positioned another patient beside her, played with the intravenous drip valve, and made some connections from wires on the gurney to monitoring devices on the bench nearby.

Technician? Bench? Why not nurse and table? Somehow, he was too fixated on the apparatus, not the patient. And he never said a word. He marched around in his Homeland Security jacket, taking care of business. The last thing he did was realign the patient's head before he left.

Something was fuzzy. Stacy figured her brain wasn't up to full rotation yet. Probably a bad radial bearing. Her attention slid from the retreating technician to the patient. A man. Sort of handsome. Kind of familiar. In fact, he…

Stacy blinked, and found she could move her hand. She was rubbing something from her eye. Aatos. He was dead. She'd seen him. He'd been so quiet, as still as Uncle Billy. He had to be dead. He...

...had looked peaceful. Not in agony. Not full of gaping holes like Uncle Billy. Sweet mercy, had she jumped to a conclusion?

Two technicians returned, one civilian, one in a strange uniform. They nodded at Stacy this time, but otherwise went about their work. One of them adjusted her own IV drip, and she faded away.

☼ ☼ ☼

Stacy and Aatos sat propped up in their beds when Chou Lee and Professor Sturdevan entered several hours later. Aatos' battered, dented birdcage perched on a bench to the side, Mr. Praline ruffling feathers as if he smelled something unpleasant. A calendar on the wall with the first couple of days of the month crossed out told them two weeks had passed since the raid. That made sense to Stacy. Her hair didn't seem much longer, and she could swear she still had the same split ends.

Aatos had eaten like he wanted to regain all his lost weight, and Stacy had nibbled from politeness. They'd been awakened and left alone long enough to pass through the brief joy of reunion, muted by memory, and enter the gloom of uncertainty. They were here, and together, for a reason. Wherever here was.

Then came Chou Lee and the professor. Strange. Not a pair she'd have expected to see together. And they didn't appear happy.

"Warning," said Mr. Praline, without much enthusiasm.

Sturdevan shut the door. He and Chou Lee kept trading looks as they approached. Sturdevan was grayer than Stacy remembered, and she could swear Chou Lee hadn't had that trace of a mustache in any of his TV interviews. When they stopped, Chou Lee gestured to the older man and stepped to the side.

"Guess you know your virus worked," said Sturdevan. "The fallout isn't what you may have hoped."

"Agents died in the raid on your drug operation," said Chou Lee. "That's murder."

"Everyone you knew there is dead or heading for prison."

"Many people are still waiting for the cure. You've ruined our relations with a dozen countries."

"So reviving you was not a kindness," said Sturdevan.

Stacy huddled into herself, wondering where this was going. Aatos studied the IV needle taped to his hand.

Chou Lee fingered his empty pipe. "What you did was unforgivable."

Sturdevan nodded, then shook his head. "And absolutely essential."

"You violated humanity, distorted nature, and abrogated the right of choice."

"Thereby ensuring the continuity of that right."

"You made decisions hard as silicon nitride," said Chou Lee. "One might say inhuman."

"Or, perhaps, the epitome of being human." Sturdevan sighed.

Chou Lee targeted Aatos. "Now it's our turn for tough choices. The world thinks you are dead."

"And you," the professor said to Stacy, "are in an incurable catatonic state."

Stacy and Aatos watched them, barely breathing.

"It wouldn't be hard to recreate those conditions on a permanent basis," said Chou Lee. "Bit of a waste, considering the price of your medicines, Ms. Romani, and the effort to hush this up. But far easier than releasing you both on the world again."

"People need peace to heal. Not controversy," said Sturdevan. "You can't go back."

Chou Lee and Sturdevan waited. They'd apparently exhausted stage one of their ammunition, whatever kind of attack they had planned.

"Okay," said Aatos, "but you didn't wake us up just to tell us that."

"They want something," said Stacy.

"Which gives us a bargaining position."

She grimaced. "You learning from my family?"

"No." Chou Lee scowled. "No bargains. This is coercion. We move you to a permanent facility and you do what we want, or we recreate the conditions the world believes."

Stacy rubbed her temple. "Moved where?"

"Can't say," said Sturdevan. "It's quite isolated."

"And then," said Chou Lee, "we have a job you must accept. That's the deal. Or game over."

Aatos and Stacy remained silent. What was there to say, at this point?

"Your inventions have become common knowledge," said Sturdevan. "The world demands equal accessibility. The United Nations is setting up a monitoring group, akin to the International Atomic Energy Agency, to oversee biogenetics research."

"We need you to oversee the overseers," said Chou Lee.

"You are the only ones with the technical competence to know subtleties to look for, to spot potential problems, to provide 'hints' we can leak to the U.N. agency when something needs investigating."

"And you are the only two people in the world who have proven you can be trusted not to abuse the power."

Stacy had never tasted this flavor of Sturdevan. Hard now to recall him as a fatherly mentor. And this whole exchange with the FBI guy sounded rehearsed, like they'd been preparing it in hopes they could wake her. They had set this up in two weeks?

Aatos digested the proposition faster than she could. "So you're offering us the one job we're most qualified to hold, doing something we can't possibly refuse. And you call it coercion?"

"This is important," said Sturdevan. "You must understand you have no choice. So that you understand you cannot change your minds later and leave."

"You know the legend," said Chou Lee. "You are the mysterious box. The weapon too powerful."

Stacy slid her fingers along the edge of the bed. "To be stashed away in a secret government warehouse."

"Pretty much," said Sturdevan. "Except we had in mind a facility with a decent laboratory, some woods, that kind of thing."

"You did what you thought you had to," said Chou Lee. "Now we're doing the same. You demonstrated your commitment once. We need it again. And this time it will be harder, because this time it never ends."

"Well, until they get old and die," said Sturdevan.

"Yes, yes, until then. So while you're at it, dream up a permanent backup system, for after you're gone. An agency with enough checks and balances to prevent abuse."

Aatos frowned. "A political invention?"

"Could be," said Chou Lee. "Could be."

Chou Lee waited, showing the patience of a police interrogator. Sturdevan waited, fidgeting like an academic who couldn't find neutral gear.

Aatos and Stacy scratched at the sheets and picked at fingernails.

When she decided she couldn't read Aatos' mind, Stacy raised an eyebrow. He lifted one hand, palm up.

"Don't look at me," said Stacy. "You're the one who pointed out I have no social life."

"With the obvious point being..."

"If neither of us ever goes anywhere anyway..."

"...why not stay here?"

It wasn't like there were a lot of options, and this was far more clement than what she deserved.

Or was it? Maybe she wasn't a butterfly, but maybe she met the professor's definition of human. Maybe, maybe, this was her final payment on a lifelong karmic debt. Maybe now she could lay some things to rest.

Aatos gave her a tiny nod. They took deep breaths and turned back as one.

"We'll do it," said Stacy.

Chou Lee drooped in relief, as if he'd been worried they might not accept. "The prof here will set you up with whatever you need in the way of equipment. Something to keep you busy when you're not reviewing others' work. Hell, once we get your location all set up, we can even ship in your dress collection. You might need one someday."

"Dress?" said Aatos.

"Collection?" said Sturdevan.

Stacy felt her cheeks turn a toasty vermilion.

"I suppose it is unfortunate." Chou Lee stuffed his pipe in a pocket. "You've heard that people need their heroes, even when the truth does not match the myth." He pivoted toward the door. "But they also need their demons."

"Or scapegoats." Sturdevan put a hand on Chou Lee's shoulder and paused. "In case no one ever says it, thank you."

The two of them left. Outside in the hall, Nadya popped off a chair and dropped a magazine. Chou Lee nodded once. Nadya got a slender gleam of triumph, the mark of someone winning a small bet. Stacy could swear she saw Chou Lee put his arm around her waist before the door shut.

For a long moment, Aatos and Stacy watched the closed door, silent.

"Um," said Aatos after a while.

"You always had a way with words."

Aatos released a nervous laugh. "Do you think they were serious?"

"Yeah. They need oversight."

"No, I mean about killing us if we didn't agree."

"Oh." Stacy pondered the question. Everything took longer today. Naturally. Her mind was still exhausted. A scratching came from the side, Mr. Praline gnawing at his cuttlebone. She tilted her head at the bird, a thought managed to filter through, and she pointed at the cage. "They brought your parrot."

"What's that—"

"I think they tried to believe they were serious, or they couldn't have asked us to hide for the rest of our lives."

Aatos reached over and let Mr. Praline nibble his finger. He nodded. "They brought my parrot." He swiveled toward Stacy, swinging his legs over the bed. "I could get you a new pencil box, and a baby slug."

"Thanks. Um..." Stacy twirled a lock of hair. She gave it a tug. "Actually, I may be ready for a parrot of my own, now."

Aatos glanced at Mr. Praline. "We could breed."

His turn. He got more red than he'd been in years. Stacy kept her attention on the bird, pretending not to notice. "We'll see." When Aatos' color faded, she pulled slack on her IV line and faced him. One foot swept out and brushed his ankle. "Sorry."

"Ha! First contact."

Stacy smiled briefly. "How soon they forget."

Aatos gave her a surprised look that blurred away when he figured out she was pulling his leg. He hopped off his gurney onto the tile floor.

Then yelped and scrambled up, rubbing a foot.

Stacy hauled a sheet off her bed and tossed it down between them. Aatos got off his gurney again and held out a hand. She took his fingers and slid her feet to the floor.

He fiddled with his IV line for slack. Stacy pulled his gurney closer, but it didn't help much. She put a hand on him, stopping his fiddling. Aatos stared into her eyes and slid his free arm around her.

And then they embraced, one arm apiece, with their other hands trailing toward IV bottles.

"Danger, danger," said Mr. Praline, springing from perch to perch. "Proximity alarm. Hull breach. Loss of containment."

Neither of them paid him any attention. After a long moment, Aatos murmured in her ear. "Welcome back, my gazelle."

"Yeah," she said. "Try not to leave again."

"Oh, all right," said Aatos. "I'll try."

Stacy hit him. Then she held him again, as hard as she could.

She would kiss him again. Soon. Of that, she was certain.

But not today.

Not until the whole thing didn't hurt so much.

THE END

About the author:

Charley Pearson started in chemistry and biology, then moved on to bioengineering, so the Navy threw in some extra training and made him a nuclear engineer. This actually made sense when his major task turned out to be overseeing chemical and radiological environmental remediation at closing Navy facilities after the end of the Cold War, releasing them for unrestricted future use. Now he writes fiction.

Catch him at www.charleypearson.com
(links there to Twitter & Facebook)

www.ingramcontent.com/pod-product-compliance
Lightning Source LLC
Chambersburg PA
CBHW060945120726
47910CB00002B/501